Running with the Devil

Plantain Series Book One

AMELIA OLIVER

DEDICATION

This book is dedicated to my hubby, and my two babes. You helped me realize my dream, and although you constantly interrupted me while I was typing and caused me to write our conversations, I still finished. I love you.

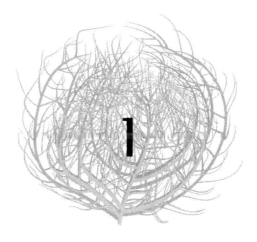

1

Let me start by saying, that running is my drug. I love it, I can't get enough of it. Often I get out a map of the area around the town I live in, and plot out where I want to go. I run whenever I have the urge, day or night. I love pushing myself, just a little further, just a little more. The feeling of reaching a distance I thought I'd not be able to achieve, only fuels the drive and passion even more. I also have the option to not run if I don't want to, but it's my choice. I crave the freedom and tranquility it gives me, there's a certain sense of gratification I feel when I'm done. That no matter what my day brings, I've at least done something for myself. I know it sounds like I'm obsessed and think way too much about it, but there's a reason for that. Running is the only thing in my life that I have consistent control over. I'm sure that sounds overly dramatic but it's true…it's *so* true.

This morning in particular is a good one, I'm headed home after a four-mile run in the nature center park. The sun is still low on the horizon, but it's already heating the air. I love the morning, it seems so clean, the sky free of smog and the air feels fresh and new. I normally run with my ear buds jammed in my ears, my music collection varies but I usually stick to classic rock since that's what I grew up on. Aside from running, music's also my escape. Always there for me and reminding me of good, and sometimes not so good times, but always a constant.

I'd shut my music off a mile back, as the day begins for most people and the cars begin to come more frequently. I don't trust most people to see me and I need my senses in order to not get hit by a distracted motorist rushing to get to work, or take the kids to school. My dog, a husky wolf mix named Bagheera, runs a few feet in front of me. Even though he's still technically a puppy, he doesn't need to run on a leash. But just as I knew I needed to be on guard as we get closer to home, he also knows to take the spot beside me as we wind our way through the side streets. I live in the heart of town, in the neighborhood that surrounds downtown, this is considered the colonial area of Plantain. Plantain is a small town set in the desert, like an oasis surrounded by endless dry land. The town is something like out of a movie. The residential streets are lined with large trees, peppered with kids riding their bikes, or walking to the ice cream shop without any fear of the outside world. I often long for that naiveté of being a child again, to be far removed from the realities of my life.

I grew up here, but not in the house I currently reside in. Although after my mom left, I did spend a majority of my days and nights here. This house had been my grandparents' and was left to me when my grandma died. It's a white two-story Victorian farm house, with wrap around porches and huge lead pane windows. I still walk in expecting to see my grandma sitting at the kitchen table, snapping peas in preparation for dinner. Growing up, my grandmother always kept the grounds flourishing with flowers and plants, and I did my best to keep them up the way she had, although I'm still waiting for my green thumb to kick in. The property is large with a yard that continues all around the house, with large trees and bushes cocooning the property from the street and neighbors. Several of the neighbors are the same as when my grandparents lived here, mostly older widowed women. They're nice to me, solely based on the fact they knew who my grandpa was and loved my grandma. They turn a blind eye to what they think I do, and who they know I associate with. On the rare occasion we did see each other, I can tell they don't really trust me, so I make sure as shit to lay on the sweet and innocent routine. All-in-all the neighborhood's fine and no one really bothers me here, it's like my Shangri-La in the crazy fucked-up-ness that is my life.

After chugging damn near a gallon of water and Bagheera doing the same, I peel off my sweaty running clothes and jump in the shower. The inside of my house is very feminine, which if you don't know me, you would think the decor doesn't fit me. My outward appearance is edgy, and maybe a little trashy in the eyes of others. I haven't changed the decor too much since my grandma, but I did update, redoing all the piping and putting in new stainless steel appliances, restoring most of the house to look fantastic but still keeping in tradition with the style. Every room has crisp white walls with hardwood floors running through the entire house. I make sure to always have fresh cut flowers in the windows and on the tables, flowers I grew, I might add. My home's a mix of my grandma and me, and I love it.

Combing out my waist length dark brown hair as I walk into my bedroom, I glance out the huge bay windows beside my bed to see Bagheera rolling around in the grass down below. Opening my dresser drawers, I pull out a pair of tight, low rise jeans, faded just enough to give it some edge, along with a tight black V-neck shirt. The hem goes down to the top of my jeans, but the V is low enough to show a lot of cleavage. After getting dressed, I apply some brown eyeshadow, which compliments my honey colored eyes, and mascara. I grab my bike keys and watch as Bagheera, who's now back inside, tilt his head and whine.

"Wanna come to work today?" I ask.

His tail wags with excitement, acting like his butt is on fire. Barely able to remain in his sitting position, and I take that as a 'yes.' I switch my keys and we head out to the garage, firing up my 1968 black Mustang. The engine roars to life as I slip on my mirrored aviators and pull out to the street, flipping on the radio to Van Halen's- "Hot for Teacher."

The large gate is open, as I pull into the long parking lot that leads to the garage. The property has several buildings, an automotive repair shop, which is where I work, along with two other outbuildings. Bikes and cars line either side of the parking lot only open to club members, and even though it's early and the shop's still closed, the garage doors are open and men are milling around near them and by their bikes. Pulling into my usual spot, I take in a deep breath and reach over to pet Bagheera, before gliding out of the car as he jumps down behind me, following as we walk towards the building.

"Morning V," Rocket smiles.

"Lookin' good as always babe," Chain adds.

My name is Maven, but everyone calls me V for the most part. Rocket and Chain are the old guys, in their sixties I guess, but they've always seemed to be that old even when I was a kid, so I'm not exactly sure their actual age. The two are drinking coffee and looking down at a bike, discussing some new modifications Chain's done on it. These two usually always beat me to work in the morning, but since they have apartments in the clubhouse, they should.

"Mornin' boys."

A huge fan blows my hair away from my face as I enter the garage and slip my sunglasses on top of my head. The Steve Miller Band blares from the speakers. Even though the morning's just beginning, it's already hot as balls inside the confined area, the smell of gasoline fumes and motor oil thick in the air. I like to think the strong stench contributes to the dumb ass mentality that seems to be an epidemic around here.

"Goddamn, how is it we've never fucked, I mean...damn."

My point exactly. Drag-strip or Drag as everyone calls him, bites his lower lip and eye the length of my body, I internally groan and grab my ID from the cubby along the wall, pressing it up to the time clock and punching in for work. Drags around my age, and he hasn't been in the club more than three years and I don't know him that well. However, I do know he's hot, and a total pig. He makes me laugh so that makes him tolerable. But sometimes I just look at him, and wonder how someone so attractive can be so revolting towards women. I know he's harmless, in that he seems to be all talk. He's never actually tried anything on me which is smart, but I still don't want to give him a reason to either. He's got longish dark brown hair he usually wears pulled back in a man-bun, and he always has the perfect amount of stubble on his chiseled jaw that never gets too long. He's built and solid, and to top it off, he's got the most uniquely stunning shade of green eyes I've ever seen. Skye totally has a thing for him. Which I understand, I also understand why she admires from afar since he's a creep.

"Because she has taste," Smokey replies.

Smokey, now there's my guy. Smokey's forty or so, but he'd been a nomad for the club for several years, which has caused him to age quicker. He did work for the club all around the west coast, before finally settling six or seven years back when his wife had their first daughter. I like Smokey, he keeps it real and keeps his dick in his pants, he's a family man and I trust him more than most. Hard to tell he's such a softy with his rough exterior, tattoos covering his exposed flesh, and a thick black handlebar mustache curling around his mouth. Along with a voice that sounds like he eats nails; hence the name Smokey, even if he doesn't smoke. I look over just in time to see Drag's long Gene Simmons-like tongue waggling, as he thrusts his hips in my direction. I roll my eyes and grab the mail sitting in front of the cubbies.

"Don't you have work to do?" I ask.

"I always have time to work on you," he quips.

Bagheera begins barking as Drag walks closer to me, even growling a little.

"Whoa, okay," Drag says, halting his movements while putting his hands up.

I smile down at Bagheera and pile the mail and packages into my arms, struggling a little with the awkward bundle. Smokey whistles and two seconds later, Spiney, a prospect, is taking the overflowing parcels and heads into my office. Spiney is barely twenty-one and about six months into patching into the club. He's sort of gangly looking, with long limbs and grown out curly blonde hair. Skye pops up from her seat at the front desk, handing me more papers accompanied with her huge smile. Skye works at the front of the shop, working the desk for customers and she's also my secretary. She's been working here for a few years, and from what little I know of her, I really like her. She has zero involvement with the club, never asking questions or seeming interested in anything she hears or sees. She's very easygoing and although we only spend a limited amount of time together, I'd like to get to know her better in the future. But it's hard to have relationships with civilians, so I know that for her and I to really be close, I'll have to change my life. Skye's gorgeous, with long blonde wavy hair highlighted from the sun. Her style's boho chic, always wearing chunky jewelry and flowing skirts. Although shorter than me, she looks long and willowy with a yoga body, and I swear she could model professionally if she really wanted to. Regardless she's always happy, with a huge megawatt grin that no matter what my temperament is during work, causes me to smile right back at her. The papers she hands me are new drop offs from overnight, I shuffle through them quickly and then smile slightly in thanks.

"Dornan and Joey were in to see you."

"Oh, okay," I nod. "Did they need something?"

"Said they'd be back around in a little bit," she shrugs.

Continuing to my office, Spiney's attempting to neatly set everything down on my perfectly organized desk. It's rather cute, but instead of telling him that, I decide to watch him struggle. Tossing my purse onto the metal chair beside my desk, I set my cellphone next to the computer before opening the only two windows and turning on the small floor fan. My office is original to the building and looks just as old as everything else on the property. Wood paneling lines the four walls, with huge metal filing cabinets against one wall. My massive metal desk positioned in the center on the worn out green carpeted floor takes up most of the room. I step in front of my chair and flip on the desk radio, Golden Earring's- "Radar Love," filters through the air out of the crackling speaker. Finally, Spiney gets everything settled and exits without a word. Taking a seat, I begin rifling through the mail. Just as I slide the letter opener through the third envelope, Spiney returns with my coffee, setting it down before speaking.

"Anything else?"

"No, thanks Spiney -Oh, wait," I begin as he turns back. "If you see Dornan and Joey, can you tell them I'm here?"

"Yep," he replies with a curt nod before leaving my office.

I know I'm supposed to be a bitch to the prospects, but the fact that they make my coffee and often get me food, causes me to treat them well. Bagheera stands up from the side of my desk, alerting me to someone coming even before I hear the deep rumbles of men. Two men, and my two oldest friends.

"I'll head up there next week," Dornan says as he enters my office first, nodding towards Bagheera and causing him to relax and sit back down.

"Alright brother, just let me know, gotta tell Katie in advance," Joey replies.

Dornan leans up against one of the filing cabinets and looks down at me, while Joey opts for the seat on the other side of the desk, lifting his heavy boots and propping them up on the corner of my desk. I grew up with these two, our dads being in the club, this place was our babysitter. Joey's beautiful, classically handsome, tall and built. He has that hair where it's longer on top, and shaved in the back and sides. Often he runs his hand through the long top to get it out of his face, and of course it looks movie star perfect afterward. He looks like he'd been locked up for years and only ever worked out. But in reality, he's just out of the military, returning six months ago from a three-year deployment. Joey's married to my good friend Katie, high school sweethearts and all that. I don't know how she did it, not only did she have to be a single mom the entire time he'd been gone, but then she had to deal with him being back in club life. Lord knows I could never be with, let alone marry, a man in the club.

Dornan's the most attractive man I've ever seen, even as a kid he was handsome. In his mid-twenties now, he only gets better with age. His face's defined with a strong jaw, small scars marring his otherwise perfectly chiseled features. He looks intense and often brooding until he smiles and can get anyone to do just about anything for him. He's definitely a charmer, which comes in handy with the business, and is why he's the main negotiator in our deals. But he also doesn't mess around, he's fierce and strong and everyone knows not to fuck with him. The three of us are thicker than blood, they're more than my brothers. I can't explain it really, but I know I'd die for them as they would die for me. I know people say that, but it's true with us, I've witnessed the lengths these two have gone numerous times to cover my back.

"Hey," Dornan nods to me.

His voice deep and intimate, his eyes locking with mine. I can't help but get a little charge inside whenever he speaks to me, or looks directly at me. I don't know why since it's clear we're only friends, but ever since becoming a woman, I notice the attraction I have to him as a man.

"Hey," I reply.

"So you know the job up in Briscoe? Happening a lot sooner than we intended, you available tomorrow night?" Dornan asks.

"Yeah, that's fine. What happened?" I ask.

"Not sure, we're going to gathering within the hour so we'll know more then," Joey says.

"Tomorrow's fine," I reply, getting back to the billing I'm doing on the computer. Joey stands at the same moment Dornan pushes away from the filing cabinet, heading towards the door.

"Need a prospect to grab you some breakfast?" Dornan asks looking back at me.

"Nah, I'm gonna finish this and I'll meet you in gathering."

"You know you should really have them doing more for you," Joey states.

"Not fucking with my food is all I need them to do for me."

"Have them go mow that football field you live on."

Dornan smiles and as our eyes lock, I feel my heart begin to beat a little faster.

I let out a 'pfft.'

"Please, the fewer of you who know where I live, the better."

"Alright girl see ya in a few," Dornan smiles again before following Joey out.

I finish my work a little while later and grab a Coke from the mini fridge, Bagheera following as we exit out to the shop. The radios still blasting, this time Gregg Allman's – "Midnight Rider." It's almost painfully loud inside the garage, on top of the music, drills whirl and wrenches crank. The sun's hot as it hits my shoulders and I take in a deep breath of fresh, slightly gas scented air, and head towards the clubhouse. The sound of the flags waving in the wind, draws my eyes up the flag poles just beside one of the supply buildings. As always, the three flags have never changed, the flag of Norway, the American flag, and the POW/MIA flag. I remember as a child, my dad explaining the importance of each of these flags, what they meant and how they needed to be respected. I loved listening to him and my grandpa take pride in where we're from, where we are, and what we've been through. My heart pinches a little at this memory, as it does with every memory that includes my dad. Halfway across the lot, Missy's champagne colored Hummer pulls up into the driveway and I hang back, taking a large gulp of my drink while waiting for her to park in front of me.

"Hey V," she smiles while exiting her vehicle.

Missy's Sven's old lady, and Dornan's mom. She's practically my mom too. When I was four my mom split and I don't remember her, not a thing. All the 'mommish' moments I've ever had, have been with Missy and Gwen, Joey's mom. They're the ones I went to when I got my first period, who I asked questions about sex, and hugged me through my first and, mind you, only heartbreak. Missy's classy and elegant, with shoulder length pale blonde hair that's always perfectly styled. She appears like an everyday citizen and unless you know her, you'd have no idea what kind of family she's part of. She's caring and generous, with the temperament of a rattle snake and the mouth of a sailor. Missy greets me with a huge hug, before stepping back and holding out my arms, looking me over.

"Girl I swear you can't pay for tits that amazing," she says looking down at her own manufactured breasts, as a result of breast cancer. "Your mom had an outstanding rack too," she adds.

I laugh slightly with a roll my eyes, not quite sure if this is true or not. Like I said, I don't remember anything about my mom, aside from knowing her name was Shine. Since we had no pictures of her in the house growing up, I had no clue what she even looked like. Resembling nothing of my dad though, I sort of figured I took after her. Everyone told me she was Native American, so I assume my dark hair and tan skin tone is a result of her genes. Missy then frees one of my hands to pet Bagheera's head.

"Please tell me you'll be over for dinner this Sunday; it's been long enough."

I sigh, knowing I've probably pushed the amount of Sunday dinner absences.

"Yeah, I think so."

"No, you better, if you don't I'm sending Dornan over to get you," she points a French manicured fingertip at me.

"Fine. I gotta go, I'll see ya Sunday," I tell her before pulling away.

"Okay, taking Skye out to lunch." She waggles her fingers in a wave over her shoulder, as she heads towards the shop.

Rocket holds the door for me as I make my way into the clubhouse, I thank him while entering the dark main area. It takes a moment for my eyes to adjust from the harsh afternoon sun, to the black painted walls inside. The front doors open into a bar, with several pool tables on the far side, while couches and assorted sitting areas pepper any open space of floor. The rest of the clubhouse is made up of apartments for members, a huge restaurant style kitchen, which comes in handy when we host other clubs or through parties. A large conference type room, rounds out the space. This room we used for gathering, or any other club business. The room has a massive wood table in the center, and everyone sits in order of rank around it. Sven, who's president sits at the head, the prospects and nomads stand along the walls and aren't allowed to sit, but are allowed to be involved in the meetings. Most everyone's already in attendance and milling about when I enter, but I don't have time to hang out and talk. I have work at the shop to finish and want to get this session done, so I walk in and take my seat alongside Sven. Sven's the same age as my dad, born only two months apart, they were practically raised as brothers. Sven's a large man, tall and solid, keeping up the physique he had as a high school football player. He practically has to turn his body sideways to let his shoulders lead him through doorways. Growing up he was a local legend, a college bound football player. People still talk about some of the plays he made all those years ago. But Vietnam came, and he was drafted, dismantling any hopes he had for a future in football. Other than his dirty blond hair graying on the sides, he still resembles the teenager he once was.

Rocket sits on the other side of me, Chain across from me. Chain's Joey's dad and beside Chain is Pipes, who's also been in the club as long as our dads. Next to them is Dornan, Joey, then Dusty, Smokey, Ace, Drag, Boo-Boo, and then Phil brings the circle back to Rocket. There's several members out on runs, but the club's made up of about one hundred and fifty guys. Thirty located here in Plantain, while the rest live within the surrounding cities.

"Okay so the matter of today's meeting is the business in Briscoe, we've had some intel from Chilly that Demons Fire MC got wind of our plans, and want a piece of the action. They want to actually buy the supplies, so we need to get there first. Which means we need to move our plan to tomorrow night," Sven announces.

There are assorted nods and grunts around the table, the air feeling uneasy. Everyone knows we're pushing these plans way ahead of schedule, and anytime we rush a job, it only inflates the tension.

"You sure we got enough info ready for that?" Chain asks.

"We know the comings and goings, what's inside, what we need. Sitting on them another month or so, isn't gonna do nothin'. Except give them time to sell to someone," Dornan answers.

Most of us nod, knowing what he's saying is true.

"V, you got the set up to get in?" Sven asks me.

"Yeah, just simple locks and the security isn't anything spectacular," I answer.

Sven looks around the room, before asking, "All in agreement for tomorrow?" he barks.

"Aye's." Go around the table.

"What's going on with the new club?" Sven questions.

"Rocket and I are going out to Woodside to meet with the builder's in a few days," I reply.

"Good, anyone have anything they need to air?" Sven asks.

When no one replies, he opens his hands to signal that gathering is over. I stand to leave and I'm almost out the door, when Sven calls after me. I stop just as Dornan looks back, and I nod for him to go ahead, which he reluctantly does after a moment. I turn to face Sven who's still sitting at the head of the table, rising as I walk closer.

"You're going out to Palm Lake after Woodside," he orders.

"Am I?"

"Need you to go out there," he repeats softening his tone.

Sometimes it freaks me out how much Sven and Dornan look alike, as if I'm looking at a younger version of Sven, and an older version of Dornan.

"To tell him about Briscoe?" I ask, confused.

"No. Not club matters, to visit."

I rub a hand over my eyebrows in aggravation, not wanting to have this conversation again. Sven's always asking me to go visit my dad. I'm not sure if Sven thinks it's something I need, or he's annoyed with the amount of times my dad begs him to get me there on his every visit.

"If it's not about the club, we don't have anything to meet about," I shrug, my voice not convincing.

But Sven's wearing me down on the subject. And honestly the more I kick the idea around, and the more time that passes, I know it's something I'm going to do eventually.

"He's your dad Maven."

"It's complicated. I'm not ready yet," I start.

"It's been five years V, how much time do you need? He really wants to see you." He pauses and takes my hand in his large rough one. "I know it's hard, but ignoring that he exists isn't good for you, or him."

Good for him? He's the one who put himself where he is. There's no point in arguing and no matter how much of a fight I put up, I know it's time I see him. I need to stop being an asshole, and come to terms with the fact that my only living parent will be behind bars for the rest of his life. I nod slightly, then turn, and Sven allows my hand to slip free as I walk out of the room.

What I just sat in on here, was a meeting of Warrior of the Gods MC, MC as in Motorcycle Club. The reason I sit in the Vice President's seat is because my dad, Owen Lofgren who was the W.G.'s V.P., is currently serving a life sentence in prison. As a deal he worked out with Sven to keep the Lofgren bloodline in the club, I'm to sit in for my Dad until Sven appoints a new V.P., which doesn't seem to be something high on Sven's to-do list. My dad's been gone for five years now, and I'm beginning to think him and Sven enjoy this slow torture they're causing on my life. As a woman, I'm not supposed to be part of the club, I'm not supposed to ride, or be a part of the things I do. Working on the business part of the club is what I'd planned to do, but no. Unfortunately for me, I'm really good at breaking into places. I'm also really good at hacking into computers. Sure, it was fun when I was a kid. Dornan, Joey, and I used to fuck around and steal shit, getting popped by the cops wasn't anything but a minor offense. But this wasn't minor anymore, these were guns we were about to steal, to rob very bad people who could come after us and kill us. My grandfather Ivan Lofgren, whose house I live in now, started this club back in the 1950's. He left the service and felt like the bond of brotherhood he loved in the army, was something he was missing in his now civilian life. So he started a club with likeminded men. Of course the other founding members were Dornan's and Joey's grandfathers, so this shit is in our blood.

"V."

Dornan's voice hits me as I exit the clubhouse with the intention to head back to my office. I stop and wait for him to come up behind me, his hand pressing on the small of my back and urging me to walk with him.

"Your dad?" he asks.

There's no need to reply, since this is usually what Sven speaks to me privately about. I don't want this life and my dad knows it, but does he care? No. He also doesn't care that he's involving me in serious illegal activities with consequences that can lead me to where he is, prison, or be killed. And for what? Bloodlines and history? But I love him, I don't understand his sacrifice to miss out on my life for the club, but I'm stubbornly dealing.

We walk in silence as Dornan leads me towards the back of the clubhouse, I know where we're going, and let him guide me there. Stopping at one of the huge oak trees that lines the perimeter of the compound, and I begin to climb up to the tree house we'd built as children. Over the years we've kept up the condition of the decent sized fort, so kids of members can still play up here during family parties. I sit with my knees bent and legs folded, Dornan digs in his pocket, his tattooed forearms flexing with the action before sitting and mocking my position. My eyes scan above the shop's rooftop and clubhouse. Being up here always makes me feel childlike again, stepping out of reality for a moment. When things got loud at the club or shit was a little too tense, we'd always come up here as kids. Dornan lights a joint and the smoke blows into my face along with the soft breeze, he hits it a few times before passing it to me. I let the smoke fill my lungs as I close my eyes for a moment, taking in the heat of the sun muted through the leaves in the trees.

"Mom texted me you're coming Sunday."

I nod, handing him back the joint.

"Still pissed about Brayden? I mean, that's why you haven't come back, right?"

There's a pang in my chest at the mention of his name, but I tamper it down and look over at Dornan, his eyes straight ahead as he looks outward. His hair's so short sometimes it seems that he cut it bald, but the sunshine reminds me there's a half-inch of blond there. I watch his beautiful profile as he smokes, his strong chiseled jaw covered in short stubble, his full lips curving around the joint, his eyes narrowed to block the brightness of the sun as he looks out towards the property.

"A little," I answer softly.

He lets out a small laugh, shaking his head.

"Fucking dumb asshole," he mumbles.

"I'm the dumb asshole who believed him," I reply.

His clear blue eyes cut over to mine, hardening with a look of annoyance at my comment.

"I mean, who knew he wouldn't leave her," I add.

Brayden is my one and only heartbreak. Brayden's dad is the President of The Children of the Reaper MC, that club and our club team up occasionally. Years ago, when his dad would go out on runs or come to Plantain for business, he'd bring Brayden. Every time he came for a visit we'd hang out, the older we got the more we hung out just the two of us. Eventually, I lost my virginity to him in one of the nasty vacant apartments at the clubhouse on a dirty mattress. Even then, I should've known that I meant nothing to him. But in my young teenage mind, I ignored the alarm bells that clearly alerted me to the fact that I was a fuck buddy, just a piece of ass for when he came to town.

He was dreamy to me, older, dangerous, from a big city across the country, something different. I believed the bullshit he told me, and he captured my heart. I wanted to give my everything to him, my devotion and faithfulness. Even though I knew he was hooking up with other girls when he wasn't with me, and sadly I allowed it to be okay in my head. We were young and he was travelling with a biker club, I didn't expect too much from the situation. But every time we had sex, it left me wanting. Not for more sex, because honestly I didn't see what the big deal was. There were no earth shattering orgasms, nothing like how I feel when I got myself off. No, it left me wanting aftercare, cuddling and lingering kisses. That flutter of anticipation when we'd see each other again, that desire for him to touch me. None of that was there with him. Regardless, he promised me things, a life with him. I would listen to plans he'd imagine as we'd talk on the phone at night, like us marrying someday. And I admit those things sounded nice, the thought of a future with someone was a settling feeling. I dreaded and had zero desire to be an old lady to someone in an MC, but always planned to work at the shop and marry a civilian. Distancing my personal life from the club as much as possible.

Three years into our 'relationship,' Brayden told me he was getting married, that he'd knocked some girl up from his neighborhood, and it was the 'right thing to do.' It broke my heart, as much as I tried to tell myself that what we had was casual and that I hadn't developed feelings for the guy, I had fallen in love with the idea of us. Of course the news of his upcoming nuptials and eventual marriage, didn't stop us from hooking up every time we got together. I knew it was wrong, but I believed the words he said when he told me he just felt bad for her, and he was all she had. I also believed him when he said once their son got older, and they were more financially set, that he'd leave her and come for me.

Years later I still waited, and like the dumbass I was, I didn't sleep with anyone else, wanting to remain faithful to Brayden. Then one Sunday a few weeks ago, I headed over to Sven's and Missy's for dinner and saw Brayden there, with his wife and kids. He never told me he had more than one baby with her, the reality hit me as I stood there in the dining room just staring wide eyed at his family. His wife was blonde and beautiful, and I could see the love they had for one another, he was using me the whole time and I believed all his lies. Since I didn't want to freak out in front of everyone, I fled for the bathroom. A few minutes later he entered and informed me he wasn't leaving his wife, and never would. That he was sorry and didn't mean to hurt me, but it didn't mean we couldn't still hook up and continue on like nothing had changed. I should have been relieved, happy I wouldn't be an old lady. Instead, I punched him in the balls and left, not returning to Sunday dinner since then. The embarrassment of being taken advantage of, my trust obliterated, I'd never felt so alone in my life. There was a sinking feeling that I would never be cherished, or a man's number one and I was coming to terms with that. I would rather be alone and never know love, than live in a delusion of love and lies.

"I just feel stupid," I mumble.

"Don't. When you want something bad enough in life you convince yourself that it will happen, if you're patient it will work out. Hindsight and all that shit. But maybe the better thing is that it didn't work out. Now you won't let another ass clown string you along like that," Dornan tells me.

I watch as my friend continues to smoke. He always got me, understood how my brain worked, and I love him for that.

"Not that I would've been any better, but it pisses me off the shit he did to you."

I give him a soft smile, wondering to myself sometimes what Dornan and I would be like as a couple. Then I always remind myself that for one, I can't ever be an old lady. Another thing, Dornan's too promiscuous, and I will never again be another disposable vagina. As gorgeous and sweet as he can be, Dornan's never had a girlfriend. I wondered why that was, assuming it's because he just doesn't want one, but who knows.

"You wouldn't have made me promises."

I smile while nudging my elbow into his, causing him to give me a smile. He wraps his arm around my neck, pulling our sides together. Breathing him in, he always smells so good, a mix of cologne, leather, and just him. Whatever the combination is, it always makes me a little hot.

"You're okay though, right? I mean, you realize you deserve better than that?"

"Yeah, it bothers me that I was so blind but, I think I know better now. Like when someone wants to be with me, I won't fall for the bullshit. So maybe it's better I went through all that so I will recognize a good man when he comes my way."

Dornan's arm squeezes me a little tighter, his rough fingertips caress my bare arm before clearing his throat.

"V, I want to talk to you about something-" he begins, before a giant bee flies past my nose.

"Oh my God!"

I shriek and begin waving my arms around while darting for the ladder, all the while Dornan's deep laughter rumbles behind me. My feet hit the ground, as I continue to flail my arms like a lunatic, then Dornan grabs my wrists.

"I think you're safe," he chuckles.

His words don't stop me from glancing around, or steadying my breathing. He continues to smile at me and hold my hands, his eyes glinting with humor.

"Stop laughing at me, asshole."

I snort and pull my hands away, smacking his shoulder, further causing him to laugh. We head back towards the clubhouse in silence, before remembering he was saying something before we were interrupted.

"What were you going to say back there?" I ask a few feet from my office.

He looks around, the parking lot's crowded with the guys and loud with laughter, along with bike engines revving. He shakes his head before giving me a long look.

"Later, we can talk later," he says and I don't like that he's holding back, important or not.

"Okay," I reluctantly reply.

"Later, V."

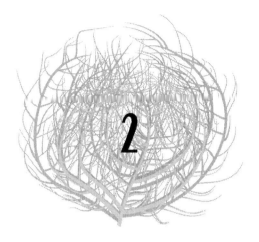

2

The next morning, I ride my bike into work. I own a fully restored 1978 Harley that Dornan and Joey fixed up for my eighteenth birthday. Bagheera stayed home much to his disappointment, but I promised him an extra-long run the next morning and that seemed to appease him. The whole day everyone lays pretty low. It's always like this the day of a job. Nerves and also running over every possible scenario of what can happen and go wrong. Needless to say, I hate the day of a job. So, I immerse myself in getting all my billing for the shop done. I also clean out my desk drawers just to keep my hands busy, and although distracting, it doesn't calm my nerves.

Finally, at ten p.m., everyone meets out in the parking lot and starts up their bikes. The whole club's going to Blades Tavern, a biker bar on the outer edge of Plantain. The point is to be seen, that anyone who passes by the bar tonight knows that the Warrior of the Gods are there, including the cops. All the other club members who live in the surrounding cities are also coming, making a huge crowd in the small establishment. We jam in and in no time, things get loud and rowdy. The jukebox blares Eddie Money's- "Shakin," as the beers begin to flow and the pool and dart games start. The Tavern's never been updated since it was built, so it looks like your typical hole in the wall dive bar circa 1970's.

An hour into the festivities, Dornan taps my shoulder, nodding at Joey who I'm having a conversation with by the back door. The idea is for the ones who are going on the run to be seen but fade into the crowd, not really conversing with anyone so no one can be certain that we left.

Joey and I casually slip out the back door and head for the black van parked in the back of the lot, hidden by trees and the bar's dumpsters. This is one of those vans that only has a driver and passenger seat, the back of the van empty, which allows us room to prepare. Sliding open the door, we grab our bags and start putting on the clothes we all wear on a job. Black pants, the same black hoodie, black beanie, black gloves and black boots that we all wear in the same size, including me. Even though I have to pack the front of my boots with socks. We could never be too careful that when the scene was examined the next day, that they'd see a small shoe print in the dirt and finger us for the job. I also wear oversized clothes, all hindering me slightly. But after doing this for years now, I know how to work with what I have. Dornan, Smokey, Drag, and Rocket all gather in the van and change their clothes.

Rocket begins to drive on our forty-minute trip, as the rest of us sit in the back and get our gear together. I braid my hair and either tuck it under my beanie or down inside the back of my sweatshirt, never wanting to look any different than the guys. Dornan grabs a pile of zip ties and passes a handful to each of us. Smokey checks the clip of his nine mm, as I finger the small metal implements in a black baggy. Making sure everything I need is there, before fishing out my laptop and firing it up. I'm not able to tap into the building's security until we get within a mile of it, finally getting the signal that I'm logged in before Rocket says, "Three minutes."

I open several screens and key in the code I hacked last week, signing in with no resistance. Setting the timer for the closed circuit TV's, security monitors, floodlights, alarms, and automatic locks to disarm in five minutes for a duration of fifteen minutes. This is all a guessing game, never knowing if someone in an outside building is hooked up to the C.C.T.V.'s and could send out the word that they're being robbed.

"Chilly says four in the warehouse and two on patrol," Dornan says, slipping his cell back into his pocket.

Chilly's like our phantom, he always does surveillance and is like a ghost, I've only actually seen him less than a handful of times. Shutting my laptop, all eyes are on me. I nod before we all take our skull bandanas and pull them over our faces, leaving only our eyes visible. Rocket parks the van along the back of the building on an industrial street, alongside some decoy vehicles we parked there earlier. One by one we exit the van, and like stealth warriors run in silence to the fence. Drag takes out the cutters from his jacket, and begins making a slit in the fence until it's large enough to squeeze through. We all follow one at a time and even in huge clunky boots, we run with minimal noise. Tucking up alongside a building, as we wait to get our bearings on the people inside. Smokey lays down on his stomach, lifting night vision goggles to his face as he peers around the corner.

"One on patrol at twelve o'clock," he whispers.

My heart beats so loud in my ears, I need to control my breathing from running to focus on Smokey and his directions.

"Other patrol also at twelve o'clock now, talking."

Waiting another minute before he signals for us to move. Without words, we split into two groups. I'm between Dornan and Joey as we head for the door and stay close to the building, while Drag and Smokey scuttle to the other side of an adjacent building, coming up opposite of us. The two patrol men are standing by a door smoking, laughing, and acting like they aren't protecting millions of dollars worth of guns, completely oblivious to us only yards away.

"Did the power go out?" one says, finally noticing the area is bathed in darkness.

"Oh man, bulb must be blown out," the other comments.

Before he can finish his sentence, Dornan and Smokey move in, grabbing both men from behind in a choke hold. Bringing them down to the ground where Joey and Drag use the zip ties to hogtie them, and duct tape their mouths shut. Pulling my black bag from my hoodie pocket, I crouch down in front of the door. I use my sense of touch, since I can't see shit, and begin to pick the default locks. Even if you disable the electronic lock, there's a default lock on most doors for security in case of a power outage, or someone trying to break in. The two patrol guys are moaning and fighting their bindings, while my brothers stand waiting for me. But I remain focused on my task. Taking only eight seconds longer than planned to hear the lock click, pushing open the heavy door. We pile in and close the door, the warehouse dark. Thankfully our eyes have adjusted outside so we're able to start, removing the large black duffel bags we shoved into our sweatshirts. There are at least fifty crates in the middle of the warehouse, all having about two machine guns in each. With practiced precision, Joey and Drag go to each crate with a crowbar and open the lids, followed by Dornan and Smokey grabbing the guns and handing them to me to put into the bags, this part takes only three minutes. When the bags are full we heave them onto our shoulders and make for the door we entered from, all stopping as voices come from outside.

"What the fuck?"

I can hear the duct tape being ripped off one of the patrol guy's face, and he pants for air.

"Inside, there's five of them, they're getting the guns."

At that same moment, we all quietly set down the bags and reach for our pieces. Smokey and Joey carry hand guns, while Drag, Dornan, and I opt for knives. We needed to be as quiet as possible, there are legit businesses around and you never know who could hear something. The door-handle jiggles and we all move to either side of the door. With a loud thump it flies open from being kicked in, the door hitting the wall beside Dornan. The four men hold small flashlights, shining them down at the bags and with guns already drawn, and walk straight into us. In a flash there's sounds of flesh being punched, groans and scuffling. One guy grabs the hood of my sweatshirt and I elbow him in the throat, dropping him to his knees. I force him onto his stomach, connecting his hands and feet with zip ties. We manage to incapacitate them in two minutes, now we really have to get a move on. We run to the fence as best we can, carrying the bags weighted down with the guns, through the fence, and into the van. The job takes us an entire thirteen minutes, not bad, but we've done better.

Rocket drives in a leisurely manner as we pull off our black oversized clothing, and return to how we looked prior to leaving the bar. Parking in the back again, we all get out of the van casually, all melding back into the tavern unnoticed. It isn't until Missy comes up and is trying to pressure me into karaoke, that I'm able to breathe, to actually take in a deep breath. It was over, until the next job.

All of us that went on the run have the same conflict of feelings, the intense high of what we've just done, coupled with trying to calm the thrumming energy pulsating under your skin. This is always hard for me, some guys like Drag and Dornan try keeping that high, partying and fucking chicks into oblivion. While Smokey and Joey get quiet and usually leave for home within the hour of a job, probably fucking their wives into oblivion also. Since I have no one to fuck, a random hook up is never something I can talk myself into no matter how charged I am. I usually go home, grab Bagheera and we run. But tonight I decide to hang out for a bit, have a beer and watch some karaoke. Missy and Gwen plead drunkenly for me to go up there, usually we do an old Motown song by The Supremes or something by Stevie Nicks. Missy always steals the show while Gwen and I are fine with doing backup. But I repeatedly shake my head 'no,' until they finally leave me alone. I absentmindedly watch as the guys from the club who hadn't gone on the run get rowdy and carefree. And wonder if they know what we've done tonight, how we sacrificed ourselves to feed them and their families.

The thoughts halt when I see Dornan leaning over a big breasted blonde, he's always favored blondes. This one has the smallest pink tank top on I've ever seen, and wonder why she shops in the kid's department. Dornan's hands wrap around her waist as she nuzzles his neck. His hands are so manly, big, his veins defined all the way up his tattooed forearms. They remain on her hips as she speaks to him and he shakes his head once, not breaking conversation with Boo-Boo beside him. I wonder what she's saying and why he's denying her, and I can't stop watching them. He turns his head to say something, causing her to giggle, which I can barely hear over the man singing to "Hair of the

Dog," by Nazareth.

"Hey V," Drag says nudging my arm and moves to my side, stopping my voyeurism as I begin to look at anyone but Dornan. I take a sip from my beer, noticing Drag doesn't have a girl with him.

"What are you up to tonight?" Drag asks as he leans over and breathes into my ear.

"I'm gonna go home and go to bed, Rocket and I have that run in the morning."

"Need me to get you home?"

"No takers tonight?" I ask raising a brow, is he hitting on me?

"Oh there was, but I've had my eye on you girl."

I don't look at him, but can see he's smiling out of the corner of my eye. This is the first time Drag's ever come on to me, and I'm not sure how I feel about it. For a moment I think how foreign an experience it is to be wanted and desired, even if he's just fucking with me.

"Oh yeah?"

"Mhmm, You're hot, but seeing you work tonight, fuck, all I want to do is get my cock so far inside your hot little pussy that you can't even think."

I feel a heat rush up my throat as he moves closer, his hand grazing my ass. I know that most these men look at me as a 'brother,' but some don't. They joke with me about being hot or whatever, but when one of them actually hits on me, it only drives the point home that I'm a woman and not one of them. It makes me feel like a piece of ass, and thinking I'm part of the club is a joke. That they use me because I'm good at something and nothing more.

"Although tempting, I'm really tired and I don't have all night to get fucked by your amazing dick so...maybe some other time."

His large hand begins to knead my butt cheek, as his fingers glide over the seam on the ass of my jeans. I like it a little too much how good it feels, and how much it's turning me on. I don't want it to, but it's been so long since I've had sex. Maybe for once I can put aside my delusions and actually hook up with someone, not Drag, but a nameless, faceless someone.

"Promise?" he purrs into my ear.

A tattooed hand grabs my arm and yanks me away, startling me as Smokey pulls me against his massive body. Flinging his arm over my shoulders, and leading me towards the door. I'm embarrassed for a moment that he will see my blushed cheeks or feel my racing heart.

"Give it a rest Drag," Smokey says.

I turn to wave goodbye to Missy and Gwen, and notice Dornan staring at me. A look in his eyes I've only seen a few times, it's the look he gets when he's about to hurt someone. His eyes move past me and towards Drag, Dornan's protective, but I don't see why this would make him so upset, he's seen men come onto me way harder than this. Whatever it is, I don't think about it too long, Dornan always gets my thoughts twisted and jumbled so I try to not think about him. Sure enough when I get home, Bagheera's chomping at the bit to go for a run. So we do, six miles. I also get myself off in the shower, imagining rough hands spreading my pussy lips. Dornan's blue eyes looking up at me, before burying his face between my legs.

3

The next day I dress in black skinny jeans, a thin gray cotton tee, my boots that lace up to my knees and of course my MC leather cut, which I fold inside my saddlebag. I'm able to get a little work done before Rocket and I have to go meet the builder, Smokey is also coming along. When we leave to head out, none of the other guys are at the shop yet, because I assume they all stayed at the tavern til the wee hours of the morning. The ride isn't long, but just long enough to enjoy. Nothing beats riding your bike on long stretches of desert. It's best when you're with a group, when we all ride out as a club, there's power in a gang that just makes you feel badass. As we approach the city outskirts, we slow and pull into a large open area, surrounded by nothing but open land. Two men and two pickup trucks sit waiting for us, I've been in contact with the contractor's Justice and Dean for weeks over the phone, but have yet to meet them in person. Because I'm in charge of the club finances and Rocket is somewhat of a businessman, we always take care of the club's business ventures. Smokey's simply here as muscle and because he has nothing better to do this morning.

RUNNING WITH THE DEVIL

We shut our bikes off and look around at the open stretch of land we've already purchased, the two men approaching us. Before I can even remove my helmet, I notice one is rather attractive. He's tall and built, around my age, with a set of beautiful dark brown eyes and a smile that gets my tummy a little fluttery. Reaching his hand out, he says, "Maven, nice to finally meet you, I'm Justice, this is Dean."

I take his hand and nod over towards my brothers.

"This is Pete and Ken."

The men shake hands and we wander over to one of the trucks. Justice, who's got a bit of a Southern accent, does most of the talking. He lays out the blueprints for the club on the open bed of his truck, and explains them in detail. I'd given specific things we wanted in the building, and he shows me everything I asked for. I'm pleased to see how well the plans came out, and everything looks good for this new place.

I can't help but notice Justice continuing to look at me, even when we aren't talking. When he's talking to Rocket, his eyes remain on me. The way he looks at me, causes a pull low in my belly. But I keep my face blank, my movements measured to not let him know that he's having an effect on me. I seriously need to get laid, Justice is hot, but so not my type. Did I have a type? Usually, it's the bad boy, but a lot of good that's done me in the past. Maybe I should switch it up a bit, take a walk on the civilian side. We review the plans for about an hour, and I tell Justice I'll relay the blueprints to the owner, and get back with him. He touches my forearm to stop me.

"Are you seeing anyone?"

The question leaves me blinking several times, and I'm glad to have my sunglasses on. The fact that he's asked me this in front of two huge tattooed guys, tells me he has some balls.

"I'm sorry?" I reply like an idiot.

Smokey chuckles slightly, but stands steadfast by my side, not giving us a moment of privacy.

"I'd like to take you out sometime and I assume a beautiful woman like you would be seeing someone. I realize this isn't maybe the right way to go about it during a business meeting but, what do you say?" he says this in a cool, calm but not cocky way. I think I admire that.

"Um...let me think about it, I have your number," I smile tightly since I'm absolutely shocked while mildly embarrassed.

"I'll call you tomorrow," he replies bluntly.

Wow, so much for letting me think about it. Justice is pushy, but I can't tell if it's just from him usually getting what he wants, or he just *really* wants to take me out. Rocket, Smokey, and I stand by our bikes and watch as Justice and Dean pull away in their trucks.

"I want to head to Beaver Falls," Rocket announces, pulling his MC vest from his saddlebag. I let out a sigh, thankful they aren't going to razz me about Justice.

"I think I'm gonna head up to Palm Lake before heading back."

They both look at me for a minute.

"I'll come with you," Smokey says. "Then we can backtrack and come get you before heading home," he adds to Rocket.

"Sounds good brother," Rocket extends his fist for Smokey to pound.

He fires up his bike and heads off towards the city, heading in the opposite direction. Nerves start to flutter in my belly, but I've already made the decision to go visit my dad, so I have to stick to it.

"You good with this V?" Smokey asks.

"Yes," I confirm, while putting my helmet on. Hopefully he didn't hear the nervousness in my voice just then, and doesn't seem to as he fires up his bike and waits for me.

Palm Lake is a fifteen-minute ride from where we are, but it seems like two seconds and we're outside the prison. But thankfully since we came for an unannounced visit, it takes a bit for us to get access to go in, and allows me some time to collect myself. As we wait, I only get more anxious, doubting the reason why I'm here. I then remember that Dornan texted me when we were meeting with the builders, and I'm about to reply when my name's called by a guard. Slipping my phone back into my pocket, I leave Smokey in the waiting area and follow one of the officers down a long hallway, to a room marked 'Visitor's Access.'

I've been sitting in a shitty plastic chair waiting for almost ten minutes, I'm the only one on either side of the room, in front of a plastic partition that separates the inmates from the visitors. A loud buzz sounds on the inmate side startles me, moments later, my dad comes into view, escorted through a steel barred door by two officers. He's wearing a yellow prison jumpsuit, looking rougher and leaner than when I last saw him years ago. Thanks to our Norwegian heritage, he looks like what you picture a Viking to be. He has long blond hair with streaks of white and grey throughout it, which he wears in a long braid down his back. His dark brown eyes study me through his black framed reading glasses, as the guards undo his handcuffs, securing a chain around his ankle to the chair. I wait until they move back towards the door, before reaching for the phone receiver. I lean forward towards the metal ledge, resting my elbows on the hard surface in front of me, and Dad mimics my movements.

"Hey baby," he says in a rough voice.

"Hi."

My eyes dart around at everything but him, and I don't know why I'm fighting the pull he has over me, of course he remains silent until my hazel eyes meet his.

"I'm so, so fucking happy you're here."

"We were close by, so…" I trail off.

"I've called a few times-"

"I know," I stop him.

"You can hate me baby, it's okay, but I'm still your dad."

I haven't been to visit him at all since he got put in here, not even when he was in lock-up awaiting trial. The only day I went to court was the day he was sentenced. I despise that I love him and would do anything for him, while he permanently removed himself from my everyday life. The feelings brought on by anything to do with my dad over the last few years is another example of how I gave someone all of me, only to be thrown aside as if I was nothing to them. There's part of what Brayden did to me that's reminiscent to those fears and inadequacies of not being important enough to stick around for. Although, obviously what my dad did was worse, abandoning me when he knew I had no family but him.

"I don't hate you Dad, I just have resentment. There's a pain in me that-" I let out a long breath. "I just, I have a problem with the fact that you were my only parent, you were all I had and you took the fall for some club shit-"

"Don't. The club is what has kept food in your belly and clothes on your back your entire life so don't fucking knock it. Yes, I know I fucked up...but baby, as a man, I did what I had to do."

"Stop. Did you even think about me? About leaving me? Not only behind but the responsibility you left on me, things I don't want, did you? A man doesn't abandon his child when he's her only parent."

"I knew the club would take care of you, that's our family."

"Fuck that. I need you, *you* Dad...and you're here and I'm left with the bullshit."

I close my eyes for a long second, opening them to see my dad's eyes regarding me wearily, before looking over his shoulder at the guards posted by the door.

"I'm sorry baby, I think about you every day...I do. I'm sorry I put you where you don't want to be, but you're doing a hell of a job, better than I ever did. I'm proud of you, the woman you've become all without a mom and I know that has something to do with me, and the club, and Missy and Gwen. If it weren't for the club you wouldn't have them...I know it's hard right now, but I think I have a good chance at a new deal I'm working on, I just need you to stick it out a little longer baby."

All the fight leaves me, at hearing he's proud. It's a start, but nowhere near concluded. It will take time to heal the wounds that still feel too fresh to stitch closed forever. Part of me knows that even though he'll be in here forever, he's somewhere. I can still talk to him and he'll be here for me, not completely gone like my mom. I know I can easily compare what my mom did to what my dad's done, but I can't give a shit about someone I never knew, or someone who never wanted to know me. I can't erase the years and bond I share with my dad, and besides, I'm a grown woman now, not a dependent four-year old. I don't know when the hell I'll ever be back here, so I decide to put my unresolved feelings aside for now, and visit with my dad.

"I'm almost done with the house," I smile.

He gives me a wide grin and nods his head. "I bet it looks amazing, you can send me photos if you want, in a letter," he suggests. "I'd love to see it."

We talk a little bit about the shop, and Bagheera. I fill him in on all the things I've done to the house he grew up in, and about my dad's other baby, his bike. Which I take out on occasion to keep her running.

"Four minutes," the guard announces.

My dad pushes his glasses down his nose and tips his head, pinning me with his eyes and narrowing them slightly before saying.

"So, Jane is having her baby in a month or so right?"

This is code for club business, what he's really asking is,

The Briscoe deal's going down in a month.

"She delivered early, this week."

"Ah," Dad runs a hand over his chin, stroking his gray goatee repeatedly.

"What's that, two for her now?"

That's a 20k gain.

"No, number four...she keeps poppin' em out."

40k gain.

"Is her old man around?"

Are we all set to turn around and sell them.

"Yeah, he's a good guy, wants to make number five and six as soon as possible."

The next job, they're offering 50-60k, in negotiations.

"Good. Fucking great," he nods and gives me a small smile.

I smile back and clear my throat.

"Dad, call me. I'll answer," I say softly.

His eyes glitter slightly as they crinkle at the corners, a smile spreading over his lips.

"Thanks for coming baby, I love you."

"I love you Dad-"

"Maven," he stops me.

His eyes serious as he glances back at the guard, before cutting his eyes back to me and leaning forward. His voice dropping when he says, "Someone might come to talk to you, I don't know how they'll contact you, but-" he stops, his eyes searching mine as he struggles for words, and I shake my head because I don't understand.

"Come on inmate, time's up," the guard announces as the two walk over and place a hand on either of his shoulders.

"Dad?"

"I've got it, just don't talk, I got this."

The last part is said through the glass, muffled by the thick barrier, as the guards remove the phone from his hand. I mouth 'I love you' and he waves as his wrists are being cuffed at his waist. His words keep replaying in my head, and I have no idea what he's trying to tell me. Or is it code? My brain still trying to download the information, even as Smokey and I exit the prison. Without a word, he takes my hand and gives a small squeeze as we walk to our bikes, but says nothing.

"Got a text from Rocket, says there's another MC at the bar and we gotta be cautious, he's gonna wait inside for us. Says if he heads out alone, there's no way he's not getting jumped."

We fire up our bikes and I follow behind as Smokey leads the way to Beaver Falls, which is twenty minutes in the opposite direction and into the city of Cordelia. When other MC's collide, there's usually a lot of shit talking, maybe some rumbling. But unless you have beef, most are cool with tolerable distance. I know Rocket wouldn't go to an MC bar, so this means that the local club is at a public bar and doesn't like a lone biker there. Because this is a civilian bar, there isn't much the MC can do to that biker, unless they want the local law enforcement to get involved. Which leaves the option for that club to wait until the biker leaves before starting shit. Even if it's just three of us, we have a better chance of getting out of there unscathed than Rocket does alone.

It's early evening when we pull up and the bar parking lot's packed, including five bikes right beside the front door, not including Rocket's. Smokey and I say nothing as we enter the dimly lit establishment. Immediately I find Rocket perched with his back to the door on a bar stool, the white Warrior of the Gods MC lettering and illustration sticking out to us on his leather back. I glance out of the corner of my eye to survey the patrons, most look like civilians and don't seem put off by our presence. The group of bikers are in the left corner, near the pool tables and watching us. Smokey claps a hand over Rocket's shoulder, expelling a puff of cigarette smoke from Rocket with the action. Both Smokey and I opt to stand on either side of him.

"You just always have to get into trouble brother," Smokey smiles.

"Hey, isn't that what being an outlaw is about?" Rocket replies dryly.

All three of us face the bar, casually resting our elbows on the polished wood. I hear the sound of heavy boots over 'Back in Black'- by AC/DC coming from the jukebox, as the bikers approach. There's a mirrored back splash behind the bar, where I get a better look at the burly men, your typical looking middle aged bikers.

"We don't allow no women with leathers on in here," one says directly behind me.

I stare at him in the mirror, I'm not short by any means, but this guy's at least six inches taller than me. He's studying the back of my cut, the metallic Scandinavian crest of a horse that's our mascot, blazes in silver and white patchwork.

"Just getting our brother and leaving," I reply, not looking at him.

I look over at Rocket who's casually drinking beer from a mug, letting his cigarette burn in between his fingers.

"Let's go," I order under my breath in his direction.

Rocket smiles with a chuckle, Smokey turning to face Rocket, showing the rest of the bikers his profile.

"It's time to get back brother."

Rocket continues to act as if we have all the time in the world, ignoring the tension mounting with every sip of that fucking beer. The man behind me suddenly grabs my bicep and squeezes, causing my jaw to tighten in reflex to not show that it hurts like a son-of-a-bitch.

"I said we don't allow bitches in here," he growls in my ear.

If a civilian calls me a bitch, it doesn't bother me. But bitch in our world has a whole other set of meanings. Bitches sit on the backs of bikes, bitches get fucked by whoever and whenever, bitches are nothing, bitches are trash, bitches are weak. I, am not weak. Smokey shakes his head and lets out a low whistle, Rocket closing his eyes as he laughs.

"Don't touch me," I hiss, still watching him in the mirror.

My voice lowered, but the biker hears me. He lets out a bark of a laugh, as his hand grows tighter around my upper arm.

"I said, bitch get the fuck out," his voice raising and drawing the attention of anyone who isn't already watching us.

Before he finishes his sentence, I pivot my body and with my other hand, reach across him and wrap my palm at the base of his neck, slamming his face down into the bar. Instantly blood gushes from his nose as he drops to his knees, effectively letting go of me. There are gasps and 'oh my Gods' from the patrons, and I look down to see the biker's eyes blinking in a daze, as he tries to focus on something. I turn to face his crew standing there, their eyes wide as they look down at their brother.

"Do we have a problem?" I ask.

None of them say a word, but one shakes his head slightly in the negative. Rocket stands, throwing cash onto the bar before smiling as he steps over the biker as he walks out. I follow while Smokey trails behind, a grin about the size of the Mississippi River covering his face, as he snaps a picture of the injured biker on the floor with his cellphone. Rocket stands in the parking lot laughing at me, as I walk past with a scowl and punch him in the gut. Not a full force hit, but enough to let him know I'm not happy. His hands cover the area immediately, but he continues to laugh.

"I'm glad I could entertain you," I growl.

"For real V, when you get all rough and shit, I store that away in my spank bank."

I make a gagging sound and mount my bike.

"You're fucking disgusting."

"That shit was some of your best work, I can't wait to show the guys," Smokey laughs.

"Come on V, I figured you needed that after seeing your pops. How is that old bastard anyway?" Rocket asks.

"Good, he said you'd fit right in, there's always someone needing their cock sucked."

Smokey let out the biggest belly laugh and swats Rocket's bicep.

"You love me," Rocket grins and I shake my head as a smile spreads over my lips.

It's dark out when we drive into the club lot, the garage doors are still open and not that anyone's still working, but the lights are on. There are clusters of men standing around both the shop area and the clubhouse entrances. Parking my bike near the shop, I enter through the front door and head to my office. Peeing and brushing my long hair free from its braid, then washing the thin film of dirt off my face from riding in the desert. Stopping at my mini fridge for a bottle of water, I go back to my bike to grab the blueprints, and head to the clubhouse. I nod 'hello's' as I hear my name being called from different directions. I roll my eyes as I enter the clubhouse to see Smokey holding out his phone, showing off the picture from the bar as he animatedly retells the story. Well, his version of the story.

"V." I hear Joey from behind me, stopping me as I whirl around with raised eyebrows to see the mountain of a man jogging up to me.

"Hey, are you busy tomorrow?"

"No, I'm not doing anything, what's up?"

"Would you be able to watch the girls? I know it's last minute but you know they were all sick last week and Katie's about to rip her hair out. Just a few hours, I want to take her out, we can even do it during the day," he offers.

"Just drop them off tomorrow whenever, they can stay overnight and you can take them after Sunday dinner."

Joey's eyes widen, before a huge grin spreads over his face.

"You know I love you right? Katie is gonna flip."

He smiles and wraps me into a hug, lifting my feet off the ground. Joey's the sweetest guy ever and I love both him and Katie. So it makes me happy to help them out, and it's easy watching the girls so I don't mind keeping them overnight. When he sets me down, I see Dornan now being told the story and shown the picture by Smokey. He's looking at me and I know exactly what that look means and why I'm receiving it, the annoyance he has with me is practically radiating off him.

"Let me go call her, see you in a minute."

As Joey passes me I watch Dornan disappear into the kitchen, feeling my chest hurt a little and know I have to remedy this. Even though I deserve the attitude for not returning his text, it still bothers me when he's unhappy with me. We always worry about each other, especially when we don't go on a run with the other, so not communicating is a dick move. When I push through the double swinging doors, the room's bathed in darkness aside from the under cabinet lights. He's standing by the sink, hands pressed on the counter, head bowed, the muscles in his back tensing under his white shirt. He's so muscular that I can see them bulging, even in the dim light.

Setting down the rolled up building blueprints and my water on the island, I walk up behind him. Hesitating for a moment before wrapping my arms around his waist, resting my cheek between his shoulder blades. His skin jumps slightly at my touch, then softens underneath me. He smells so good and I rub my cheek over his shirt, hoping it will transfer onto my skin. He lets out a long sigh before placing an arm over mine, his palm over my hand, his fingers slipping in between mine. The action causes my heart to flutter, and heat my flesh.

"I went to see my dad," I speak in a whisper, lifting my head.

His fingers tighten as his arm presses harder, lifting his head and turning it to show me I have his attention.

"We were close by and I knew I'd beat myself up if I didn't. He looked good, seemed good. We talked a little about, ya know everything...it's a start I guess."

"How do you feel?"

"I feel a little better, yeah."

He turns in my arms, and wraps his arms over my shoulders. Pulling me closer as he plants a kiss on the top of my head, resting my head once more against his strong body. I close my eyes and hug him just as fiercely, letting his strong form cocoon me.

Our bodies press together, lining up and fitting. Dornan always makes me feel feminine and small when he touches me like this, intimately, well, intimate to me. Even though I definitely look like a woman, sometimes the things I do, i.e. the bar incident earlier, make me feel masculine and too strong. I'm tall for a girl, almost 5'9". I'm slender and toned, but still curvy. With large breasts and an ass that I assume I inherited from my mom.

Dornan runs a hand over my hair and continues to pet me, both of us silent. It takes me a minute to feel the press of something against my stomach, another second to register it's his erection. The urge to reach down and cup him is overwhelming, to feel him like this, and I'm instantly feeling it between my legs. Before I can think about it, my body instinctively presses closer. My pelvis rubbing against him, causing him to inhale a quick breath. The feel of him mixed with the smell of him, his strong hands caressing me, is a heady combination. My breathing picks up, my breasts push against his rib cage, his heart thundering beneath my ear. His hand stops at the small of my back and tightens, as he tugs my hips even closer, making sure I feel his hardness. Slowly, I lift my head and stare at his chest. As his hands slide up my back, tangling in my hair to cradle my head, my eyes meeting his. Normally they're a shade of crystal clear blue, but now they appear almost black with the intensity, the pupils dilated as he watches me. My palms run up his stomach, bumping along the muscles that line his torso, to rest on his large pecs. My index finger absently finds the pendant he wears underneath his shirt, and knowing it's there causes my heart to pick up its pace, the blood to pump loudly in my ears. Never once do our eyes leave the other's, his hands tightening slightly in my hair as he looks down at my lips. Oh God I want him to kiss me, but I know by the look in his eyes and the way he's holding back, that he wants me to make that move. Like I've given up fighting the pull, stopped resisting, my head leans towards him as he bows his to meet me. We pause as his breath lashes across my lips, so close, so fucking close. My eyes drift shut while my lips part, waiting with held breath for the contact.

"Guys, meeting!" Joey yells from the other side of the door.

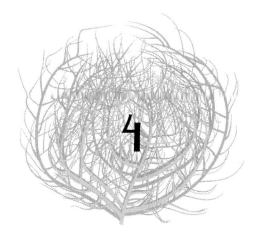

4

I pull away and put a hand to my throat, what...the...fuck?

"Maven," Dornan says huskily as I back away.

No seriously, what the fuck is happening? With shaky hands, I grab my papers and bolt for the door. Not looking back, I can't believe I almost kissed him. He's my friend, he's off limits. I know if I let myself go there, I'll be hurt, I'll be just another notch on his bedpost...right? We have too good of a friendship to fuck this up by letting feelings like this get in the way. Do I have feelings like that for him? I mean we were hugging and he got hard, doesn't that happen to a lot of guys whether they're attracted to a girl or not? In a still lust-filled fog, I make it to the room we hold gathering at. Sven's sitting in his President's place at the head of the table, as the other guys stand around various parts of the room. He's talking with Chain and I toss the prints down between them, interrupting their conversation, and two sets of eyes slowly look up at me.

"Here's the blueprints. Everything looks good," I rush the words out, my breathing still a little too rapid.

The two shoot one another a look at my odd behavior, before focusing on the papers. While I try to ignore that I was completely rude just then, and also that Dornan's entered the room behind me. Fuck I can feel him, his heat and energy, and I wonder if he's kicking himself also for what almost just happened.

"And we're on board for the deadline?" Sven asks.

"We have a rough timeline yes, mid-June. Once we finalize the drawings we can get a firmer date."

"Oh, speaking of date," Smokey says. "Fucking dude asked V out," he announces to the room.

"What dude?" Joey asks beside me.

I look over my shoulder to see, that once again I'm making Smokey laugh as he answers for me.

"Contractor. Had the balls to ask her in front of us."

I try to ignore the look on Dornan's face, his very pissed off looking face. Not sure if the date talk is causing it, or the fact that I almost let us make a huge mistake only moments ago.

"What did you tell him?" Dornan asks me, like we aren't in a room full of people. His tone hard but intimate, and I can't ignore the fact that the room falls quiet.

"I told him I'd think about it." I attempt to make my voice seem nonchalant, but it comes off a little raspy and strained.

Everyone knows Dornan and Joey are protective of me, and I hope no one notes the added tension between us during this exchange. After a long moment, Dornan clicks his tongue and looks away from me. So I return my attention to Sven, as if nothing weird just happened. We discuss more about the blueprints, while slowly the chatter amongst the guys resumes. Eventually, the pool games start, and I'm able to get out of there without Dornan noticing and get home.

***

Saturday, Joey and Katie drop off their three daughters, and Katie is nonstop thanking me for their night off. The girls ages range from eight to four, and although they demand all my attention, we have fun. We spend most our day playing dress up, then making dinner, and finally watching a movie before they all crash in my bed. By the time we get to Missy and Sven's Sunday evening however, I'm about over being a mom for the weekend. I'm more than happy when the girls take off as soon as we get there, meeting up with Smokey and Emily's kids in the backyard. Missy wraps me in a big hug when I enter the kitchen, and Emily gives me a one arm embrace as she holds her and Smokey's two-week old son Evan to her chest.

"You better gimme that baby," I order.

She smiles, kissing Evan on the cheek before passing over the sleeping bundle. He snuggles right in as I begin swaying back and forth, his warm little body giving me comfort. We chit chat as the kids play outside and the guys talk in the living room, watching some sporting event and drinking beer. There are about ten of us that always come to dinner on Sunday's, and since I see the guys on a daily basis, this is time for me to catch up with the women.

"Ugh that girl is on my last nerve. I swear, if I see her touch Smokey one more time, I'll break her face," Emily sighs, fixing the black hair knot on top of her head.

She's talking about some sweet bottom at the club, and both Missy and I laugh at her. Emily's a small woman, soft spoken and sweet as can be. So when she says shit like this, it's comical. Immediately, I feel Dornan enter the kitchen and my eyes meet his. He doesn't smile or show warmth in his eyes, just looks at Evan for a moment then back at me. Then he moves past us and towards his mom, kissing her cheek and exchanging hello's. My body engulfs in heat, although he's clearly mad at me. Rightly so, we did something dumb. And me being the one who always wants to act like things aren't a big deal, avoided his calls and texts all day yesterday and today. But we did need to talk, no matter how long I brushed it off. Having the girls over yesterday distracted me and I needed time to sort all this out, all the feelings and shit before Dornan and I have that talk. Katie and Joey arrive just before we all sit to eat, looking smiley and well-sexed. The table fills with chatter as the kids talk about things kids talk about, while the grown-ups laugh and joke. Dornan sits across from me, and I do everything in my power to avoid those blue eyes willing me to look up.

"A man called aunt V last night," Natasha, Katie and Joey's oldest daughter comments. The table gets a little quiet just as I feel everyone's eyes on me.

"Oh?" Katie asks excitedly with a smile.

"Who?" Joey asks in a stern tone.

I take a sip of my beer in an attempt to stall.

"No one," I shake my head, taking a massive forkful of mashed potatoes and shoving it into my mouth.

"Justin or something, what was his name Auntie?" Natasha asks.

"Justice?" Smokey questions, his eyes wide as that Cheshire Cat grin begins.

I look down at my plate, at the food I'm picking at with my fork.

"It was about the blueprints," I state, thinking that will shut it down.

"Nooo it wasn't," Natasha beams.

I shoot her a look with raised brows, then narrow my eyes to let her know I mean business, she just smiles and giggles in reaction.

"You got all flustered and we heard him asking you out."

Dornan's fork clatters onto his plate, as he sits back in his chair. The look on his face is like nothing he's ever directed at me before. He's mad as hell now, and I still don't understand why exactly.

"Well?" Katie asks.

"Did you say yes?" Emily adds, the two of them look like they're about to burst with anticipation for my answer.

While the women are looking at me with wide eyes, the guys...not so much.

"I told him I'd let him know," I reply quietly.

"Oh my God, is he hot?" Katie gushes.

"Ya know, I don't really want to talk about this right now." I look at my friend, giving her a tone of voice I hope she will interpret as; *this is really awkward for me to talk about in front of everyone.* Eventually, when I don't answer any of the questions, the topic of conversation changes. I can sense the tension pouring out of Dornan, but still I refuse to look at him.

After dinner the guys and I leave for the MC's owned topless bar. The building is two levels, upstairs is the titty club, while the downstairs is a dance club. The upstairs is packed, and I make my way through the stages for the dancers to the manager's office. We talk about how business's been and look through finances for the month, while also discussing his possible move over to the new club. When I go back out to the main floor, the party's in full swing and reminds me of a Motley Crue video. Scantily clad women hanging all over the guys under neon lights, while others perform on the stages for their dollar bills. I recognize the blonde sweet bottom who was trying to get Dornan's attention at the tavern the other night, sitting on his lap. Straddling him actually, and she's in a G-string...only in a G-string. Her breasts are pressed in his face, but again he isn't paying too much attention to her. She touches his chest and leans down to whisper in his ear, the urge to stomp over and yank the skank off him causes my vision to blaze red.

That's my cue to head downstairs to the civilian club, because I'm not going to torture myself by watching them. I don't want to think of what she's telling him or what his reaction will be. Halfway down the steps I realize that what is happening up there is probably for the best, he needs a distraction from thinking he wants me. I meet with the manager downstairs, looking over numbers and chatting a little, before deciding I need a drink and to dance. For a Sunday night, the club's packed and the music's pumping. It was my first decision as V.P. to turn the main floor of the building into a civilian club. We're the only dance club within forty miles, so it's a popular place with the younger crowd. I head to the bar and down a few shots of tequila in a row. I'm in a pair of white booty shorts, and a black halter-top. When we got to the club, I'd swapped out my boots for the pair of black strappy heels I usually keep in my saddle bag.

As the liquor begins to warm my blood, the dance floor seems much more appealing. So I make my way into the massive crowd of bodies, moving along to the music. A few songs in, and I'm feeling good. When Rhianna's- "Skin" comes on, the people dancing move together to the sexy song. Even though I have my mind open to maybe meeting someone tonight, I'm not drunk enough to allow just anyone to dance with me. So, I decide to maybe hit the bar again, when I feel hands gripping on my hips from behind, small hands and know they belong to a woman.

The hands press tentatively against me, then harder as a masculine pair cover the smaller ones. One glance down at this pair of hands, and I know who it is. My head shoots around, looking over my shoulder and wondering what the hell is going on, and I lock eyes with Dornan. He's dancing with a girl in front of him, their joined hands roaming over my body. She's shorter than both of us, and I can't focus on her as they press closer to me, their fingers running along the waistline of my shorts. His hands guide them, directing where they go. I face forward and allow them to get closer, my heart beating in time to the music as our bodies move. Rough and soft fingertips graze under the hem of my tank top to touch bare skin, as Dornan's breath ruffles my hair. I'm relieved neither can see that my eyes have drifted closed so I can focus solely on that rough touch. Their hands run up along my ribs, right under the swells of my breasts. Causing my back to arch, pushing my chest out and ass back. Even through my bra, I can feel Dornan's thumbs graze my nipples, and I exhale a shuddering breath. Fuck, he's turning me inside out, my pussy is wet and throbbing, all from just his hands on me. I swear his touch makes me think crazy things and wanting things, things I never thought about with Brayden.

They push closer to me, and the girl's hands leave Dornan's as she begins to rub my hips. Her leg pushes between mine, as his hand slowly creeps up to my neck, his other remaining on my breast as he fondles me over my shirt. The hand at my neck slides back and up into my hair, which I've left down. Allowing him to grab a handful, to tug my head back and to the side. His breath pounds against my cheek, as his tongue tastes the sweat behind my ear. My body trembles at the movement, and the existence of everyone around us melts away. The feel of his tongue, him just breathing on my skin, sends goosebumps all over and my body instinctively pivots to face him.

The poor girl in between us doesn't seem to mind, or even notice that she's being used as a means for him to get close to me. She also turns and faces him, her back pressing into my front. Her lips kiss against the base of his neck, then trail along his collarbone, but he only seems to notice me. His fingers are still coiled tightly in my hair, as he pulls my face closer. His eyes liquid heat as I suck on my bottom lip, and beg with my eyes and body for him to kiss me. Leaning forward, Dornan brings my face closer. Just as the girl between us knocks her head into my chin, leaning up and planting a kiss on his lips, sealing around them as he opens and instinctively accepts.

I pull back and again gather my senses, his head jerks away from her and I'm jostled by a man beside me as the music changes to a more up-tempo song. Effectively pushing me further away, regardless Dornan tries to reach for me, but I'm too far. I just stare at him, probably like a deer in headlights, as the girl continues to try and get his attention back on her lips. Fuck, fuck, fuck. In a fight or flight reaction, I take off. Pushing my way through the patrons, out the door, and to my bike.

***

Monday morning is hell, I barely slept last night and feel like a zombie. My mind and body racing over the events at the club, hell the shit from all week actually. I don't understand Dornan's sudden interest in me, or is at least now acting on it. So after I got home, I spent the next six hours thinking about my entire life. All the subtle things Dornan does every day and wonder, has he been like this with me always and I'm just now noticing? Yes, of course he's always been touchy feely with me, always shooting me knowing glances and winks. But never, never has he tried to kiss me. Never tried to touch me like he did on the dance floor, never seemed pissed that a guy was showing interest in me. How insanely pissed he seemed when Drag came on to me, or livid about Justice asking me out. I just don't know what to make of it all. Of course I slept maybe four hours, eventually rolling into work at noon.

Relieved to make it to my office with no notice from the guys, as I sit down at my desk to skim over the papers sitting there, before reading my messages. Missy called a bunch of times, she also called my cellphone earlier, but I ignored them. Under the note to call Missy, there's another piece of smaller post-it paper in Dornan's handwriting, that says,

'Come find me when you get in.'

I crumple up the papers and toss them into the trash with a sigh, not sure if I'm ready to have this conversation with him yet. The one we definitely need to have, but part of me is terrified. Yes, terrified. Do I ignore the blatantly obvious quest Dornan is on to sleep with me, and go on like I don't notice it to not risk our friendship? Because surely all he wants is sex, and there's no way I can be friends with him after if we ever do that. Even if he wants a fuck buddy, a continuous arrangement to hook up, that's all I was to Brayden, a convenient piece of ass that he knew was always willing and able. Like a fucking sweet bottom, and I will never *ever* put myself in that situation again. Part of me knows I can't possibly come up with a solution, without knowing exactly what Dornan's intentions are. I have to sort these feelings out, but wonder if I procrastinate enough, Dornan will get bored and drop it.

On the flip side of that coin though, what really scares me, is what if he tells me he's always wanted me and wants to settle down, to be with only me. I'm not cut out to be an old lady, I know this. Being on the inside, I see what goes on at the MC parties with the girls, and the dangerous shit we do on runs. I would go insane with doubt and worry. Can I handle sitting at home waiting for him knowing he might not come back alive, or that he's going home with someone else? My cellphone begins to chime and at first I ignore it, but then notice Justice's name on my display.

"Hello?" I answer holding the phone to my ear.

"Maven, it's Justice, are you busy?"

I let out a long breath, his slight southern accent just does something to me.

"No. Nothing major, what's up?"

"Good, I'm in the area, wanna get lunch?"

Do I want to get lunch? It's just a date-was this a date? No, this is lunch, a day date, friend zone status...safe. Maybe he just wants to discuss work stuff, but no that's probably not the case, since he's been so pushy about seeing me on a non-work related occasion. My eyes land on Dornan's note crumpled in the garbage. Why does seeing this make me feel bad for talking to Justice? I need to nip this thing in the bud with me and Dornan. Forget that he makes me feel electric, and sexy, and his hands on me feels fucking awesome, or the way he looks at me makes me want to do stupid things.

"Yes, lunch sounds good," I reply quickly.

"Okay, I'm just around the corner, meet me out front?"

"Yes, perfect."

Maybe a little space from the grounds and with another man will help clear my head. I grab my purse and stop by Skye's desk to let her know I'll be back in an hour. Ignoring the look she gives since I just got here, and head towards the front gate. When I get out to the street, Justice is already sitting in his truck waiting for me.

"Wow," he says as I close the passenger door after climbing up into the massive truck.

"What's that?" I ask.

"You wear that to work?"

I cock my head slightly. Yes, okay maybe I wear things that aren't business appropriate, but I work at a mechanic's for God's sake. Either way, I look down to make sure my shirt isn't too low. Hating myself the instant I do it, because who the fuck is he to make me question myself.

"No, you look pretty," he hurries out at seeing my reaction.

I don't say anything for a moment, not wanting to really tell him to go fuck himself. Reminding myself repeatedly, that he's a business associate, and I need to be professional and ignore his comment.

"It's fine," I reply with a small smile.

He returns the smile, while turning the volume of the radio up with his fingers on the steering wheel controls.

"Oh I love this song," I comment as "Stranglehold" by Ted Nugent fills the awkward silence in the truck.

We drive down Main Street and pull into a spot just in front of the Plantain Diner, I guess he doesn't want my opinion on where I want to eat. There are plenty of restaurants and cafes in Plantain so it's not like we're limited in options, something I note but tuck away. He opens my door and lets me walk in first, doing all the gentlemanly things girls go gaga over. But everything just seems off to me, almost forced. I can't pinpoint it, but there's a vibe. I'm also not sure if it's on my end or his, but again I place it in the back of my mind. We're seated by the windows looking out onto Main Street, and begin looking over the menus.

"Ever been here?" he asks.

"Yeah of course."

"What's good?" his eyes scanning above the menu, but mine remain down.

"Never had anything bad," I smile.

The waitress fills our glasses with water as I set my menu down. Justice thanks her but never takes his eyes off me. He's in a white dress shirt, the sleeves rolled up, and a pair of black dress pants. Justice is tan and looks active, with dark wavy brown hair and permanent five o'clock shadow. He's definitely attractive, but he seems very edgy at the moment, like there's something just under the surface he's trying to tamper down.

"Did you grow up here?" he asks.

"Yes. Where are you from?"

"Montana originally, came out here for college and loved it, so I stayed."

Montana? His accent is definitely southern, so that makes no sense.

"You live in San Falls now?" I ask, remembering that's where his contracting company is based in.

"Yeah. Did you go to college?" he asks.

What is this? Twenty questions? I kept trying to make conversation, and push the topic away from me, but he just keeps volleying it back.

"No," I shake my head slightly.

"Really? How did you get the job as Chief Financial Officer at Frederickson and Co.?"

I guess no one can accuse him of being subtle.

"Just applied there when I was in high school for an internship, moved my way up with on the job training."

It didn't dawn on me until just now, that he wouldn't have known to pick me up at the shop. The address on my card I'd given him, is for the titty bar. Yet he didn't call me thinking he was near that address, he knew I'd be at the shop, a shop he shouldn't even know exists. Justice shouldn't have any knowledge of the auto body shop, since the club and the dealerships appear to be under separate ownerships, and by all accounts on paper, it is. Being from out of town, he wouldn't know that The Warrior of the Gods own everything. Again it's just a hunch, maybe I'm looking too much into it, so I tuck all this into the back of my head.

"Are you okay? You seem a little tense or something," I ask, giving him a raised brow and again trying to deflect the topic.

He lets out a long breath and nods.

"Yeah sorry, just before I called you I had a disagreement with an associate. I'm trying not to think about it, so I thought what better way to distract myself than by taking a beautiful woman out to lunch. So I'm sorry if I seem distracted, it's not you."

I give him a sweet smile, the same one I give to my neighbors, ya know *that* smile.

"So how did you come to work with the Warrior of the Gods?"

Hello! My spine straightens, but I cover up my sudden movement by grabbing my water glass and sipping from it. So I guess he knows more than I thought he did. When we met at the building site, none of us had our MC leathers on, so how would he put two and two together?

"Excuse me?" I question.

"The day we met at the site, you were with bikers, rumor has it Warrior of the Gods are from around here."

"Actually, Pete is Chief Business Coordinator for Frederickson and Co. and Ken is a trainee. We happen to love bikes and when we have to ride in the desert, prefer them. Might not be the most professional but we own strip clubs, so people don't usually question it. The Warrior of the Gods, I don't know anything about them. I thought they were an urban legend."

He narrows his eyes slightly, and I mean for a millisecond. Thankfully the waitress comes back and we order. Placing my arms on the table, I lean forward slightly. I'm about to ask something in regards to business, since that's a neutral topic, but he beats me to it.

"Did your dad or grandpa teach you to ride?"

That's pretty specific, my dad or grandpa? Why not just ask if someone in my family? Unless he knows about my family's history with the club. I can't imagine why he would be interested in this, and why he's hinting to the fact that he knows or thinks he knows my involvement in the MC. He's a contractor, is he trying to find out if he wants to be working for us if that's the case? Reputation and all that. Part of me wants to reply, 'If there's something you want to ask, then why don't you come out and ask?' He's been blunt with me before, so why tip toe around this subject?

"No," I state. "They hated that sort of thing," I add for good measure.

If he's going to be evasive with me, then back at ya.

"Hmm. How did you get into motorcycles then?"

The question irritates me, like women aren't allowed to just like motorcycles.

"Growing up my neighbor had one and I just wandered over the fence and watched him fix his bike up. It was a real piece of shit, a hunk of scraps when he started. Seeing what it became and the power that it possesses, I fell in love," I smile through the bullshit.

"Wow, that's a great memory," Justice says almost sarcastically with a smile, before his eyes dart out the window then back to me. Showing a hint of annoyance there.

The rest of the lunch is void of any more awkward family talk, or personal questions. Still we don't have much to talk about, other than the building site. Even if he asked me straight out, what the connection is between the business and the MC, I'd lie. I never talk to anyone outside the club about personal shit, and even then, they just always knew my shit because I grew up there. I don't want to lie to Justice. But with that, realization dawns on me that I can never be with someone outside the club as long as I'm a part of it. Or at least someone that I couldn't tell things to about my life until I knew for sure I could trust them. Even then, who the fuck would put up with that? My dreams of one day being with a civilian are saved for when I'm cleared from my obligation to the club, even though that seems like light years away. But more importantly, why the entire time I was out with Justice, was I thinking of Dornan? It seems like lately every time my mind wanders to my future, his face comes to me. I know once we talk and I tell him my guidelines, that it will stop. Once I lay my parameters out, he'll realize this whole thing that's going on with us the last few days, is implausible. Justice pulls up to the entrance for the shop, just as I turn to him.

"It was really nice talking with you, you took my mind off things," he says, giving me a tight smile.

"Thank you for lunch, I'm glad we could meet up…" I take a deep breath, "Justice-"

"I get it, you're not into me," he smiles sweetly.

"It's not that," I shake my head. "I just recently got out of a long relationship, and I just need some time before I jump into something. I don't want to lead you on, or give you the wrong impression of where I am at in my life by agreeing to go out with you. Does that make sense?"

"Of course, I have no problem being cool with you, maybe we can do lunch another day soon."

"Sure," I reply, but I don't really think he understands what I'm saying.

When I return through the gate, the lot of the club is empty. The temperature's gone up, and the guys who normally just hang out usually like to chill inside this time of day. I'm sure someone saw me leave with Justice, and word will get to Dornan in no time. This idea makes my stomach knot and there's that damn guilt again. I'm not in my office two minutes, before the door bangs open and I startle. Looking to see Missy in all her pissed off glory, standing with her hands on her hips in the doorway. She enters and swings the door shut behind her with a kick of her heel. Tossing her bag onto one of the chairs as she walks over to place her hands on my desk and leaning forward.

"You know I don't like being ignored, what the fuck Maven?"

I sigh and sit back in my chair, looking up at her in contemplation.

"I think I'm falling for Dornan."

I don't even pretend to have control over my mouth, the words just come out. Her face softens, as she removes her sunglasses and her eyes narrow.

"Well, it's about fucking time," she retorts.

I groan and rest my head in my hands, as she takes the seat in front of my desk.

"What happened to make you suddenly notice?" her voice is now taking on the tone of a mom.

I tell her about everything, *everything*. The attempted kisses, the groping at the dance club, how he invades my every waking moment, how all I could do was think of him when I was with Justice. All the while she just looks at me with a small smile on her lips.

"Dornan's had it bad for you forever, I'd say since birth, but I don't think that's actually possible."

"I don't know what to do," I huff.

"I know he's a slut, but I know that if you expressed your feelings to him, he'd cut all that shit out. If your heart is telling you to go for it, go for it," she lifts a shoulder like this isn't the biggest deal ever.

"What if we try and it fails, and then I've lost my friend?"

"You won't. Dornan will always be there; we'll all always be there for you. Lord knows none of us are perfect, we've all fucked up... but you take the chance and that's life, babe," she smiles.

I open my mouth to reply, when my office phone rings and I know it's Skye. I raise my index finger in a 'hold that thought' gesture to Missy as I answer.

"Yeah?"

"Milton's talking with Sven in the lot."

Fuck.

"Thanks."

I stand as I put the receiver back into its cradle, while trying to peer out the window from my desk, but can't see anything. What the hell could he be here for? Surely not the Briscoe job, we were clean and efficient, no way the law has anything on us for that.

"What?" Missy asks.

"Officer Milton."

"Shit," she mumbles. "Let me go see what's up."

She groans and stands, making her way to the door before turning back to me.

"Good luck."

She smiles and I know she's referring to Dornan, and not the cops. I roll my eyes in response, and begin shuffling papers on my desk. Mentally check listing that none of the MC files are on this computer, none of our papers are in here, everything's in the safe or not on the premises. Not like it matters, we aren't being raided, but I still like to know where all the dirty shit is. Suddenly, my door opens again and I glance up, expecting it to be Milton or Sven, but it's Dornan. I try to peer out the open door over his shoulder, to once again see what's going on in the front of the shop. But he closes it quickly, blocking my view. I'm not sure if he's here to tell me Milton's outside or what, but he appears agitated.

"Did you get my note?"

Unsure why he's picking right now to talk about this, I reply, "I did. Got in late and your mom caught me right away…sorry."

I resume pretending to now have something important on my desk, my heart quickening as he walks closer and around to the side of my desk. His hands stop mine, and I watch his thick fingers wrap gently around my small wrists. Pulling them slightly towards him, causing me to raise my head and he's right there. His body so close, and I begin breathing in his scent. His warm touch, his tall frame, all envelop me and my mind blanks in reaction. His blue eyes search my face, I mean really takes me in, as he tries to read me.

"Why did you leave last night?" his voice a husky whisper.

My mouth opens but nothing happens, what the fuck do I say?

"I can't."

My eyes trail from his eyes to his lips, and he lets out a small groan, bringing my eyes back to his.

"I can't be a fuck buddy, I *won't* be another fuck buddy," I add defiantly.

"That's what you think?"

There's irritation in his features, as his brows furrow slightly.

"I've never seen you with a girl longer than a week. Yeah, that's what I think."

I can hear Milton and Sven's voices now in the reception area, but can't make out the words. Dornan removes his hands from my wrists, the loss of contact leaves me feeling needy. But then he cups my jaw, his thumb running under my lower lip.

"Why do you think I never had a girlfriend? I've only ever wanted that designation to be for you, you've been my only girl ever. The others were killing time until you realized you were mine."

He leans his head in closer, and softly speaks against my lips.

"I didn't want them. I've always wanted you."

My heart skips a beat.

"Then why didn't you ever tell me, why now? Why the sudden interest?" my tone's clipped as I try to step back and distance myself from him, but his hands cup my neck to keep me close.

"Sudden interest? Seriously?" His eyes search mine as if he's trying to see if I have a clue about his feelings for me.

"I've been trying to get you alone to talk, to try and tell you how I feel. I waited too long and Brayden came along, I thought he made you happy and that's all I ever wanted for you, I was scared to tell you how I felt even when I knew he was jerking you around but I couldn't risk you laughing off my confession because you were in a Brayden delusion."

He swallows thickly, and I can see the pulse racing in his neck. Lifting my hand, I place my palm over the throbbing, his eyes closing as his lips part.

"Now the contractor is interested and I can't go on anymore waiting. It's my turn now, it's been years and I'm done waiting."

We're inhaling one another's exhales, my hands caressing him in a way I've never touched him, connecting in ways we never have before. His thumbs stroke my cheeks, his eyes staring down at my lips.

"Waiting for what?" my voice coming out a little breathy.

"Maven!" I hear Sven yell from the other side of my door.

I turn my head in the direction of his voice, but Dornan tightens his grip and brings my attention back to him.

"Waiting for you to realize, that you're meant to be with me."

Oh. My. God.

"Dorn-" I begin, but I'm cut off by my office door opening, and Sven standing beside Officer Milton. Even though Dornan's still holding my face, his hands loosen, and I'm able to turn towards them. However, Dornan's eyes never leave my face.

"I need you to come down to the station," Milton says.

My eyes shift as I take a deep breath, trying to calm myself from Dornan's words and touch, and come back to reality. Sven gives me a small nod, and I know this business with Milton is nothing to worry about.

"Sure," I reply, placing my hands over Dornan's to remove them from my face. I hate it, the feeling that he's not touching me, and instantly I'm pissed off at Milton and his bullshit interrupting this monumental conversation between us. Milton smiles at me in that no-teeth-cop-polite-grin, and nods his head slightly. I just look at him as I walk past, and out to the squad SUV. He opens the door for me and as I wait for him to get in, I notice the guys standing around in clusters in the lot as I sit. Milton closes his door and I look over towards the shop entrance, seeing Sven and Dornan facing me. Both have their arms crossed over their chests, as Sven talks and Dornan's eyes stay fixed on mine. I've been in the back of a squad vehicle before, but this time I'm not handcuffed, so the ride isn't that unbearable. Milton grew up here too, but he's a couple of years older than me. We're friendly every time we come into contact, as much as a cop can be to someone like me. He's attractive in a very clean cut, all-American kind of way. With brown hair he keeps short in a military cut, he's tall and still in good shape from playing football in high school and college.

"How ya been Maven?" he asks, looking back at me over his shoulder.

"I've been better."

He gives me a quick smile in the rearview mirror.

"I see you've put work in on your grandma's house...looks nice."

I give him a small nod in acknowledgement, then hear the roar of a bike behind us as Milton drives down the Main Street to the police station. When we park I see Smokey's followed us and stops the bike in front of the station, leaning back and talking on his cellphone. Milton leads me inside and through a row of desks that have other officers sitting at them. The office is newly renovated and looks updated and clean, and still smells slightly of paint. We stop beside a door and Milton ushers me in, where I take a seat in a metal chair behind a metal table pushed against the wall. The room's white and the lights are harsh and bright, there's a two-way mirror to my right and I wonder who's behind it. There are other interrogation rooms here with no mirrors, but closed circuit cameras so others can watch the interview live and also be recorded. This room has the closed circuit TV's too, but there must be a reason I'm in this particular room with the mirror.

"Coffee?" Milton asks, still in the doorway.

I shake my head and he closes the door, leaving me alone. I stare straight ahead, still not knowing what I'm here for and who could be behind the mirror. For whatever reason, a certain person keeps making all this seem inconsequential. Someone with a set of pale blue eyes who's touch I can still feel on my skin like an electric current. Dornan's words replay in my mind, the way he looked at me like I was a cherished possession, while cupping my face with a gentle yet powerful grasp. He said he was tired of waiting, waiting for me to realize I was meant for him...meant for him...for him...him. Dornan, who I've always looked at one way, is now being seen in a totally different light. But the more I think about things, memories, pondering if I've always had more than friend feelings for him. Maybe I pushed them back so far because the fact that I'd be an old lady, was too scary to think about most of the time. But as things dawn on me, they don't scare me like I thought they would. Dornan's always loved me, and I've always loved him. We still need to talk more, because he says he's always wanted me but Brayden was in the way. I don't know what he means by that, and with Dornan, it could mean anything.

Milton walks back in and sets a folder on the table, along with a mug of coffee for himself. He sits in front of me, clicking his pen repeatedly as he opens the folder to read over the papers.

"I need your side of what happened in Beaver Falls," he says, never looking up from the papers.

Ah, the biker bar.

"I was accosted," I state.

He keeps clicking his pen and nodding.

"What were you doing in Beaver Falls?" he looks up, locking eyes on me.

"Business."

One corner of his mouth pulls up.

"Which business?"

"I don't know what you mean," I smile.

The relationship between the Plantain Police and Warrior of the Gods is an odd one, we need each other but dislike each other too. We keep the city safe really, we don't allow shit to go down here and we never shit on our doorstep. Regardless, sometimes trouble followed us here. We needed the cops who inadvertently fed us information, because any news was spread around here like a wild fire. Although I'm not sure who exactly, I know we have insiders. When my dad got busted, I knew Sr. Milton purposely withheld evidence when the FBI took the case. Despite Sr. Milton and Dad hating one another, he owed him. In their early twenties Sr. Milton's sister was raped in Coral Groves, a town not far from here. It's where all the college kids hang out, and my dad stumbled onto it while in progress, and beat the shit out of the guy. My dad took Milton's sister to the hospital, and called her parents. I won't go as far as to say that my dad tracked the guy down and killed him, but we all know that guy did end up in an abandoned building with his throat slit. Generations don't forget that shit, time can go on but bloodlines don't erase the history. So whether we don't like each other or not, our pasts won't let us forget we're linked.

"Would you like to file charges against the man in Beaver Falls?" he asks.

"No."

Milton writes on the paper and clicks his pen...again.

"A patron called the police at the bar, of course they saw the guy with the blood pouring from his face, cops took it upon themselves to watch the security video, saw you, Rocket, and Smokey and thought I might want to take care of it. The guy's not pressing charges."

"I wouldn't think so."

Like what biker is about to take a woman to court for kicking his ass?

"Do anything else while you were there? See anyone I mean."

I look in his eyes, my expression blank and he begins to look uncomfortable after a moment, his eyes diverting from mine.

"No."

The fact that he can check the prison records, if he hasn't already to see if I'd been there, was silly to lie about, but it wasn't any of his business.

"Okay, thanks Maven, appreciate you coming down on short notice, just didn't want to have this sitting on my desk."

This is all he wanted to talk about? This could have been asked at my office or calling me and asking me to come up, this didn't require an escorted meeting in an interrogation room. Which further makes me wonder who's behind the mirror.

"I'll give you a ride back," Milton says as we walk out the front doors.

I see Smokey still sitting on his bike. He's leaning against a black Ford F150, with his arms bent on the open window talking to the driver.

"No, I'm good."

Without looking back, I walk over to the passenger side of the truck and get in. Sven and Smokey both look at me for a second, before Smokey moves away and starts his bike. The Who's – "My Generation" is playing on the radio as we begin down Main Street, and Sven turns it down as he speaks.

"All good?"

"Yup," I reply, looking out the window.

"Beaver Falls?"

"Patron called the cops."

He then turns the radio back up, and we sit in comfortable silence the rest of the ride. When we pull into the president's reserved spot, I reach for the door handle, but his hand covers mine. I look over but he's not looking at me, his eyes on the clubhouse in front of us.

"He's a good guy. A man," he tells me.

I furrow my brows, unclear on who 'he' is. My eyes then follow his line of sight to see Dornan standing with Joey talking. They both seem anxious, Dornan's brows are furrowed, something he does when he's stressed. The urge to rush to him, to know what's wrong, overwhelms me.

"I know," I reply.

Sven finally looks over at me.

"You're good for him, always have been. You put his head in the right space, he needs that."

Did Missy tell Sven about our talk earlier? Or has Dornan confided in his dad like I had with his mom? I really don't know what to say, but I nod and Sven lets go of my hand, giving me a soft smile. As soon as we exit the truck, Joey and Dornan approach us, the worry on both their faces now.

"We've got a problem," Dornan says. "The Steel Axes want seven hundred guns now, not five hundred. They want the other two by tonight or there's no deal."

Steel Axes are a black gang, they're who we sell guns to, and they in turn sell to whoever's demanding.

"Shit," I sigh.

"We got any insight on the Durango compound?" Sven asks.

"Just talked to Chilly and he's going to get all the intel he has and get back to me. We gotta do this job quick."

"Let everyone know we're going to gathering," Sven replies.

5

With a long look Dornan watches me, before heading around the club to corral everyone. I go inside and make my way for the basement, this is where most of our equipment for jobs is stored, including my laptop. Heading into the gathering room, I plop down in my seat and begin trying to hack into Durango. This is a bad idea, I don't like doing a job on a rush, no one does, but going in basically blind is scary as fuck. I'm so engrossed in what I'm working on, that I don't notice the room fill and draw quiet until Sven begins to talk. Still I remain focused on making progress, and not liking what I'm seeing.

"What's the word from Chilly?" Sven asks.

"Says the place usually has twenty-five to thirty people there at all times, heavy security but there's a shift change at midnight. Our best bet is to try and get in then," Dornan answers.

"Maven," Sven says.

"Security is heavy for sure. Cameras, dogs, fences, key code entry to all the doors, looks like the guards patrol one certain building which I assume holds the goods, the area is so large there is a possibility for us to get in when the two guards are on opposite sides of the building, but we just need to coordinate our exit with that too."

Sven heaves a heavy sigh. "This is gonna be dangerous, more dangerous than usual. I need everyone who's on board to be in this one hundred percent, I need everyone on alert, if you think you can't, say it now."

Looking up to notice for the first time, that Drag's here...with two black eyes and a cut on the bridge of his nose. He hasn't been around much lately, and thinking back to the last time I saw him was at the tavern after our last job...when he tried getting me to go home with him. When Dornan looks around the table and locks eyes with Drag, Drag immediately looks away. There's my answer, Dornan must've beat him up. It can't be over him trying to pick me up, or could it? But I don't have the time to analyze that now, or my head will explode.

"Everyone be ready by eleven," Sven ends.

I continue to work on the security as the guys wander out. Unsure how much later, Dornan walks in again and sets a bottle of water beside my laptop, placing his hand on my shoulder and giving it a squeeze. I look up at him and there's something in his eyes, like he wants to say something, but is debating on whether he should or not.

"Not sure I want you on this one," he says softly.

The tone of his voice hits straight to my gut, and instantly makes me ache. "But we need you," he adds, his eyes trailing down my face to my lips.

"I'm good for tonight," Joey says entering and sitting down across from us. "Katie was cool with it."

Both Dornan and I look at him with question.

"Well, she doesn't know the job but she was fine with me not being home 'til later," he amends.

The three of us sit in silence, the sound of my keyboard clicking and Dornan's text messages firing off fill the space.

"I think I got it," I suddenly say, causing the two men to lean closer.

"There's a thirty-five second window for us to get in the door to the warehouse, I can set it up on my phone to unlock when we're there. But the doors lock automatically from the inside too so when we leave I have to manually do it."

Dornan runs a hand over his face and takes a long look at me, then Joey.

"We got this man," Joey shrugs.

There's a rock in the pit of my stomach, I'm still not happy about this. We don't know the layout of the grounds or the inside, and we can't be certain the building we're going to actually stores the guns.

The three of us, Smokey, Rocket, and Drag, go down to the basement and get our gear together. Unlike normal jobs, we all grab a gun and some clips of ammo. There's an uneasiness hanging in the air, and no one talks as we prepare for the unknown. Even as we leave the club, Sven has a look of worry etching his features. Chain who is normally quiet and rarely speaks, tells us 'good luck,' and that just freaks me out even more.

Just as we've always done, we double check our gear as I hack into the Durango server. Turning on our pre-paid unregistered burner phone, to set up the system for the automatic locks, then we wait as Rocket drives us. We sit in the van until midnight, Rocket's parked up a hill on the back end of the warehouse, out of the view of cameras. I'm not able to get into the system to shut those down, but make sure the flood lights go off when we make our way down to the doors, and hopefully no one will notice since it will be a shift change. Drag scales the cement block wall and clips the barbwire, before jumping down and running low towards the massive building at the bottom of the hill. Joey goes next and waits for me on the other side of the wall to make sure I clear it, before we both run down to meet Drag. I remove my glove to work the touch screen of my phone, making sure to cover the screen the best I can to not bring attention to ourselves, even though I don't see anyone on the grounds. The door clicks, and Drag holds it open as we make our way in. Smokey just makes it, but Dornan's still ten feet away and running towards us as a red light begins to flash beside the door, signaling that the alarm's about to go off if it stays open any longer. Dornan signals for us to go and Smokey closes the door, leaving Dornan outside and we all stand still for a moment taking in the surroundings. The building appears empty, but we can hear men talking somewhere not far from us, the voices echoing in the large space. At first glance, the inside mimics a massive home improvement store. With its rows of huge steel storage shelves that have to be at least fifty feet high and seventy feet long, filled with wood freight containers. Joey signals for us to split up and meet back in ten minutes, this is going to be difficult since we don't know where the hell we're going.

Smokey and I split to the left, quickly glancing down the aisles, looking for crates that will signal us to where the guns are. The Durango people use color coded labels on their crates, and Chilly told Dornan the ones we need have a blue and green mark of spray paint on the front. We've gone down twenty or more rows before my eyes land on the colors, I tap Smokey's arm and we halt. Moving down the aisle towards the crates, they've already been opened, and the tops are just sitting on the boxes thank God. As I reach for the bag inside my sweatshirt, I'm startled as I hear a pop then a zip and another pop…gunfire. Smokey pushes me back and out into the main aisle, as he removes his gun from the back of his pants and aims to fire. But before he can get a round off, he grunts and steps back, falling onto his ass. Grabbing the sleeve of his sweatshirt, I try pulling him towards me but he's too heavy. He groans and has his hand pressed to his chest, blood seeping over it.

The gunfire stops and I look down the row at two men reloading their handguns, a good fifty feet from us. I take that moment to put my forearms under Smokey's armpits and pull him back, but before I can make any progress, they start firing again. Smokey groans at the same time I feel the impact of another bullet entering his body. There's shrapnel from the bullets hitting the crates, sending fragmented chunks of wood everywhere, the scent of gunpowder thick in the air as the shots intensify. Smokey's arms are limp so he can't return fire, instead, I grab his gun while removing mine from the back of my jeans and stand. Walking forward a few steps as the men approach, still aiming and firing their weapons towards us. Bullets ricochet all around me. Hoping no more hit Smokey, my fingers squeeze the trigger four times in total. Hitting both their chests and the center of their foreheads, and dropping them immediately.

When I turn back, Smokey has blood coming from his mouth. With renewed strength and adrenaline, I'm able to crouch down and pull him back towards a door behind us, while he uses his legs to help me. I hear other voices and gunshots, along with dog's barking in the direction Joey and Drag had gone, it's like the sound is all around us. The doors are locked, so without thinking, I grab my black baggie and in two seconds the locks are picked and we're in a dark room. There's a window too high for me to lift Smokey, maybe if I push a table under it, I can try to get him up to it.

"V," I hear Smokey choke out, before I can turn, huge arms wrap around my chest and pull me away from the window. Someone grabs me, lifting my feet off the ground with their strength. One arm moves up around my neck in an attempt to put me in a chokehold, and I kick the person in the knee with my heel, then slam my fist into his crotch. He drops me to my knees, as he staggers back a few feet. My back is still to him when he comes at me again, my hand wraps around the handle on my knife inside the ankle of my boot. With all my might, I swing back, lodging my blade into the side of his neck. The man begins to choke and drops onto me, blood pouring into my hair and face. Removing my knife, before I can roll him off me, and tuck it back into my boot. I first go to the door and lock it, before going back to the window and pounding on it with my fists. Trying to break the glass, or alert Dornan to where we are. There's a wheezing sound followed by struggling breaths, and I'm not sure if it's Smokey or the other guy. I run back over to Smokey who looks really bad, a pool of blood forming beneath him.

"We gotta try to get out another way."

"Go V," he whispers.

"Fuck you. No," I mutter.

A crash of glass comes from behind us, then Joey and Drag are dropping in from the window. Rushing over and lifting Smokey up and carrying him to Dornan, who's leaning down through the window to grab him. Banging starts on the other side of the door, then gunshots as they try to shoot the lock off. My adrenaline's spiking, and I'm not sure if this is actually real it's happening so fast. Joey grabs the front of my sweatshirt and yanks me towards the window, practically throwing me into Dornan's hands. Once out of the building, Joey puts Smokey onto his shoulders in a fireman's hold, and we all begin making our way up the hill towards the van. As we reach the grass, I then notice the blaring wale of the alarms going off, all the lights in the area are on and shining on us like beacons. Gunshots go off around us, as bullets deflect off the ground in front of and around our feet, we just keep running. Dornan's a few feet behind me, using his body to shield me from the oncoming fire.

Time flashes by, and events of our escape blur together in my head. Getting to the top of the hill, making it over the fence and into the van… but then we're safe and it's quiet as we drive off. Smokey grabs my wrist as he lays across Joey's lap, and his touch finally brings me back to reality. My hands cover his chest, Dornan's hands underneath him and putting pressure on the other wound.

"Tell Emily-" Smokey begins.

"Shut up," I snap angrily.

He smiles a little and blinks his eyes long and slow, he's pale and looks worse than I want to acknowledge. I can't think about this being it for him, I just can't. I don't want to be aware that he might die before we even get to the clubhouse, that I'll have to go to his house and tell his family he's gone. Drag's in the front seat on his cellphone, talking rapidly and looking back between us and the road. There's just so much blood, it's everywhere, and it just won't stop. The van door slides open, and the guys who didn't go on the run are there, reaching in to carry Smokey inside the clubhouse. *We're back, everything's going to be okay*, I tell myself. We all follow in after them, as they put Smokey on a long table inside the door. Master, who's one of the brothers and an EMT, begins examining him. I can't stand here, my adrenaline's still too strong, and pushing my body to keep moving. My feet begin to walk, my mind absent. I've shot people before, hurt them, but I don't think

I've ever killed anyone, at least I sleep at night telling myself I haven't.

I end up in the long apartment hallway, leaning against the wall. I bend over and put my hands on my knees, taking in deep breaths. It's then I notice my hands and clothes covered in blood. I rip off my hoodie and run the clean material of the inside over my face, my chest heaving with labored breaths the more I frantically try to wipe the blood. Dornan's heavy footsteps alert me to his presence before he grabs my hands and holds them between us, causing me to straighten. His eyes look over my body, assessing if I'm hurt. Then our eyes lock, moments before his lips crash against mine, my lips part and welcome him. But this is more than just a kiss, it's comfort and reassurance. Being shot at, Smokey, the fact we all could've been fucked. His teeth bite into my lower lip and I whimper, his hands tangle in my hair as my fingers grip the front of his sweatshirt, trying to get him as close to me as possible. My fingers brush against the medallion he always wears, and my heart flutters. His body presses my back against the wall as he slides a leg between mine, pushing his hips against me. Our breaths heavy and fast, I want to cry it's so gut wrenching, so soul shattering. I've never been kissed like this before, nor will I ever again. My throat tightens with emotion and a small sob escapes before the kiss ends. Dornan's strong arms wrap around me, my eyes burning as I shake slightly, while he holds me tightly against his equally trembling body.

"We're going to emergency, call Em, V," Joey's voice comes booming down the hall from the front room.

Dornan cups my face, his eyes glassy as they look into mine once again. He swallows hard and leans his forehead down to mine.

"We have to go," his whisper caressing my face.

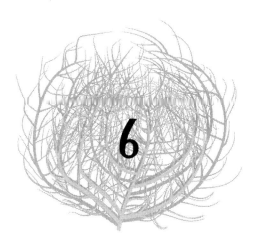

6

He slips his hand down to take mine, leading us through the hallway and back to the chaos in the main room. But Smokey isn't there and just then I hear a vehicle take off out front, blood and gauze cover the floor and the table he'd been on. All the gear from the job is laying on the floor by the door, and I pull my hand free as we pass, reaching down for my laptop.

I set the computer on the bar and quickly hack into Durango, searching through the files, finally finding the security camera feed. Highlighting all the files to erase them, then I clear the hard drive, assuring that there was no video of us from tonight. I mean they'll have Smokey's blood, and for a moment I fear that if Durango, like us, has someone in the police force, they can run tests and find out who's blood it is and trace it back to us. But then I realize that no cop would stick their neck out with expensive testing that would raise red flags, just for a crooked company. I have to believe they won't go that far to get it analyzed for a botched robbery, fuck...my gloves are gone. Shit, when the fuck did that happen? I rack my brain to try and remember at what point I lost them. It's out of any of our hands, I just have to hope that Durango doesn't look too much into this one.

Dornan takes my hand and pulls me out the door and to his Charger. I call Emily as Dornan drives us to the hospital, her two sisters have been staying with them to help with the older kids, since she just gave birth.

"Smokey's been shot."

Taking in a deep breath as soon as the words leave me, my heart cracking as she asks me to repeat myself. Dornan reaches over and un-balls my fist on my lap, linking his fingers with mine. Emily's surprisingly strong, she asks me if he's okay in a weak voice. When I tell her he's headed to the hospital, she clears her throat and tells me she'll be waiting for Joey and Chain to pick her up.

This is one of the many reasons I can never be an old lady, the dreaded call of your man being hurt or even killed. Turning my head against the seat, I look over at Dornan. His free hand grips the top of the steering wheel tight, his brows furrowed slightly, as the edginess radiates off him. Something shifts in me, even though Dornan could eventually be hurt or worse, the need to be with him seems worth attempting. Everything relating to Dornan seems worth it. The feelings I have about being with someone who's in an MC, I realize, is slowly dissipating. No one knows me like this man does, he knows what I haven't yet come to terms with. That we're going to be together, it's inevitable. Out of the corner of his eye he notices me looking, and smiles that sexy half grin I feel in my gut, his hand tightening with mine as we ride in silence.

Entering the hospital, Dornan does all the talking at the front desk, finding out where we need to go and leads us there. The guys are standing in the hall, all looking nervous. Missy and Sven are hugging, it seems as if she just got there also, they both turn to look at us. Missy rushes towards me, grabbing my shoulders before turning me, breaking my hand away from Dornan's.

"Bathroom babe."

She leads me to the bathroom and when we enter, I catch sight of myself in the mirror and see why she wants me in here. I turn the water on and rub it over my face, my neck, my hands, and arms, in an attempt to clean the dry blood off. My shirt's fine since I had my hoodie on during the run, but my pants are covered. Even though their black, you can still see dark stains covering them. Dornan's and Joey's clothes are also covered, which causes me to cringe thinking of Emily having to see her husband's blood all over us.

"You're not hurt right?" Missy asks.

"No," I reply softly.

After a long pause, she asks, "Job went bad, huh?"

Missy's cool, but she's still an old lady. I know for certain Sven tells her things in regards to the club, but not details, not facts or too much information. That's more than most other old ladies are privy to, but she's no equal by any means.

"Uh huh," I answer as I dry my face with paper towels.

The night and early morning is spent waiting, since we have such a large group we get moved to a private waiting area. Emily holds herself together, not crying, but anxiously wrings her hands on her lap. Officer Milton came by since the hospital reported a gunshot wound, and he talked with Sven in the hallway, telling him it was an accident at the club with a prospect. Finally, after what seems like days, the surgeon came out and told us that Smokey will be fine. The bullets had ruptured his spleen, and the one in his chest had just missed his lung and heart, but he would recover. The sun's already coming up by the time Dornan and I leave, the fog of no sleep and all the night's events, has me on the verge of delirium.

Luckily, my house is a short distance from the hospital, but it seems like we get stopped at every light, and the trip's taking an eternity. I'm so out of it I don't even think anything of it when Dornan pulls up my driveway, turning off the car and following me into the house. Bagheera excitedly jumps up to me, his paws on my hips as I pet his head and bend down to kiss his head. Dornan dumps dry food in his bowl and refills his water as I go upstairs. Stripping my clothes off and getting in the shower, the water pink from the blood I wasn't able to get out of my hair earlier. Walking into my bedroom in only a towel, Dornan passes by shirtless, with his jeans unbuttoned as he enters the bathroom after me. I slip on a vintage Grateful Dead tee and some panties, before closing the drapes to darken the room from the sun that will be rising shortly. Knowing my thoughts are going to be running rampant, regardless of how tired I am, I turn on my iPod on the dock and put Bob Seger's- "Night Moves" album on.

I stand at the dresser and comb out my wet hair, when Dornan walks into the room, I watch him in the mirror and pause. I've seen him shirtless many times, but something about seeing him in my room, knowing he's just been naked in my shower...does things to me. He's tall, tan and lean. His black and grey tattoos shiny on his still damp skin and muscles, oh and his muscles are a work of art. I can see the pendant that lays between his pecs, and as usual when I think about it or see it, the feeling it gives me is deep in my heart. Dornan wears a necklace with a pendant of Saint Christopher that I gave him on his twenty-first birthday. Since then, I always see the chain peeking out from the collar of his shirts, but haven't seen the actual pendant in so long. Dornan arranges the pillows before dropping onto the bed, stretching his legs out as he throws his arms over his head, oblivious of my ogling.

It's like I have to remind myself how to actually pull the brush through my hair, because even a task like this seems impossible when looking at all this Dornan flesh on my bed. Setting the brush on the dresser and without thinking, I crawl in beside him. Pressing my body into his side, and snaking my hand around his waist. Before I can get comfortable though, he rolls onto his side, maneuvering me so my back is to his front. He slides an arm under my neck and under my pillow, as his other arm wraps tightly around my midsection. Both my hands connect to his, and he links our fingers while nestling his face into my hair, his legs tangling with mine. I've never spooned with anyone, cuddled even, and shit I can get used to this. When the song "Night Moves" comes on, he begins to hum. The vibration of his chest against my back, his soft exhales playing with my hair, makes my whole body tighten.

"She was a black haired beauty with big dark eyes," he sings softly.

This causes me to smile at his voice singing, I melt. Melt. As Dornan continues to sing, I try to fight the sleep that's quickly approaching just to keep hearing him, but by the time the song ends, I'm out.

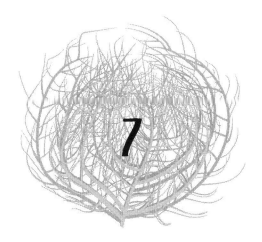

7

It only seems like minutes later when I hear my phone ringing in the distance. It takes me a while to realize I'm on my stomach, and Dornan's laying with half his body over mine. Then his phone begins to ring on the bed side table, and with a groan his warmth leaves me.

"Yeah?" he asks in a gruff voice. "Okay... yeah, we're coming... no, she's with me."

My eyes still struggle to open as Dornan smacks my butt cheek lightly.

"Smokey's awake," he whispers.

I roll onto my back as he stands, showing me his amazing toned back. The muscles defined and flexing under his tattooed flesh as he stretches, the top curve of his ass also showing above his boxer briefs. He adjusts himself and wanders into the bathroom, while I head downstairs and let Bagheera out and start a pot of coffee. The bathroom's empty when I go back up, so I wash my face and braid my hair before returning to the bedroom. Dornan's standing at the dresser, and I notice he's set clothes out for me on my bed. A pair of faded jeans, purple tank top, along with a matching black lacy bra and panties. I slip the bra on under my shirt, while Dornan seems more interested in my jewelry box than checking me out in the mirror, although he does glance up before I put the tank top on.

"You still have this?"

He asks, turning and holding something in between his fingers. I slip my jeans on as he steps closer, showing me the ruby ring.

When we were fifteen, Dornan told me he found this ring mowing the clubhouse grass one day. But the ring looked brand new, and I often wondered if he lied and bought it for me. It was too big at the time, so I used to wear it on my right middle finger.

"Of course I do."

His eyes transfix on the ring, not looking at me when he says, "You stopped wearing it and I thought maybe, you got rid of it."

The tone of his voice takes me back to when he was a kid, and showed emotion or expressed his feelings. A little embarrassed, but hopeful.

"No, never...but I started...with Brayden and it didn't seem right to wear something you gave me - to him or you."

He lifts his eyes and his blues meet my honey, his fingers toying with the ring.

"You're not with him anymore," he states.

I reach out to take it from him, now it's too tight on my middle finger, so I slide it onto my right ring finger. The ring's really beautiful, there's a small ruby in the center and two diamonds on either side. Dornan lets out a breath and presses his forehead to mine, nuzzling my nose along his as I bite my lower lip. We're both breathing fast, and my fingers trace down his cheek. His hands grip my hips, flexing into the material of my shirt.

"We should go," he groans in a pained voice.

I nod and close my eyes a moment, inhaling him and really feeling him against me. We listen to Tom Petty on the drive to the hospital, and I check my work emails on my cellphone along the way. There's one from Justice, asking if we can meet at the building site sometime next week. Which I reply with an, 'I'll let you know at the end of this week.' Justice is nice and all, and hasn't done anything in particular to turn me off. But not being able to be honest with someone about the simplest things like, 'What did you do last night?' or not being trusting enough to talk about my dad with, made me think. Yes, I just met the guy, but would I or could I ever trust someone not in the circle of the MC? With Dornan I don't have to get into the pain over my dad, or why my neighbors don't like me, or how I got the scar on my knee when I was nine. Dornan and I make sense, even if this life we're living is anything but normal, I'm realizing that life for me will never be cookie cutter. As much as I hate the MC part of my life, hate it and fear every day that I'll get thrown in jail or murdered. I can never escape it; it will always be there no matter how far away I try to distance myself.

We swing by the clubhouse so Dornan can change his clothes since he lives in an apartment there, which takes him all of five minutes before we're back on the road. Even though it's still very early and we probably only slept three hours, it was the best sleep I've had in a long time, and I knew it was because Dornan was with me. Katie and Joey are waiting at the elevator doors on Smokey's floor, and we exchange hugs.

"I've got to get to work so I just wanted to come by and see Emily, but then Smokey woke up," Katie tells me.

"The doctor says he's doing really good, did well through the night and is optimistic that he can get released in a few days," Joey says.

"Good brother. You coming back?" Dornan asks.

"Yeah, just gonna walk Katie to the car."

Katie and I hug again before the two enter the elevator, and the door slides shut. Dornan takes my hand as we walk down the hallway and around a few turns, before I see Emily leaning against the wall on her cellphone. As we approach she smiles, giving us a small wave.

"Yeah, I'll be home in the hour. Don't forget Eva has her school project due today...okay, love you too, bye."

She ends the call just as we near the room, instantly she hugs Dornan.

"Thanks for coming, Smokey's been asking for you since he woke up," she says looking weary as she takes my hands.

Her eyes water as they connect with mine. "He told me what you did... how you got him out of there."

"He's family Em, of course-" I state.

"No, I know but he said you got into that room and, we're so grateful," she nods, swallowing hard.

I pull her in a one armed hug as she covers her mouth with her hand, before pulling herself together and giving me a watery smile.

"Are you going to stay in the hall all day?" Smokey yells from inside his room.

"Well, you heard the man, better go before he climbs out of the bed to get you," Em smiles with a sniffle.

Smokey looks too big for the bed he's in, the white sheet pulled up to his waist. He's pale and aside from the IV's in his hand, he looks okay. Sven stands on the opposite side of the bed, pacing in front of the window on his cellphone, as Dornan and I greet our injured brother.

"How ya feelin brother?" Dornan asks.

"Like I've been shot," Smokey groans.

His eyes move down and notices my hand in Dornan's, and that signature shit eating grin begins to creep over his lips.

"Ah shit, who knew me being shot would finally get you two fuckers together...'bout damn time, if I had to see this dude wanting to pile drive every guy who ever looked at you one more time, I was about to beg you to date him."

"Just because you're in this bed doesn't mean I won't fuckin hurt you," Dornan states.

I smile and roll my eyes at Smokey, noticing Sven run his hand over his hair, worry etching his features.

"Joey said something about you goin' home in a few days," Dornan says.

"Yeah, thank fuck, one night in here is good enough for me," Smokey shakes his head.

Sven ends his call and finally seems to realize Dornan and I are in the room, he winks at me but it does nothing to soften his features. He looks to Dornan, before lifting his chin towards the door and walking out, causing Dornan to follow.

Smokey keeps smiling and then asks, "Seriously, I'm glad you are together...that's what it is right? I know that kid wouldn't just go halfway when he finally got you, he's probably already planning the wedding."

"You know I wish you got shot in the mouth," I reply sarcastically.

"I'm just sayin, I thought maybe you were needing to get your head checked if you kept ignoring him."

"How about you stop worrying about us and worry about yourself and going home."

Smokey clears his throat, his facial expression turning serious. I'm

RUNNING WITH THE DEVIL

not sure if he's in pain and I need to get a nurse or something.

"For real though V. You could have left me, gotten out, but you didn't. I owe you."

"Smokey. God, between you and Em you act like I did something that you wouldn't have done. You're my brother, if shit went down, it would go down for both of us, simple as that, so stop."

"Yeah, yeah. But just know that because of you I'll be seeing my kids and woman another day."

Dornan and Sven's heavy boots shuffle in behind us, before Dornan takes my hand, causing me to turn to him. His face taking on that same worried expression his dad has.

"It was good seeing you brother," Dornan says while outstretching his fist, Smokey holds his arm up limply and nods as they bump knuckles.

Smokey blinks long and I wonder if medicines just been administered through his IV Dornan pulls me towards the door, leaving Sven sitting in the plastic chair beside Smokey to watch TV. Emily's still in the hallway but down at the end looking out the window, talking on her cellphone again.

"I gotta go, Dad worked something out with The Steel Axes, and we got a few more days to work out getting the guns. Me, Joey, and Boo-Boo are heading out to Milestone, they owe us and hopefully it will be just a night or two."

"Why am I not going?" I ask, my brows furrowing.

"Stop thinking whatever it is you're thinking right now-"

"Because I fucked up at Durango?" I state more than question.

"Stop." Dornan cups my face and tips my head up to lock eyes with him.

"We all fucked up, the job was fucked up, it wasn't anyone's fault.

Dad needs you to run the shop; he can't have you gone for days. You do have an actual job, remember?"

I swallow hard because he's right, but I also feel annoyed that they'll be going into the unknown again with this one. Annoyance melds into fear, fear gripping my gut and my heart.

"Text me when you get there, keep me updated with what's going on," I tell him.

He wraps his arm around my shoulder to pull me close, as I slip my arms around him. His lips press against the top of my head, while his other hand rubs my back.

"This is gonna be a hell, especially knowing what you've got on under your clothes," by his tone I can tell he's smiling.

I playfully dig my finger into his ribs, causing him to groan, slapping my ass before squeezing it hard and pulling my hips into his.

"Keep me updated on Smokey. I'll leave the car for you, Joey can take me to get my bike," he says, pulling away and placing the keys in my palm.

"And try not to miss me too much," he smiles before turning and heading down the hall to meet Joey near the elevators.

I spent the rest of the morning at the hospital talking with Emily and Sven as Smokey went in and out of sleep, before I finally decide I should get to work.

Something about sitting in Dornan's car makes me feel, special. He never lets anyone drive his Charger, no one. I slip his aviator sunglasses on and blast Heart's- "Magic Man" as I cruise back home to get Bagheera, then to the shop. About three hours later Dornan texts me with a simple- 'Here.' I text back a 'Thanks' and don't hear from him again until after my run that night.

Dornan: Looks like it's going to be a few days...staying at the Devil's Backbone clubhouse in the meantime, place is a shit hole, smells like straight up ass.

The Devil's Backbone is a club we're affiliated with, and often do business together. I've been to their clubhouse briefly once, and knew exactly what he means, the sweet bottoms that hang out there also smell like straight up ass.

Me: Just got home from a run, sorry I didn't have my phone, few days? (Frowny face).

He replies immediately.

Dornan: A run huh? So you're all sweaty and in tight clothes?

Me: Sweaty yes, tight clothes no. Those are on the floor, about to shower.

Dornan: Fuck V, I'm at a table with the brothers and thinking of you nude is making me hard.

I smile and bite my lower lip.

Me: Too bad you're not closer, I could help you with that.

Dornan: Seriously stop. Thinking about those lips of yours wrapped around my cock with your eyes looking up at me...fuck.

Envisioning that very thing myself had me pressing my thighs together, and licking my lips. I've seen Dornan in some compromising positions with females, but never got a glimpse of the goods. I can only imagine what it would be like to have his dick in my hands, my mouth, my pussy.

Me: Shower time, later lover boy.

Dornan: You better think of me in the shower.

Yes, I did think about him in my shower. His tongue on my clit to be exact, using my fingers and pretending they're his. When I get out of the shower there's another text from him.

Dornan: Did you think about me?

My fingers hover over the keypad, as I think of how to reply.

Me: Yes, but I think my fingers won't hold a candle to yours.

Two seconds after the texts sent, my phone begins to ring.

"Hey," I answer.

"Are you trying to make me beat off in public?" his tone low and growly.

"You asked," I chuckle, and can hear loud voices in the background.

"What exactly were your fingers doing?"

I feel heat rush up my neck, and my insides tightening.

"Um, you were, ya know," I stop, feeling embarrassed, I was never, *never* embarrassed, but shit I can't say the actual words to him.

"That won't do."

Then he's silent, I take a deep breath and close my eyes.

"I thought about you eating me out and fingering me," I reply.

Still silence, as my face grows hotter.

"Jesus Christ." he says through gritted teeth. "You're going to fucking kill me, when I get home-"

"D come on," I hear Joey in the background.

"One second," Dornan replies. "We gotta meet with the Pres then I'm going to bed, I'm fucking exhausted...but now I have to beat off first," he says in a low tone almost as if it's not meant for me to hear.

"Yeah, we didn't get much sleep this morning," I reply.

"Best sleep I've ever had," he whispers.

My heart flutters, my smile hurting my cheeks.

"Sweet dreams babe," he adds before hanging up.

The next few days I'm back into my routine, morning runs with

Bagheera and then work. After work and sometimes at lunch, I'd head over to the hospital to see Smokey. Then he was discharged only three days after being admitted. Throughout the day Dornan texts me, everything from asking how I am, to what I'm wearing. No matter the message, it causes me to smile and turn my insides to goo. By Friday, I'm so anxious to see Dornan I'm snappy and irritated, especially when he's been calling me at night, and his deep voice making more than my insides gooey.

We're having a club get together tonight, a barbecue with the families that usually turns into a pretty hardcore party after the kids and most of the old ladies leave. I'm not particularly looking forward to this since Dornan and Joey still aren't back, and don't know when they will be. But I'll be getting to spend time with Missy, Gwen, Katie, Emily, and Smokey, who's feeling well enough to come out for a little while. I make salad and help get all the food together with the old ladies and girlfriends in the club's massive kitchen, all the while Katie fills me in on what her and Joey did on their night without the kids last weekend. It's nice to have female bonding time, since I spend more than enough time with men, and like all girls, I enjoy the gossip.

"You know," Missy begins, as we walk side by side with bowls of food out towards the picnic tables. The air's cooling down and the sun is low in the sky, perfect weather for a party. The bonfires are already beginning, as kids run around and play on the playground set up on the back lawn.

"Children of the Reaper are gonna be here."

I try not to falter in my steps, but my breath stutters as my words catch in my throat, so I remain silent.

"I mean, I'm not sure if Brayden's coming, but..." she trails off.

I know that Brayden will be here if that's the case, he never misses a party and all I can wonder is if he'll bring his wife. I wish for nothing more than to have Dornan here, not for protection or to make Brayden jealous, but just to have that touchstone. The stability and comfort of his presence, with that I know I can face anything.

We all eat and I decide to get royally fucked up, it's been a crazy few weeks and I want to just relax and enjoy my family. Missy and Katie go shot for shot of tequila with me, and by the time the kids are all gone home and the music begins blaring, I'm well on my way to sloppy. There's still no sign of Brayden, but there are at least two hundred people here, and it's possible we just haven't crossed paths yet. I ran into his dad Judas however, and he asks about my dad and we chat briefly, before a sweet bottom passes by and catches his eye. I know for certain if Judas is here, then so is Brayden. But at this point in my drunken state, I don't really care.

The sky's dark now and the bonfires light up all around the compound, casting an orange glow on everyone and everything. Led Zeppelin's- "When the Levee Breaks," is blasting through the speakers. While I sit at a picnic table with Katie, talking about her eldest daughter having her first crush. I saw Drag when he first arrived, but ever since he had the alleged altercation with Dornan, he's kept his distance. For whatever reason, I want to talk to him tonight and find out what really happened, if him being distant has something to do with Dornan. Rocket, Chain, and Dusty sit at the same table as us, discussing whose bike has better modifications. When in mid-sentence Katie squeals, "Baby!"

Launching herself off the bench, I turn to see Joey, Boo-Boo, and Dornan all walking up. Katie literally jumps into Joey's arms, before kissing him sloppily in front of everyone. Blue eyes suck me in, and I just sit there staring, unsure what to do. Do I go to him? Were we going to show everyone we're a thing?

Dornan never takes off the necklace I gave him, but normally it's tucked under his shirt, tonight it's laying over his shirt. Well, I'm not really sure what that means, but I know it makes my insides heat and liquefy. The muted metal nestles between his pecs and rests on the bright white of his V-neck t-shirt, and the sight makes me a little weak in the knees. His jeans fit him just right, he even makes his unlaced dirty boots look fucking delicious. His lips quirk into a grin as he starts for me, I finally stand and take two steps to meet him. I'm about to take his hand and lead him to his apartment, when he surprises me by grabbing my thighs, lifting me up to wrap my legs around his hips.

"Hey there," he says softly as he runs his nose along mine.

"Hi," I reply breathlessly.

Tenderly he places his lips on mine, sucking and gently coaxing my lips to part, as he slides his tongue inside to stroke mine. My heart pounds and distantly I can make out cheering at the kiss Dornan is laying down on me, glad he's picked me up because I'm positive my knees would give way from this. My hands cup his jaw before one trails down to the medallion on his chest, running my fingertip over the raised metal. Dornan groans into my mouth while pulling my hips against him firmly, causing me to gasp before I feel a swat on my ass, not from Dornan.

"Jesus, get a room," Joey says loudly.

"Awe, babe, leave them alone," Katie adds, swatting my ass again.

Our lips part and we pull away, looking down at him to notice his eyes are glazed, appearing just as turned on as I feel.

"Having fun?" He asks licking his lips, oblivious to everyone around us.

Surely he can taste the alcohol transferred from my tongue.

"I missed you," I smile.

He pecks my lips again before his eyes leave mine to scan the partygoers, his eyes stopping, taking a long look across the lot.

"Children of the Reaper are here?"

I set my feet on the ground and look in the same direction, and see Judas and Sven are talking near a fire pit. There's an unasked question in Dornan's tone; have you seen Brayden? But he doesn't ask and I don't tell him, not wanting to even think about Brayden. After a few tense minutes, Dornan relaxes as Joey hands him a beer and they join in on the bike modification conversation, while Katie and I resume ours.

A few beers later and I'm beyond drunk. I've always been able to handle alcohol and know I'm drunker than I appear. Dornan and I keep exchanging glances and often I feel his eyes on me, not looking away when I catch him. However, when he catches me, I blush and avert my eyes. Stopping Katie mid-sentence, I stand,

"I gotta pee, hold that thought."

I wander through the drunken groups of people, making it to the clubhouse after what seems like forever, since I can't walk a straight line to save my life. Several times I have to push my way through people in the main area to get to the apartment's hallway. I'm not about to use the public bathrooms, so I head to Dornan's apartment. I know he has a spare key somewhere around the door, I just have to find it. Attempting to rise up on my tip toes and run my fingertips along the door frame, I stumble for a few seconds before finally toppling over, and landing on my ass. Then I fumble to lift the floor mat and search underneath for it, when I finally do find it, it takes me several times and needing to really focus to get the key off the floor. I'm dizzy when I stand and after letting myself in, I trip towards the bed and land face down on the mattress. On the verge of almost passing out, my bladder urges me to get up and go pee. I practically have to crawl there, sighing deeply when I finally get my ass onto the toilet. Closing my eyes to stop the spins and taking a few deep breaths to stop the pre-vomit taste in my mouth, I sit there a little longer than necessary. Washing my hands, I cup some water and splash my face, using Dornan's toothbrush to brush my teeth in hopes to settle my stomach.

Reemerging from the wash room, I feel marginally better. I haven't been in his room in a long time, but it's orderly and neat. His king size bed's made and there are no dirty clothes on the floor, even the bathrooms clean. I wander around the small space and see a framed picture of Missy, Dornan, and Sven, along with Dornan's older sister Kendall who lives in Montana now, sitting on his bookshelf. There are books and an old baseball along with another photo sitting on the shelf. This one's of me, Joey, and Dornan when we were about twelve or so.

As I enter the hallway, closing the door behind me and awkwardly dropping the key onto the floor, which causes me to fall to my knees in order to get it back into its hiding spot. When I stand back up, dizziness washes over me again, just as someone grabs my hips and instantly I know it's not Dornan. Pulling away just as fast, the action turns my stomach. Brayden stands there, a beer in his hand. He's tall and muscular from working out every day. He's got the body to prove it, but looks larger than I remember. I feel the hairs on the back of my neck stand and an uncomfortable tension begin to run through me. The churning bile returns in the pit of my stomach, as he smiles before taking a pull from his beer. Even though the clubhouse is packed, there's no one back here but us.

"Hey honey. Were you gonna come say hi to me?" he slurs, stepping closer causing me to step back.

"I wasn't planning on it."

Thankfully my words aren't also slurred. He lets out a groan and places a hand over his heart.

"I'm crushed."

I narrow my eyes.

"What do you want?" I ask.

"Same thing I always want from you."

My jaw tenses, as my vision goes a little foggy, and I have to put a hand against the wall to balance myself.

"I'm not available for that anymore."

His dark brown eyes scan my body. I'm wearing a pair of jean shorts, a long sleeve shirt, and my bike boots.

"You sure honey?"

Brayden always calls me honey because of my eye color, and I used to like the endearment, but now it just makes me feel icky.

"Yes, I'm sure. There's probably fifty or so sweet bottoms out there willing to get nailed against a wall, or fucked on the sink in the bathroom," I shrug.

The first time Brayden and I had sex was slow, delicate, and in a bed, dirty, but nevertheless a bed. From there on out, it was anything but. The only times we ever saw each other was at club meetings or parties where we had to sneak off for a quick fuck, leaving me feeling nothing but disgusting and used.

"What's this all about, you got no love for me now?"

He opens his arms, stepping closer. Again I step back, my steadiness wavering.

"Are you serious? Uh, how about when you told me you weren't leaving your wife...that's what this," I motion a finger between the two of us, "is all about."

"That doesn't mean we still can't hook up-"

He finishes his beer, tossing the empty can down onto the floor.

"Actually asshole, that's exactly what it means."

Since I'm drunk and my reflexes are a little slow, he's able to grab my wrist and yank me towards him, causing me to trip over my own feet and fall into his chest.

"What the fuck did you just call me?" he growls.

"Asshole," I reply, trying to jerk my arm free.

His nostrils flare and his jaw ticks, eyes darkening.

"You're nothing but a sweet bottom, I fuck you wherever and whenever I want, don't you forget that...just because you wear the leather cut and play with the boys doesn't make you a brother or fuckin V.P."

My back hits the wall as he draws closer, the grip on my wrist tightening as he pins my arm to my side.

"You're nothing but a worthless bitch," he breathes into my face.

His other hand roughly cups my breast, and I jerk to the side in an attempt to get him to stop. My free hand flying to his but he breaks free from my grasp, and wraps his fingers around my jaw.

"You're my bitch, I own that ass and if you don't play nice well then I get to share you with my brothers."

"Fuck you, you dick-less piece of shit," I growl.

I begin to push my body against his, which just causes him to laugh. When both my arms get free and I punch him in the jaw, then he really begins to fight me. Before I can get my arm back to hit him again, he lifts me and tosses me like a rag doll against the wall. The back of my head hits the cement hard with a thud, and leaves me seeing black before stars fill my eyes. The impact drops me to my knees, then his hands are gripping my shirt and bringing me to my feet, my legs unstable leave me slouching and limp. When his fingers begin to fumble with the button on my shorts, I feel my disorientation lift slightly as I attempt to bring my leg and try to knock his hand away. But then he presses his forearm against my throat, pinning my head against the wall. My nails claw at his skin as the hit to my head, combined with the light headed feeling I have from lack of oxygen, and the alcohol in my system, is winning. Panic takes over and I never let the fear win, but the realization that I'm about to be raped, that this is really happening, scares me more than anything ever has. Brayden slips his hand down the front of my shorts and I gasp, while struggling for air as he touches bare skin. His arm presses harder, allowing me only short small inhales of air.

"Dick-less, huh. I'll show you how dick-less I am."

He's looking at me like I'm nothing, like he's looking through me. I close my eyes as stars dance under my lids, my lungs burn, my body beginning to lose the strength to fight. When suddenly the pressure leaves, and I'm finally able to gasp in a huge lungful of air. There's thumping and groans beside me as I fall to the floor, my hands bracing myself as I try to stand, my vision slowly coming back to a watery distorted view. I cough and bring my knees under me, slumping into the wall as I continue to try and get up. My body's shaking uncontrollably, my lungs and throat feel like they're on fire, and I can't inhale without coughing.

"Maven."

I hear Joey's voice and then big rough hands touch my face, but I can't see him, not being able to focus.

"Shit," he growls.

Then his hands are gone and I feel alone again.

"Stop brother!" Joey yells and I hear boots scuffling on the cement floor, heavy breathing and someone coughing.

"I'm gonna kill this motherfucker," Dornan growls.

"No, V needs you, take care of her. We got this," Joey says.

There's a long pause, more coughing and then I hear someone spit.

"If you ever so much as look at her, if you even think about her and I find out, I'll fucking kill you. Get the fuck outta here and take your shitty ass club with you before I kill every one of them," Dornan tells Brayden.

A searing pain shoots through the back of my head, as finally the injury from hitting the wall registers in my body. My eyes are barely able to stay open, when someone lifts me and presses my head onto their shoulder. Knowing instantly it's Dornan. He holds me with my legs wrapped around his hips, placing my arms over his shoulders, since I can't manage to do it myself. My body trembles against him as I gasp in his smell, and fight the urge to cry. But I won't, there's no need, I'm safe now and Dornan won't let anything happen to me.

"I got you babe," he whispers and begins walking.

I don't know why but I say, "No."

Thinking maybe he's about to walk me through the party, and everyone will see me. He continues to walk us and places a hand on the back of my head, covering the pain that's throbbing there. Almost like he's connected to me, and knows exactly where I hurt.

"We're going out the back," he replies.

Dornan and Joey converse as he tucks me into the car, another male voice I wanna say is Drag and a female voice I recognize as Skye joining them. Skye? Why is Skye here? Or maybe I hit my head harder than I thought, and I'm delusional. There's vague awareness when we get to my house, Bagheera's whining and licking my hand, as Dornan carries me in his arms.

"It's okay boy," Dornan tells him as he lays me onto the bed, and I finally pass out.

8

My head feels like it's in a vise, my eyes burning and they feel too big in my skull. My throat's sore and dry, other parts of me ache and it takes me a minute after waking up to realize why. The previous night's events rush back to me and cause a sinking feeling in my chest. I'm alone in bed, and when I finally manage to open my eyes fully, the sun's shining and it seems late. Sure enough when I raise my head to see the clock, it's already two p.m.

I hear Bagheera's nails clicking on the wood floor downstairs and a low rumble of a male voice. It takes me a while longer to sit up and shuffle to the bathroom. Immediately, I'm vomiting into the toilet, which at least stops the room from spinning. I recall that during the night, Dornan woke me to take some headache medicine, but he didn't stay with me. I take a hot shower, scrubbing away the shame and regret from last night. Yes, things could've been a lot worse, Brayden could have...but didn't. No thanks to my inebriated state, he almost did. I've taken a beating before, probably worse than this one. I'm not sure if these feelings are magnified because Brayden's someone I thought I loved at one time. But never have I felt so violated, and vulnerable, so defenseless. The guilt eats me up that I put myself in that position, and I promise myself I never will again.

After my shower, I slip panties on and a long t-shirt over my head before walking downstairs. I want to eat, take more meds, and go back to bed, and I assume Dornan will leave once he realizes I'm fine. When I see Dornan in the kitchen, arms braced on the counter with his head down, my heart pauses. Bagheera comes in through the doggy door to greet me.

"Hey buddy," I say softly, leaning down to kiss his head.

When I stand, pain and blood rush to my head, causing me to wince and press a palm against my forehead. Without a word, Dornan hands me two white pills and a glass of water. I take them, his eyes flickering up to mine for a moment, before he turns to face the window to the backyard again. I don't know what to say, 'thanks for beating Brayden up, thanks for stopping me from getting raped, sorry I got so drunk.'

"I'm sorry," I finally muster.

Dornan lets out a breath and shakes his head slightly.

"Sorry?" He questions, his tone annoyed.

"Yes, sorry," I lift a shoulder, my voice raising almost in defense.

"For what?" His eyes turn to mine, then dip down to the marks on my neck.

"For...everything-for getting drunk and not being able to get myself out of a situation, that you had to beat someone up for me, that I put you in that position-"

"Trust me, I've been wanting to get into a fight with that asshole for a long time," he states. "And what if I hadn't come back there V... then what?"

"Then I would've had to deal with that for the rest of my life, accept what I did and what happened and move on," I state adamantly.

His eyes harden then narrow.

"Please tell me that's never happened to you before."

"No," I rush out. "Brayden's never been like that with me-"

"I don't mean Brayden, I mean anyone, anytime."

The pain and fear in his eyes causes my eyes to water, swallowing hard as I shake my head.

"No," I finally whisper.

Dornan lets out a long hard breath and bows his head, closing his eyes. We stand there in silence and I can't stop the tears from pooling in my eyes, the overwhelming heaviness of the situation taking over.

"How the hell did you think you were gonna get home if I wasn't there?" He stops and shakes his head again.

"I was," my voice wavers and I stop. "Sven said he'd take me, or I was gonna stay at your apartment. I'm sorry Dornan, I fucked up, I know it. Stop trying to make me feel worse, I've already beat myself up enough this morning."

His eyes open and shoot to me, faltering slightly when he notices the tears falling down my cheeks.

"It's all I can see...him touching you and you not able to do shit."

I can't take this, the intensity. The need to distance myself, has me walking backwards towards the dining room.

"Try not to act like a stupid bitch next time you drink," he mumbles.

I halt, is he being serious? Did he just call me a bitch? My self-pity turns to anger in an instant, like he thinks he's going to throw that at me and I won't respond. Is he trying to piss me off? Because it works.

"Oh like you're one to talk, how many fights have you gotten into when you're drunk? How many times have you been locked up when you're drunk? Or the countless other mistakes you've made... so don't you dare fucking lecture me because I fuck up *one* time and you think it's a free pass to make me the asshole! Stupid bitch my ass, you goddamn fucking piece of shit!" I yell while whirling around, away from him.

"Maven," he growls.

And if his tone of voice didn't alert me to his temperament, the use of my full name sure does.

"We're not done talking."

I stop and turn to face him again, his brows furrowed as he stares me down with that hardened expression I've seen him give enemies before. I've seen grown men crumble at this look, but not me, nope. He's about to lay into me, but I'm going to cut him off at the pass.

"No, you're not gonna talk down to me like I don't know I did something stupid or last night couldn't have changed my life forever... if all you're gonna do is make me feel more like shit than I already do, you can just fucking leave," I huff and again turn away.

I get one foot in the hallway, planning on heading back to my room to sleep. When suddenly Dornan's hands grab my arms, whirling me around and pushing my ass against the wall. Then he grasps my hips as his face comes within inches of mine, our noses touching, our lips a hair's-breath away. I lean closer wanting his lips on mine but he retreats, pulling his head back and then closer to toy with me. His breathing is labored as he yanks my hips towards him using my panties, before pulling them down my thighs. He drops to his knees, and guides my panties off my feet before tossing them aside. I need this, yes, something terrible happened last night to me, but I need Dornan to show me worship and erase all the touches Brayden has ever placed on my skin. His palms lift under my thighs, draping my legs over his shoulders as he plants his lips on my clit, his mouth devouring my pussy.

"Oh God," I pant. "Oh God."

Slapping my opened hands onto the wall beside me to brace myself, but Dornan's body and strength keep me upright, and my back firmly against the wall. My hair falls over my shoulders in long curtains, as I look down at his tongue lapping my flesh, my chest heaving under my shirt. His fingers dig into my ass cheeks as he pulls me against his mouth, licking, sucking, and fucking my pussy with his tongue.

"So good, so perfect-" Dornan chants against my pussy.

Nothing's ever felt this good, no one has ever shown such profuse attention to my body like this before. Dornan groans as he eats me, my eyes closing as my head hits the wall, all pain from my injury seeming nonexistent as he takes me...he fucking *takes me*. He maneuvers my leg over his shoulder as he frees one of his hands, and I hear the rustling of fabric. Blinking to clear my vision and look down to see him struggling to free the button on his jeans. Finally, his magnificent dick comes free, and he moans as he takes himself in hand, beginning to stroke it.

"Swear to Christ tasting you is gonna make me come."

Oh. My. God.

I'm so wet and getting wetter as I feel my orgasm approaching, the unreachable reaction no man has ever given me. His lips latch onto my clit to push me over the edge. Stomach trembling, thighs quivering in an all-out explosion of my senses. I swear I've never come so hard in my life, not even on my own. As colors dance behind my eyelids, Dornan whispers things to me as he softly kisses my clit one last time, causing me to shudder at the sensitive flesh he's still toying with.

Urgently he sets me on my feet, my skin still thrumming with orgasm and excitement, wanting the feelings to never end. The need only intensifies, as his cock presses against my clit. With shaking hands, I grip the hem of his shirt at the same instant he reaches back with one hand to pull it over his head. When all that bare chiseled flesh comes into view, my mouth goes to it. Kissing down his neck to his collarbone, dragging my tongue down the center of his abs while I sink to my knees. Dornan growls and puts both his palms against the wall in front of him, bowing his head to watch me. Not that I've seen many cocks in real life, but Dornan's is beautiful. Standing thick and proud and hard, the veins defined, the flushed head huge and bobbing before my lips. I want to play, study it, but not now, right now I want to make him come. My fingers wrap around the base as I suck him into my mouth.

"Maven," he moans.

His eyes blink lazily, looking down at me with excitement and lust. There's never been an urge on my part to suck a dick before, I never thought I was particularly good at it either, but the way he's watching me drives me blow job crazy. I suck hard as I pull back, liking the sensation of my lips slipping over the thick skin of the head. Bumping the wall with the back of my skull with a thud, Dornan hurriedly places a hand over the tender spot to protect it. My hand pumps and squeezes as my mouth takes him deep, my tongue dancing along the underside, my other hand cups and massages his balls. Then both of his hands are on my head as he begins to thrust into my mouth. At first slow, but when he realizes he can go further into my throat, and I can take it, he moves faster. Frantically he thrusts as he pushes into me, my grip tightening at the base along with my mouth. My watery eyes never leave his, as warm spurts of semen shoot onto my tongue.

"Jesus-fuck fuck fuck fuck."

He groans long as his jaw tightens, before his lips part and he begins panting. His hands loosen their hold on my head, his hips slowing, his body jerking slightly as the last remnants from his orgasm leave him.

I swallow and remove my mouth from him, feeling totally bad ass that I just made him come. But then the pain from my head injury returns, or maybe my high's wearing off, because now I can barely keep my eyes open. Dornan lifts me, cradling me in his arms as he carries me upstairs to bed. He situates me on my side, facing him as he lays down beside me. His arm curling over my torso to press his hand onto my lower back, bringing our bodies as close as possible. My face nuzzles into his neck, and I inhale him with a deep breath before falling asleep.

When I wake, there's warmth between my legs. I'm on my back. A strong hand massaging my breasts underneath my shirt, while Dornan's tongue runs back and forth along my folds. My legs are bent at the knees as he pushes my thighs open with his shoulders, his fingers spreading my lips so he can delve deeper. I'm thrusting and grinding my hips up to his face, my fingers clawing into the sheets as I come while his name escapes in a moan from my mouth. As my breathing slows and my head clears, Dornan kisses up my torso. Showing attention to each breast, sucking on my nipples over my shirt, before kissing up to my bare neck.

"Well, hello." I smile, running my hands through his short hair, before wrapping my arms around his wide shoulders.

"How are you feeling?" he whispers in my ear.

"Uh, besides amazingly fantastic...hungry," I smile even wider.

The sun's setting and I feel better, my head's still sore but after two earth shattering orgasms, I feel like a new woman. Who knew that this is what I've been missing all my life, that Dornan and I could've been having this for years now, but instead I wasted time with Brayden.

Dornan lays between my legs, his erection pressing into my thigh, but he makes no move to push for anything more. Instead, he kisses me softly, my neck, my cheeks, my face, treasuring me. The intimacy makes my eyes burn, the feelings he's conjuring in me, are ones I've never experienced before. It makes me thankful that I can say that Brayden never made me feel this way, that this is something for Dornan and Dornan only. Finally, he rises up from the bed, shooting me a sweet smile before kicking the sheet off his jean clad legs and walking out of the room. When he bypasses the bathroom, I begin to ask what he's doing when he beats me to it.

"Don't get up, I'll be right back," he says.

There's going to be no problem with that because I'm limp and languid. I hear Dornan talking to Bagheera, and the sound of dog food being poured into his bowl before letting him out the back door. Sneaking into the bathroom I look at myself in the mirror, the marks on my neck from Brayden are still red and visible but easy to cover with my hair. My hair's a rumpled and wild looking mess that shouts 'I just got some.' Slickness coats between my legs, as my pussy still trembles with the aftermath of orgasm. This new sensation of being thoroughly worked over, totally wrung out, it's foreign but so welcomed.

"I told you not to get up," Dornan says from the doorway, knocking me from my thoughts and scaring the shit out of me.

I smile at not obeying him.

"Come on."

Reaching his hand out for me to take it, gladly I follow his bare back and low riding jeans down the steps. I'm still in a t-shirt and nothing else, the house is dark except for the light over the sink in the kitchen. When we walk into the dining room, there's two bowls of cereal sitting there. I smile and press a kiss on the back of his shoulder before sitting down, scooping a large amount of the chocolatey puffs onto my spoon and shoveling it into my mouth. Dornan smiles at my unladylike way of eating, but I'm so hungry that I don't care.

"You have quite the cereal collection, I thought you grew out of that." he says, walking over to the fridge and grabbing juice from the door.

"Never," I mumble around another mouthful. All my life cereal has been my favorite meal, mainly since growing up with a dad who never cooked. Dornan sets three headache pills on the table along with the jug of juice beside me, then he begins eating. We sit in comfortable silence, as we scarf down our food. After my second bowl, I sit back with a contented sigh and look at him.

"I feel better now," I state.

"How's your head?"

"Okay, it comes and goes," I shrug.

"Do you want me to take you to the doctor?"

"No, I'll be okay. Thank you though," I tell him.

Bagheera wanders in from outside and sits at my feet, nudging his nose into my hands for me to pet him. I scratch the fur on his cheeks, and lean down to kiss his nose. Excitedly he sits up, putting his front paws on my lap and pushes closer as his tail wags like crazy along the floor.

"Did you want me to go?" Dornan asks.

I raise my head and furrow my brows.

"No. Why?"

Honestly confused as to why he's asking.

"You told me to leave earlier," he says, still looking down at his food.

I slide my hand across the table, and flick his wrist with my index finger.

"Hey," I say softly.

He turns his head to look at me. The thought that I might say 'yes' is all over his face.

"I was mad. I want you to stay," I smile.

That night we spent time in the living room, sprawled in a tangle of limbs on the couch, watching mindless television and snacking. Other than the occasional kiss, things remain PG, and I'm not sure why. The thrum of sexual tension pulses between us, my insides feel fluttery, my skin so aware when he touches me. Never has someone made me feel like this, it's like electricity is flowing through my veins, lighting me up from the inside.

The next morning, I wake up alone and hear music coming from one of the spare bedrooms. I get out of bed and run my hands through my hair as I walk down the hall, seeing Bagheera laying on the floor by one of the open doors. When I enter the room I see Dornan in the en-suite bathroom, lights on as he paints... he's painting the bathroom. The house still isn't finished and I work on it when I can, all I have left to do is paint the four spare bedrooms and bathrooms upstairs.

"Hey there."

I say over the music, as I pet Bagheera's head. Dornan has a paint can in one hand, his other raised above his head holding the paintbrush, as he looks over his shoulder at me.

"Hey...did I wake you?" he asks, his eyes look me up and down with that little side smirk.

"No. But-you don't have to do that," I state, walking to the doorway

116

of the bathroom. I feel slightly embarrassed that he either thinks I need his help, or that he thinks I'm lazy for it not to be finished yet.

"I was bored, there's only so long I can watch you sleep. You needed the rest, and I'm not into necrophilia, so… you've got a lot of painting to do still."

"Yeah I know, but I'm in the home stretch of being done so…" I reply rather defensively.

"You did a really great job on the house babe."

I feel my cheeks flush as I bite my lower lip and smile, I have put a lot of work into the house. But I never have anyone over to see the inside, so this is the first compliment on all my hard work.

"Thank you," I smile wider as my anxiety defuses.

I watch his muscles flex under his shirt, as he continues to paint and look fucking hot in the process.

"Are you just gonna watch me all day, or are you gonna help?" he asks, not looking back at me.

"Oh yeah, yeah," I reply quickly as his words knock me out of my trance.

"Let me just change."

I push away from the door.

"Okay, we're gonna do this...we're gonna paint."

And it's then I realize I'd hoped to wake up another way, more like Dornan on top of me in bed. I change into the ratty clothes I wear when I work on the house, and we spend hours painting. There's the occasional kiss here and there, ass smacking, and long looks as we work, but no more. I stop at five and get us bowls of cereal, and as soon as we finish eating we get right back into painting. It's around nine when we finish. My arms, shoulders, and neck scream with pain, but it's worth it to know my house is finally finished. Dornan washes out the brushes, as I fold up the drop cloth. Van Morrison's- "Into the Mystic" is playing over my iPod. When suddenly, Dornan grabs me and plants a kiss on my lips. My hands drop the cloth in order to place my hands over his, as he cups my cheeks. He presses soft kisses to my lips as we begin swaying to the song, and I look up into his eyes before he kisses the tip of my nose.

"I wanna rock your gypsy soul," he sings. "Just like back in the days of old, and together we will flow into the mystic."

I close my eyes and take in this moment. I never want to forget any time with Dornan, especially when he's like this. Even though I've known him all my life, this part of him is new and I'm cherishing this unexplored side to him. My heart pangs at these awakening sensations, he makes me feel sexy and desirable, but also cared for and protected.

"Shower?" he asks in between kisses on my neck.

"I have something better," I whisper, biting my lower lip as he sends goosebumps all over my skin.

"What could be better than seeing me wet and naked?"

I snort and turn, tugging his hand as I lead him out the backdoor. Bagheera runs out into the night ahead of us, as I take Dornan to the edge of the property just before the thick tree line. It's fairly dark back here, the only illumination is from Mrs. Kendall's porch lights, which gives off just enough to let me know I'm about to really enjoy this.

"Oh shit, I forgot about this. I remember when we'd come over in the summer, and your grams would let us swim here all day. Then she'd make us peanut butter and jelly sandwiches," Dornan smiles.

We both look out at the man-made pool that my grandpa put in when my dad was a kid, it's nothing spectacular just a huge hole in the ground, but I have some great memories here. Bagheera runs around the yard at full speed as Dornan and I both inspect the dark water. I watch Dornan look over at me because I'm stripping my clothes off. He blinks at what my hands are doing, then his eyes widen when I slip my shorts and panties off. Then I'm pretty sure he stops breathing, when I fling off my t-shirt and unclasp my bra.

"Don't you wanna swim?" I tease, before jumping into the water.

It's freezing cold which causes me to gasp when I come up for air, running my hands over my wet hair to smooth it back. Dornan's still standing there, pulling his shirt over his head when I re-emerge. Our eyes meet and the smile slowly disappears from my lips as he strips for me... strips... for... me. His blue eyes watch me treading water as he slowly unbuttons the fly of his jeans, kicking his boots off, before bending down to remove them. His perfect body on display, paint covering his hands and forearms, and even at rest, a thick massive cock that I can already feel between my legs. He stands there, naked as a jaybird. The light from next door shining on him, and making the yard look black beyond his form. I just stare, taking in every inch of him, he's beautiful.

Then I lift a hand and splash water forward, he raises his brows before stepping into the water up to his waist, and using both arms to send tidal waves of water towards me. We're both laughing and suddenly Bagheera jumps in and we're all splashing and being loud. At one point I glance up at the neighbor's house and see someone looking at us through the drapes, which makes me laugh even harder. What a sight we must be and how surely Mrs. Kendall's debating calling the cops, or an ambulance over the heart attack I'm sure we're giving her. Suddenly, Dornan grabs my waist, causing me to cry out as he pulls me onto his lap, my legs wrapping around his hips as he treads water. Droplets of water drip from our faces as he runs his fingers over my hairline, down behind my ears to my neck and shoulders, wiping my hair back as he clears my eyes. My smile fades when I take in his serious expression.

"I don't ever want there to be apologies between us, we get shit out and say what we need to each other because we're closer than other people, you understand?"

I nod.

"But I'm sorry for what I said the other night. You didn't do anything wrong. He did. You have every right to do what you want, if you want to get drunk you can. I know you're smart enough to have had a way to get home, and I'm sorry. I would never blame you for something that wasn't your fault, I didn't mean to make you feel worse," he says softly.

"I know," I swallow hard. "I know you were just upset."

He cups my cheeks and meets my eyes.

"You're always so strong and you don't take shit, and that's what I've always relied on from you, you to be the one that I can talk to, to reason with me. But I never forget," he stops and runs his thumb under my lip. "That you have always been the most beautiful girl I've ever laid eyes on, you're smart and independent and you don't need me. You could live without me and be fine... but you want me, you want *me*." He ran his nose along mine. "Do you know how that makes me feel?"

I shake my head as a smile spreads over my lips, and my eyes water, a single tear spilling down my cheeks.

"It makes me feel like fucking Superman."

I let out a small watery laugh.

"I want you to be mine V."

I place my hands on his shoulders, my heart pounding even harder in my chest. Can I do this? Can I be Dornan's old lady? I'll always be tied to this life I'm beginning to realize, old lady or not, this is it for me. The reality is I need to face, well, reality. Dornan's better to me and for me than I could ever want a man to be. He makes me feel like I'm the only woman he's ever really seen, the only woman he's ever let in. Watching the hesitation in my eyes, he sighs.

"And I don't mean old lady like it is with my mom, or Gwen, or Katie even...you're my equal. I can't keep anything from you, even if you decide to hang your cut and leave the MC, there'll never be a time I won't talk to you about shit. I won't be able to go on a job, or run and not tell you what for. I respect you too much to treat you lesser than you deserve. You're it for me V, I've always known that. I trust you with my life, with my past and my future-"

"Yes," I rush out, cutting him off. "I want to be yours Dornan."

His eyes light up before he pulls me into his lips, taking my breath away as he stands. Lifting me as he walks us out of the water and up the massive lawn towards the house, never once stopping our kiss. My ass hits the backdoor as Dornan fumbles with the handle, kicking it open once the latch gives. Water drips off us and onto the wood floors, as he carries me through the house to my bedroom. With a strong arm he guides me onto the bed, our skin still wet but now hot from kissing, and the excitement of what we're about to do is palpable. He lays over me as I spread my legs so his hips can rest in between, soft kisses placed on my face as my hands run up and down his back. My insides are fluttering with anticipation, never in my life have I wanted someone so badly. I almost feel like I will explode with the anticipation if he doesn't fuck me this instant. His hands clasp mine, linking our fingers and bringing them over our heads. My hips push up, cradling his erection between us, hoping that this might hint that I'm ready. But he just keeps kissing me, slow and unhurried.

"Dornan," I growl in frustration, because clearly we're on two different pages about the urgency here.

He chuckles softly against my neck before nipping the skin there, so I arch my back to press my chest to his. My hard nipples graze along his skin, which causes him to groan and push his hips down against mine.

"I've waited forever for this, but I don't think I can wait... later, later I will worship you the way you deserve, but now I just need to fuck you," he pants against my face.

I smile and lean up to kiss him, quickly it turns hot and wet, tongues tasting and teasing. I untangle my hand from his, slipping down between us, taking his engorged cock in my palm and squeezing. He moans, resting his forehead on mine. My closed fist runs down and up his dick, twisting my wrist at the head, as his shuddering breath dances over my lips.

"I have an IUD, we always used condoms," I blurt out. 'We' in reference to me and Brayden.

His eyes meet mine as he swallows loudly, in realization that I want him bare.

"I'm clean V, condoms always, always."

I can't give Dornan my virginity, but I can give him this, and we can experience this first together. Pushing my hips up once more, the head of him kisses my wetness and we both freeze. Our breaths come fast and labored as Dornan reaches down to take my hand from his cock, kissing my palm before placing it over my head again. His body lifts, the head of his dick finding my entrance without any assistance. As he pushes in, every hot inch of him scorches me with no barrier. My breathing halts as my body stills and tenses, the fit's snug and my body tightens even more in an involuntary reaction. I want him so badly, but I can't get my body to focus. His smell, sounds, taste, and feel, all overloading my brain. The fact that this is actually even happening…it's all too much.

"Hey," he whispers.

His soft low voice brings me out of my head. With this I realize my eyes are tightly closed, and I blink them open when I realize he's stopped moving.

"Hey," he repeats and my eyes connect to his.

My breath comes out shaky, an apology on my lips but no words produce.

"It's okay…just kiss me," he whispers, running his nose up along mine.

My lips touch his, my body's shivering, my shoulders jerking as my nerves fire off with adrenaline. He's trembling too, but probably with restraint since half his cock's sitting inside me. He kisses me slow and deep, with every lap of his tongue my body melts and accepts him. All while nodding my head over and over in silent submission that he can continue, but he just keeps kissing me until I soften even more. Then his hands grip mine tighter, as his upper body lifts and he thrusts hard into me. I let out a strangled moan that turns into a gasp, the head of his cock hitting something so deep, I swear it's never been touched before.

"Good?" he asks in a thick voice.

"Yes, very good," I rush out.

He looks down at me as I tilt my head up, his cock is so huge, causing sensations I've never felt before. This is what I'd been missing with Brayden, Dornan makes me feel cherished and loved. My pleasure is his, and the way his face changes as he nestles deep inside me. His eyes happy under the glassiness, as a smile spreads over his lips and he kisses me again.

Slowly, he begins to thrust in and out of my body, my moans growing louder as his hand runs down my arm to cup my breast, bringing his lips to my nipple. My thighs flex around his torso while I bring my hands to his head, pressing him down to suck harder. Leaving my chest with a pop, he sits up on his knees and pulls my hips onto him. I lean up, resting back on my hands as I ground down. He grabs the back of my neck to pull me closer and kiss me savagely, his cock rubbing deep, my hips begin to circle faster over him, almost frantically.

"Fuck yes, come for me V," Dornan pants against my lips.

He looks down at where we join, his muscles flexed and sweaty. Never in all my imaginings of him like this, did I ever picture him looking this gorgeous. The way he's holding onto me, the way his eyes scan up and zero on my lips before kissing me tenderly. His hips move fast, as his lips move slow.

My arms give way, sending me back onto the bed. He follows, never breaking the kiss. Resting his elbows beside my head, he thrusts into me hard and powerful, but slow and rhythmic. He slides his hands up into my hair, cocooning his body over mine and making me feel so small beneath his massive frame. He palms the back of my head to kiss me deeper, his tongue tangling with mine. Reaching down I begin to rub my clit vigorously, my pussy tightening around him and urging his pace faster as his hips slam into me. My insides grip him hard as I come and my muscles tighten, while my mouth opens in a silent cry before whimpers break free. Dornan groans as he buries his face in my neck, every muscle in his body flexes and hardens just before he comes inside me. I bite my lip and feel totally drained, physically and emotionally. We both heave for air as his weight lay comfortably on top of me, and I pull his shoulders closer against me.

"That was-" he stops and swallows. "Damn woman."

"Yeah," I sigh dreamily.

We both chuckle before he leans up, and kisses me silly. We get up and take a shower together, I've never showered with someone else before, let alone a man and it's...pretty counterproductive. Something shifts between us that I like, we've now had sex, we've crossed the line of the point of no return...and it feels right. I thought it would terrify me that afterwards Dornan would realize he'd made a mistake in lusting after me all these years, he'd get a piece then try like hell to get away. Instead, we enjoy this new closeness without our clothes on. Dornan seems more, if it's possible, into me. He keeps touching me and kissing me, and whispering sweet dirty things into my ear that make my toes curl. Going from never having anyone in my house, to him fitting into it perfectly made sense, everything made sense. Again I had several 'duh' moments to which I caught myself wondering why in the world we hadn't started this sooner in life.

"Oh God don't stop," I moan as Dornan plunges his tongue inside me, he'd woken me up on my stomach, his hands lifting my ass in the air as he eats me out from behind. My cheek presses against the mattress, as my fingers claw at the pillows above my head. He has a glorious tongue and a wonderful mouth that when it locks onto my clit, the elation pulses through my entire body. His tongue takes long licks from my clit to my asshole, that have me shuddering and grinding against his mouth in seconds. As he crawls over my body, his hips push down on my rear, pinning me to the bed as he uses his legs to press mine together. His thick hard cock slides into me and I swear I hear angels singing, sex can't be this good for everyone or else no one would leave their houses.

When he's to the hilt, he plants kisses on my neck, while his arms cage my shoulders. He starts to slam into me, his massive biceps hold me in place and I can get the full force of his dick fucking me. He moves hard and deep, not overly fast but the pace has me biting my lip, and white knuckling the sheets. My forehead presses into the bed, as the intensity from this is quickly driving me mad.

"Take it," he groans.

I raise my head and let out a cry, one of his hands grabs my hair and pulls my head back causing another whimpered cry to leave me. He begins to kiss me, his tongue and lips driving me madder. His hips slap against my ass as his thighs tighten beside my legs, his biceps bulge and I picture looking at us like this. Him completely over me and pushing his big rigid cock into me over and over, as I lay there immobile and receive what he gives me.

"Perfection," he says into my ear. "Your tight pussy squeezing my dick, my dick making you wet and hot, wanting more," his hand tightens in my hair.

"Oh...Dornan," I plead.

"You like when I pull your hair and fuck you like this, fuck you from behind and you fucking take it?"

"Yes," I sigh, nodding my head frantically.

I feel out of control, my body taking over and reaching for release. I push onto my elbows and begin to thrust my ass up to meet him.

"Dornan," I whimper.

"Tell me what you want, babe."

"Make me come," I pant.

"You want to come on my cock. You want to feel me come inside that perfect little cunt?"

I moan and bite my lip. Dornan slips a hand under me and presses his fingers to my clit.

"Fuck," I moan and slam my hand onto the bed, chanting. "Oh God."

"Say my name when you come. Scream it."

So I do, I scream his name with an orgasm that has me grinding into his hand as my pussy clenches around him before he stills and comes too. We both pant and lay there, our bodies jerking and shuddering with the aftershocks of our orgasms. Soft kisses press on my shoulders and neck, as Dornan gathers my hair over one shoulder. Running his nose along my ear, and causing me to shiver.

"Can we stay in bed all day?" he asks.

I groan slightly.

"No... I have so much work to do today, it's the end of the month so billing's a bitch."

His lips still dance over my skin and Jesus he's making this hard, his hands moving under me to cup my breasts.

"Dornan...don't start this again."

"Just one more time," he mumbles against my shoulder.

Pushing his hips into me and making sure I can feel his cock thickening inside me.

"You said that last time," I groan playfully.

Just then Bagheera walks into the room and sits in the doorway. Both Dornan and I look at him as he cocks his head and makes a displeased sound. After a moment Dornan rolls off me, I reach down and grab my t-shirt from the floor, slipping it over my head before following Bagheera downstairs to feed him. It's already nine a.m. and I don't have time for a run, but I'm fairly sure I've done enough cardio in the last twelve hours that I feel okay with skipping it.

I walk back into my bedroom after a shower, surprised to see Dornan dressing since he seemed more than content with laying in bed all day. He's laid clothes out for me again this morning. A pair of black khaki shorts that are plenty short, a black and white striped tank top with a racerback, that has a low dip in the front. Is he trying to get other guys to notice me? Because this top always does. I dress as he sits on the edge of the bed, putting his boots on while turning his head to watch me.

"Uh, you forgot panties," I state.

"No, I didn't," he shoots me that half grin that makes me want to climb back into bed with him,

I shake my head and finish getting dressed. As I walk over to my dresser he catches me by the wrist, pulling me onto his lap. He presses his nose and lips into the crook of my neck, where there's still faint marks from Brayden's assault, while wrapping his arms loosely around my waist. The embrace isn't sexual, just comforting and intimate, almost like a moment to take in all the things that happened the night before. Slipping my arms around his broad shoulders, I rest my cheek on his head and we sit there for a while, neither wanting to break the contact. Finally, one of our cellphones ringing constantly downstairs breaks us from our physical connection, and gets us moving.

As I get my purse and phone together at the kitchen table, Dornan listening to his voicemails. He disappears to the entryway of the house, returning with my black chunky bike boots and setting them down beside my feet. I smile at the gesture, and the fact that he really likes picking my clothes. After zipping up my boots, I grab my car keys just as Dornan swipes the screen of his phone, ending the call.

"I'm driving."

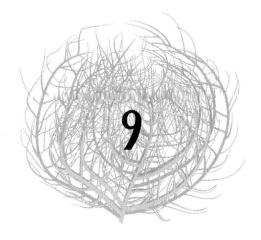

9

Dornan opens my door as we park in the lot of the shop, Bagheera immediately takes off running towards the back grounds with grass. Dornan takes my hand and we begin walking, only a few feet after we start, he begins pulling to the right as I walk to the left. He's heading for the clubhouse and me to the shop. Just before our hands part, he pulls me back into his arms. Cupping my throat and chin with his hand, he plants a kiss on me that causes between my legs to throb. A few whistles and catcalls come from around the clubhouse and the shop, which makes me giggle into his lips before he smacks my ass and we part ways. I can't hide my smile as I walk towards the shop, glancing back to see Dornan looking back at me with a smile and a wink, as we walk away from each other.

"That lucky fuckin' bastard," Drag states as I clock in.

"Please. Like you ever had a fucking chance," Smokey replies.

Smokey's back to work on a part time basis, not really doing any mechanic work but helping me with office stuff, or if Skye needs help with anything at the front desk.

"She never even gave me a shot," Drag adds.

I look at him over my shoulder, and by the smile he's giving me I know he's teasing.

"Sorry, he's got a better bike than you," I shrug slightly.

"Ohh shit," Smokey laughs, then coughs.

"Take it easy old man," Drag furrows his brows at Smokey.

I shake my head and turn towards my office, Skye's on the phone but hands me my messages and other paperwork. Sitting down at my desk I see there's several messages from Justice, what the fuck? Seriously, how does he know about the shop and its connection or that I even work here? He always called my cellphone before picking me up from here, what was going on with this guy? I toss the messages in the trash and knew I'd eventually have to speak with him, since the foundation for the new strip club is being poured today, and planned to meet him out there Friday to check on progress.

There's also a letter from Dad, which causes me to smile as I study my father's handwriting. For whatever reason, maybe since so much shit has happened in the last week with Brayden, the wonderfulness of Dornan, or maybe just because I miss him, my eyes pool with tears. I fan my face with my hands in an attempt to dry them and not let myself cry. Finally, I take a few deep cleansing breaths and clear my throat, before slipping the letter into my purse to read at home later.

Sometime later, Spiney the prospect knocks on the frame of my open office door. The office is sweltering in the mid afternoon heat. Combined with the smell and noise from the shop, is making me irritated and edgy. On top of that, I hadn't seen Dornan since this morning, and about two hours ago I'd received a text from him saying he's heading out with Joey and Chain. That he would come see me when he gets back.

"Yeah?" I say without looking up.

It's so hot, even Bagheera doesn't move, just lays there panting.

"Pres is callin' gathering," he says in his deep voice.

"Okay."

Still Spiney stands there.

"Need something?" I ask as I stand.

His eyes dart to the ground, then to Bagheera, then to my desk.

"I'm supposed to give you a piggy back ride over to the clubhouse," he says quickly.

Raising an eyebrow, I ask, "What did you do?"

"I may or may not have forgotten to fill Rocket's bike with gas, and it may or may not have stalled on him in the middle of nowhere."

I cock my head to the side.

"It's not my fault the old bastard never takes a cellphone," he shrugs.

"Well," I begin while rounding my desk. "I'm not going to make you carry me, but Bagheera would love to run through the hose and kiddie pool in the back. You can go ahead and do that for me, cool?"

"Fuck yes," he replies. "Not that I don't want to carry you," he amends. "I do. But the guys only told me to do this because they want to see Dornan pissed, and I don't want to start shit with him. Besides you have those little shorts on and..." he trails off looking up and down my bare legs.

"Hello, I can make another arrangement for you, like putting all of my dog's shit in your car for a week. Or do you want to go ahead and pull your head out of your ass?"

His eyes shoot up to mine.

"No, no, the doggy water park is fine."

The open air of outside, even though still hot, feels amazing as I make the short walk over to the clubhouse. I notice all bikes are accounted for including Dornan's, so he'd come back and not come to see me. I groan as I enter the stifling hot building, the smell of sweat and leather hanging in the air like a thick curtain, notching my irritation level up higher. Joey squeezes my shoulder as I walk towards the meeting room and look up at him with a smile. The last time I'd seen him, he was pulling Dornan off of Brayden. He studies my face and I give him a genuine smile to convey I'm alright, and thankful he'd been there. His arm slides over my shoulders and pulls me into his side with a squeeze, before kissing my temple and leading me through the door beside him. Dornan's sitting at his seat already, eyes downcast at the table as he appears deep in thought. The instant I walk in, his eyes shoot to me and I can tell something serious is going on. Taking my seat beside Sven, who waits until everyone's seated before he begins speaking.

"Thank you everyone for getting together on short notice… few things we need to discuss." He pauses before leaning forward, resting his forearms on the oak table.

"Business between us and Children of the Reaper is no more. We no longer associate with them from here on out."

I'm not sure who knows what happened at the party, but my eyes stay on Sven's profile, his eyes scanning the faces around me. I'm hyperaware of my body language, and concentrate on keeping my senses in check. To not allow my posture to change, or cheeks to flush with embarrassment.

"Of course this means we need to prepare for the inevitable retaliation, because Judas and his council were not happy about this as you can imagine. We all know weapons aren't their main source of income, but we need to possibly transfer what we have to another location. Including what's in the clubhouse, and out at the galaxy field."

Galaxy field is a piece of property the club owns out in the middle of nowhere desert, it has an underground bunker where we hide all reserves, and just in case shit that we might need as leverage in some situations. We could've dipped into the few guns we had store there to fix the mess with The Steel Axes, but we mainly kept club papers, drugs, and more serious weaponry than guns there. Including grenades, machine guns, and even a rocket launcher we'd gotten in a trade. There are nods and mumbles around the table.

"Also the situation with The Steel Axes has been taken care of, we owe Milestone but they are usually willing to take narcotics off our hands in payment."

Our club mainly deals with weapons, but we confiscate drugs when they fall into our laps and only use those to barter or trade. I glance over at Dornan who's staring at me, and seems less concerned now as he makes eye contact with me, like he's decompressed with each of his dad's words. The longer I look at him, for whatever reason, the more annoyed I get. And by the way he raises his eyebrows a fraction in question, tells me he notices.

"Alright, that's all I have," Sven nods and chairs push back from the table.

I squeeze through the huge men standing around the room, and get the hell out of this hot ass building, before I have heat stroke or puke from the smell. Spiney's already hosing Bagheera down in the back, and by the look of it, both seem to be enjoying themselves. I run my hand through my long hair, gathering it in my hands and twisting it up into a bun and off my neck, which instantly begins to unravel as I inhale a deep breath of semi fresh air.

"Maven, Justice called for you again," Skye announces as I enter the shop.

I nod while giving the customer standing at the front counter a smile, even though Skye's propped the doors open and has several fans blowing, the permanent boob sweat is again adding to my annoyance. Once entering my office, I bend down towards my desk fan, pulling the front of my shirt down to let the cool air blow over me, when the door behind me opens and slams shut.

"What's your problem?" Dornan asks.

I stand and turn.

"Weren't you supposed to come see me when you got back?" I ask.

I realize it's dumb, as soon as I say it. This isn't even my problem; I don't know what my problem is actually.

He raises his brows, resting his hands on his narrow hips.

"Seriously?"

I shrug slightly.

"Yeah, seriously."

"I'd just gotten back and saw Spiney heading to your office, I assumed to get you for gathering, where I would see you."

"Why didn't you come anyway?"

"I had to talk to Dad," he replies, annoyance beginning in his eyes.

"About?"

"We went to the Children of the Reapers, Dad wanted us to reiterate to Judas that if they didn't exile Brayden from the club, that we weren't cool anymore. Obviously, they disagreed."

I nod, looking down.

"So your dad knows what happened at the party?" I ask, my voice quiet.

"Of course...Joey went to get him after I nearly beat Brayden to death, and they took care of getting the CR out of the party. Dad told Judas they had 'til today to decide what their next move was, kick Brayden out or cut ties with us."

I'm not sure how I feel knowing Sven knows about that night, he doesn't seem to act like he knows and I'm fine with that. There's something about the club looking at me as powerless or a weak link that niggles at me. I want to be dependable, unbreakable and reliable. Not some chick who gets wasted at parties, and makes herself an easy target. Dornan steps closer, his scent filling my lungs, his hand slides under my hair and rests at the base of my neck.

"Now what's really wrong?" he asks, his voice low.

I sigh, hating yet loving that he knows me so well.

"I don't know," I exhale. "Shit with Brayden and the club, Justice's been calling me, my dad sent a letter, and its fucking hot as hell in here-" I say in a rush.

Dornan pulls me to him, my knees and feet knocking into his, his hand at my nape keeps me upright as he slams my body against his.

"I think your problem is you need to come, babe," he growls and begins walking me backwards until my ass hits the lip of the desk.

His hips part my legs as he lifts me onto the top. His fingertips trail down the exposed skin of my legs, all the way to my boots. Grasping me at the ankles, before bringing my feet up to plant them on the desk, causing my legs to spread even wider.

"No, there's customers out there," I gasp into his lips.

"Then I guess you'll have to be quiet."

"Dornan," I plead as his tongue slips into my mouth.

"I'll make it feel better," he whispers.

I whimper and bite his lower lip, my hands fisting the sleeves of his t-shirt.

"Are you addicted to my cock?"

I shudder as his fingertips graze my inner thigh, and slide down inside the crotch of my shorts. Touching directly onto my bare skin, his fingers rubbing in circles over my clit.

"Are you?" he asks, pulling his hand away from my flesh.

"Yes," I pant. "So-so addicted to you oohh," my words cut off by a moan as he returns to rubbing me.

"No, babe, not as addicted as I am to your face when you come."

My breath sputters against his lips as he finds the right spot and quickly begins to drive me into oblivion. Closing my eyes as he runs his nose along mine and begins whispering dirty words against my lips as my back arches, my hips inching closer into his touch.

"You're sloppy wet for me...oh Jesus and swollen, you're swollen from me inside you all night," he says to himself in awe. I moan and bite my lower lip, fuck, this man. He runs his fingers up and down my folds, dipping his middle finger inside me before moving back up and circling my clit again.

"I can smell how much you want it, smells so fucking good...when I eat your pussy I can't get enough, when I'm inside you I can't get enough...you're so tight and hot and wet for me."

My lips part and I gasp, whimpering as my orgasm begins to build. My hips circle and buck forward into his hand in a jerky motion.

"You look so gorgeous when you come from me."

His fingers quicken as my hands wrap tight around his biceps, my nails digging into his flesh as I try to muffle my cries of pleasure.

"Do you want to come? Fuck, I can feel it on my fingers, your muscles squeezing and wanting my cock...fuck Maven."

He groans and in hearing him say my name, I come. His lips sealing over mine as my body tightens and trembles with the force, his fingers slow right before he jerks my ass off the desk. His strong hands yank my shorts down and off, leaving me in my boots before pushing my legs back into position. My hands help his as we undo his jeans, then push his boxer briefs down to set his erection free. He slides a hand under my knee, propping my leg in the crook of his arm, before his eyes lock on mine, and he's pushing into me again.

"Dornan, oh God please, yes fuck me," I whimper, my eyes unfocusing as he slides deeper.

I press my hands back on the desk behind me, to hold myself up as he seats himself completely. Our breaths labored and fast. He runs his free hand over my cheek, before moving to the back of my neck and bringing my face closer to his.

"So fucking good," he chants. "You see what you do to me? Make me feel like a man, knowing my cock fucks your tight little body until you come."

My pussy gets wetter at his words and he really begins to move, pushing in and pulling out slowly at first, because yes, I'm swollen from last night. Our bodies make obscene sounds with how wet I am. He pulls out almost completely to let the thick crest of his head rub just inside my opening. I swear to God I go cross eyed, just before I'm about to come he slams into me. Maybe remembering we're in my office and probably don't have much time, he begins to move, his hips slam against my ass over and over. Bending my leg back further as he slides his hand from my neck up into my hair, grabbing a handful to keep me in place.

"Do you want to come again? You want my cock to make you

come?" he asks.

My lips part and I nod, holding my hair tighter as he fucks me, causing the desk to rattle with the movements.

"Yes I want to come, make me come," I gasp out.

"You like to scream my name, and be loud but you can't do that right? Everyone will know what I'm doing to you in here."

"Mmmm," is all I can say.

The hand that's bracing us up on the desk, slides up my torso and two fingers slip into my mouth, the same two fingers he used to fuck my pussy. I taste my sweet flavor and begin to suck on them as he delves deeper, searching for his own release. All of a sudden I come, increasing the pressure of my mouth around him as my body jerks.

"I'm coming Maven," he groans and lets out a growl as he spills inside me, feeling every hot burst of his come.

We're both covered in sweat, my office reeks of sex, but I don't care. This man makes me feel like the sexiest woman alive, powerful, that I can make him lose control with me. Lifting his head from my shoulder, he caresses my face with his fingers, smoothing my hair back and kissing my lips. He sets my feet down and heads into my attached bathroom, returning with his pants still unbuttoned but his cock tucked away. Kneeling before me, and with a warm wash cloth, he runs it between my legs. Cleaning me of any remnants of our love making, because it was love making. It doesn't matter that he'd just fucked me on a desk, it's the connection we share. Brayden could fuck me against a wall or even a bed, but it was just fucking, we didn't share anything, there was no intimacy in what we had. With me and Dornan, everything is done with love.

"Feel better now?" he asks after sliding my shorts on and standing.

I wrap my arms around his shoulders, pressing my face into his chest.

"I do actually," I smile and let out a sigh. "This better not be something I'm always going to need."

I tease lifting my head to meet his blue gaze, a look of confusion on his face.

"Because that tight little pussy you like so much, won't be that tight anymore."

Dornan growls and grabs my ass with both hands, tugging me closer.

"I'll take you with droopy titties, wrinkles, gray hair, and blown out," he smiles.

I tilt my head back and laugh, causing him to laugh, before he pulls my head back up and kisses me.

****

The next few days are uneventful, thank God. I needed time to decompress and get my shit together. It's a few days before I read my dad's letter, it wasn't about anything interesting, because he doesn't have much going on these days. Still, it's nice to have that connection to him and I decide that I'll go visit him sometime next week. There's no mention of what he meant when he said someone was going to come to me and that I shouldn't tell them anything, hoping that on my next visit he could tell me more.

Dornan and I are inseparable, when I'm home, he's there. When I'm at the shop, he's at the club. He's practically moved in with me. One morning I noticed his things in the shower, then a few days later he cleared two drawers in my dresser for his stuff. I don't mind since he does stay over every night, and the house is big enough for the both of us, besides I like having him in my space. Sometimes he runs with us in the morning, or leaves the club before I'm done at work and I'd come home to dinner made, and him telling me I 'deserve to be treated like gold.' He does laundry and helps me grocery shop, he's literally joined my life seamlessly, and I love it. Needless to say, the sex is amazing and keeps getting better. The fact that I've trusted him for so long, and with my life, strengthens our connection.

It's only this morning when I wake up to go for a run, that I notice my ruby ring's been moved from my right hand ring finger...to my left. He must've done this while I was asleep, and I'm not sure what this means. We haven't talked about the future really, Dornan always said he'd never make me promises. But he did ask me to be his old lady, and that was the extent of it. Knowing him for so long, I think part of it was he thought I'd still reject him, or tell him this meant more to him than me.

He got up before I left for my morning run, telling me he has to meet Drag and Sven at the clubhouse, and they'll be gone on a run all day. I know the job he's going on and it's nothing major, meeting with a business we've worked with before many times. I wait for him to be ready before Bagheera and I leave, his Charger pulling out the long driveway ahead of us as I blow him a kiss and head in the opposite direction. We run five miles in the foothills of the mountains, before heading home. It's late morning by the time Bagheera and I turn onto our street, and all seems quiet. Already today's beautiful, a breeze blows through the huge oak trees that line either side of the street, and it seems as if our heat wave might be letting up today.

"Maven!" I hear being called to my left, looking over to see my neighbor Mrs. Clayton walking towards me down her front walk. I slow and jog over towards her, I rarely ever talk to her, because like all the other neighbors she doesn't seem to like me. But she was one of my grandma's best friends, and is the eyes and ears of Plantain. The little old lady is dressed like it's winter in Colorado, as I stand there sweating and practically naked.

"Maven, I'm glad I saw you. I wanted to tell you, I saw a man on your property a few days ago."

"Oh, well I've had someone move in with me recently-"

"Not Dornan Frederiksen, this was someone I've never seen before."

I look over towards my house. I hadn't noticed anything out of place, like someone had tried to break in.

"He was in a dark SUV with another man driving, but only the one got out. He walked around the house, and looked in some of the windows. He was only there a few minutes before Bagheera," she nods down at him sitting beside me, "came out and chased him to the car."

I reach over to pet Bagheera's head, as I try to remember what day I left him home. But then it occurs to me, if Bagheera was outside, then that means that Dornan or myself had to be home at the time in order to let him outside. I place a hand on my throat, someone had been at my house with us there and we didn't even know it.

"I was about to call Officer Milton, but I didn't get a good look at the license plate, and I didn't see anyone come back. I only worried because they didn't come to the door, and I saw Dornan's Charger in the drive."

I'm not sure how to feel about this, no club members know where I live, except for Dornan, and Joey. But Mrs. Clayton knows Joey and would recognize him easily, and he would tell me if he'd been there.

"Thank you Mrs. Clayton," I reply monotone and start to walk towards my house when she begins talking again.

"I did see something though on the back windshield...you know." She lifts her arm and bends her hand inwards. "The thing the grim reaper holds?"

I feel my stomach drop, I mean, literally drop. A wave of nausea crashing over me, as I feel my knees weaken slightly.

"Scythe," I say to myself.

"What dear?" she narrows her eyes in not hearing me.

"Nothing," I lift my hand in a wave and turn around. "Thank you," I repeat.

I barely make it into my house, my bloods rushing and I feel faint. Robotically I fill Bagheera's water and grab my cellphone, seeing Dornan's texted me to tell me he made it there safely. My fingers hover over his name to call, fuck what am I supposed to say? 'Hey, just FYI Children of the Reaper were at our house.' Fuck. Grabbing a bag from one of the spare bedroom closets, and throw in a days worth of clothes. Dornan still has stuff at his clubhouse apartment, so I don't need to pack for him. I lock my doors, which I've never had to be mindful of, and for once wished I had some awesome security system or complicated locks. But this is my house, my sanctuary, things like this shouldn't be what I think about here.

We load into the car and head for the clubhouse, where no one seems to notice my arrival as I head to Dornan's apartment. I shower there and get dressed for the day, my nerves still fucking with me, my mind racing. What the fuck did they want at my house? Were they looking for me? Was it Brayden that had been there?

Dornan texts me again mid-afternoon, saying he doesn't think he'll be back until after midnight. A while later, I reply that I'm not feeling that great, and I'm probably going to crash in his apartment. I really don't feel well, but not bad enough to be unable to drive, I just need an excuse to keep Dornan and myself from the house. He immediately calls me and asks a hundred and one questions about what's wrong, and if I want Spiney to drive me home. I tell him I just need some sleep, and it isn't some awful thing that I'll be staying at his place.

"I fucked chicks on that bed V, I don't want to sleep with you there," he replies bluntly.

"Well, I'll be sure to change the sheets," I smile and cut him off as he starts to protest again. "Okay, see you when you get back, be safe," I rush out before hanging up.

Of course he calls me back, and I repeat that I don't care. His sweetness about it makes me forget, for a moment, the reason we're staying there to begin with. It's not that I'm avoiding telling him, but I'm not sure what the visit means or what they wanted...and really could I be certain it's even anyone from that MC? Granted, all Children of the Reaper have the reaper's scythe symbol on their leathers, their bikes, their flags, their tattoos. Maybe it's a coincidence, and some random person has it for a bumper sticker. Regardless, I don't want to cause a big thing if it's nothing, and I want more information before I tell anyone.

I page Chilly, yes page. He's so secretive and wants off the grid as far as possible, I'm surprised we don't use carrier pigeons to get in contact with him. The pager number's listed as a plumbing company in Texas, and he returns the call on a very complicated, untraceable setup he uses on a laptop. It's so complicated, I don't even understand it.

"Are you watching CR?" I ask.

"I got eyes on them, yeah."

143

His voice is gruffer than Smokey's, but he's actually a smoker.

"I'm not sure, but I have reason to believe, they might be attempting to collect personal information on members."

He makes a noise that I think is intended to be 'hmmm,' but it's so low and gravely, it comes out like a groan.

"Anyone in particular?" he asks.

"Not sure yet, just wanted to give you a heads up."

"Got it kid... if I find anything like that, I'll make sure D relays it."

Fuck.

"Sure, thanks brother."

I exhale deeply as I hang up the receiver, trying to focus back to the pile of work on my desk. But I can't concentrate due to my mind running over a million scenarios. Just as I'm about to give up and call it a day, my phone pings with a text, and I smile for the first time in hours to see it's from Dornan.

"Every time I hear this song I think of you babe...heading back, see ya soon."

Below is a link to Billy Joel's- "Always a Woman to Me." I bite my lip and let out a little giggle. Of course I've heard this song more than enough times to know it by heart. But knowing the lyrics connects me to him, causes me to stop and really listen. This is Dornan's way of telling me what he thinks of me. I guess some chicks would maybe not like the words, but every line makes me think of an instance in our lives together. When the song ends, I begin searching through my songs. One in particular I know will tell him everything I want to, the unspoken feelings I have for him, the one's I can't put into words for myself.

"Thank you for my song dedication, I plan to listen to it on repeat...here's a song for you, have a safe trip. XX"

Then the link for Led Zeppelin's- "All of My Love."

I press send and try to picture his reaction to hearing the song, hoping he'll listen to the words and understand how I feel about him.

10

DORNAN

I open the text from Maven and click the link for the song she sent, cranking the volume as I start up my bike. We stopped to fill up before the four hour trip back home, and knowing V's in my bed waiting for me, surely means that this will be the longest four fucking hours of my life. She drives me crazy, in all the good ways of course. Even in the not good ways, I love that she challenges me and calls me on my bullshit. She's the only girl I've ever wanted. Sure I was obviously attracted to other women, I slept around and tried to curb the appetite I had for V since I was fifteen. But still, no one compares to what she does to me. The way she looks at me, and shoots me devilish grins at meetings. The way she rides her motorcycle even, not to mention watching her do the shit with computers and things we do on runs. She's smart and feisty and doesn't take shit. But she's still sweet and thoughtful, always classy, and always too damn sexy for her own good. She never knew how much the other guys ribbed me about how crazy I am for her. But I always took the jokes and comments, because I knew one day she'd be mine.

I watched and waited for her to figure out Brayden was an asshole, of course I didn't want her to be hurt by him. But knew it was only a matter of time, and that was the only way she'd get over him. I still don't really get their relationship, she became this pliant dumbed down version of who she really is, like she just accepted him being married and him treating her like a sweet bottom. I hated watching her waste a smile on him, a touch, a kiss, all the while he was jerking her around. It sucked even more when I knew I would never treat her that way. She deserves to be treated like a fucking gem, because that's what she is. A one of a kind woman who should never settle, or put up with the shit that Brayden pulled on her. I never understood how she didn't know I'm into her. Maybe because I've always treated her the same since we were little, with respect and love. Maybe she just came to think that friends were what we'd always be, since Joey also shows her nothing but respect.

Once Brayden was out of the picture, I had to restrain myself from following her home after their confrontation at my parents, to tell her then and there that she was mine. Instead I gave her some time, to let her realize she's better than what he made her, hoping she'd see that in me. But for someone so smart, she really was dumb about us. Then finally when I did tell her, tell her what I wanted, that I was done waiting, I could see the blinders fall off and she started to see me in a totally different way. She finally saw the way I looked at her, the way I cherished her, the way she made me hard with one look.

I listen to the song she sent me the entire trip home, the words hitting me in the heart, and fuck I love her so goddamn much. I want to tell her, but what's love to us? We'd been through hell and back, been through shit, seen shit- times where we both put ourselves in danger for the other. What the fuck did love mean in all that? We're beyond that, those words seem meaningless in the story of our life.

When we pull into the club's lot it's after three am, a few hours later than we planned. But Chain had some bike issues we had to stop a few times to take care of. I nod my goodnights as they both get into Joey's truck, and drive off towards home. The clubhouse is quiet, but there are brothers and a few sweet bottoms in the main area, playing pool and drinking at the bar. The Eagles- "Life in the Fastlane," is playing over the speakers, as the smell of cigarette and pot smoke hangs thick in the air. I slide my beanie off as Rocket waves two fingers in my direction from the bar, and I stretch my arms in the air while making my way over.

"V made you dinner, in the first fridge on the right," he says over the music with a nod.

I tilt my chin in thanks and head for the kitchen, unzipping my leather jacket as I flip a light on. I half expect to see a bowl of cereal there, but opening the fridge I see a plate covered with tinfoil along with a note:

"Microwave for 2 minutes x."

Removing the tinfoil and tossing it onto the counter, I place the plate of chicken, rice, and broccoli in the microwave and go back to the fridge for a bottle of water. All I want to do is go to my girl, but I'm fucking starving and she's asleep. That's not going to stop me from waking her ass up, and showing her how that song she sent makes me feel though.

I shovel my food down and chug my water, before heading out the other entrance to the kitchen, which leads to the back hallways and the apartments. My eyes glance over to where Brayden had Maven up against the wall by her neck, and feel my anger spark. I don't think

I'll ever be able to get the vision of that, and him touching her, out of my head. The feelings I have about that will stay with me for a long time, the fear for her and the murderous rage I feel for him. I know if Joey hadn't stopped me, I would've killed Brayden that night. Even on runs or when fucked up shit happens with Maven there, I know she can handle herself. But to see her the way she was in that moment, unable to fight him, makes me sick. I stayed up all that night with her sleeping upstairs, replaying the scene and what could've happened if I didn't notice she'd been gone too long for the bathroom. I've never had something linger with me like this, I couldn't shake the sight all night or next morning. When she came downstairs, and I saw her neck marred with angry red marks, I knew Brayden would pay for this. But then seeing in her eyes that she was okay, I almost cried from the stress. She turns me inside out, but frustrates the hell out of me. Even more that she seemed accepting of what happened, well, what almost happened. The thought of her maybe being assaulted in the past by some other MC asshole made me want to murder. What I did to Drag at the Tavern after he'd tried to pick her up, would be mild to what I want to do to someone at the thought of her being hurt. When she confirmed nothing like that had ever happened before, the weight of the world lifted off my chest. But no matter her words or resolve, the events from that night will always be with me.

I open the door to the apartment slowly, the light from the hallway filters in and Bagheera raises his head as I enter. The moonlight streams in through the old sheer curtains, glowing off the bare back of my girl. V's lying on her stomach, the thin white sheet barely covering her fine plump ass. Her long dark hair's all over the pillows, *my* pillows, and for whatever reason I feel it in my dick. I slip into the bathroom to shower, knowing I stink from being in the sun and on my bike for hours today. When I re-emerge, she's still sound asleep in the same position. Lifting the sheet, I get in bed and lean down to kiss between her shoulder blades, inhaling her scent of woman and something sweet and flowery that's just V. She hums in reaction, but doesn't move. I lay down beside her and run my hand over her hair, before kissing the tip of her nose, causing another hum and making my dick hard as fuck. I kiss the little crease between her eyebrows as she stirs slightly, my lips planting kisses on her face. Finally, she sighs and rolls onto her side, showing me her beautiful full tits. My hand moves to her cheek as I kiss her lips, and she begins mumbling something.

"Shhh," I whisper against her lips.

"I need you," she replies softly.

Since V's become mine, I can't get enough of her. Not just sex, but kissing and touching her, watching her, and talking with her. She stimulates every one of my senses. With sex though, she never objects and always lets me take her anytime and any way. Just like she does with me, seeking me out at work to take me into her office and fuck me. With a shiver, she rolls onto her back, her dark mauve nipples tighten while my hand moves to cup one of her tits. To see her like this, naked and open to me, I never imagined how it would make me feel to actually have this, to have her in real life. She takes care of herself, and it does all the right things, toning her sleek long body. She's always had an amazing rack, even when she first developed boobs. It was like one day she was a kid, and then boom the next day she was a woman. I wanted to tell her that her tits had been the first images I'd ever jerked off to, but I'm not sure how she'd take that.

I kiss her neck and collarbone, licking and sucking the sweet flesh.

My fingertips dance down her torso, running my index fingers over the little blonde hairs around her navel. Before venturing further to her clit, which is already budded up and hard. I look up to see she's biting her lip in response to my touch, looking down at me through the valley of her tits. Her eyes always do something to me, even before we were together. She would look at me like she wanted me, like she daydreamed about me, and I fucking love it.

Just as my fingers graze over the tiny bud of skin, she rolls over on top of me, pushing me onto my back. She kisses my neck and down the center of my chest, her fingers running over the necklace she gave me forever ago. Her lips move to each nipple and circle them with her tongue until they respond. My hands move into her hair, gathering the thick mane back into one fist as she kisses lower, down my happy trail to my cock, which is straining just waiting for her mouth.

Her eyes flicker up to mine as she licks her full lips, her tiny hands wrapping around my base and shaft. While she sticks her delicate pink tongue out to tease the head, causing me to groan a sound I swear comes deep from my balls. The moonlight shining in is just enough light for me to see her, to watch her suck my dick. No matter how many times I pictured her doing this or pretended it was her when some chick gave me head, nothing *ever* could or would compare to the real thing. To have her worshiping my cock like her mouth's made specifically to give my dick mind blowing pleasure. She literally makes love to me with her mouth, all her focus on me and giving pleasure, and I love every second of it. She deep throats me a few times, cheeks hollowing as she sucks, but stops just before I'm going to come.

Running fingers under her swollen bottom lip, she catches her breath before smiling sweetly. Kissing up my body, and positioning herself on my lap, aligning over me and allowing my cock inside her pussy. She's so wet and slick, the instant heat sends a shock down to my balls, that has me consciously restraining my hips from bucking up into her.

"Jesus Maven," I groan before my jaw goes slack.

She lets out a whimper and furrows her brows, as her succulent lips part and her head tilts, her hair tumbling to one side. V is every school boy and grown man fantasy I've ever had; she's absolutely the most beautiful creature I've ever seen. Something about the way she looks when we're having sex is indescribable. She's always hot, but seeing her like this, everything she does, from the faces and sounds she makes, to the reactions she has is a hot wire straight to my soul. Every time we're together, it doesn't go unnoticed by me that it feels like we're made for each other. Honestly, it may sound cheesy but true. Even if she wasn't the most stunning being alive, our insides are the lovers. Our souls recognize one another's as the same, connected and bonded, born from the same spirit. She begins to ride me, lifting her ass up and down. Teasing my cock with her tight pussy, my eyes locked on where our bodies meet. My cock looks too big and swollen to fit inside her, her thigh muscles defined with strain as she rides the head and first three inches of my dick several times. Then relaxing and sitting fully, only to repeat the movement again.

"Ride my dick babe, fuck, fuck, squeeze me with that beautiful cunt," I groan.

Her hands press her tits against her chest, obstructing my view. So I push her shoulders back, before pulling her hands away and onto the bed beside my shoulders. Lifting my head to suck one perfect nipple into my mouth. One hand kneads her tit while my other hand smacks her ass then splays over it, my index finger massaging the puckered flesh of her asshole.

"Oh God!" V shouts as her pussy clamps around me and her back arches.

"You like that? You want me in your ass, my cock in your ass and finger your pussy?"

"Dornan, Dornan," she chants, and I can tell she likes that idea.

I suck her other nipple into my mouth, her thighs tightening against my hips. Her eyes close as she bows her head, her shoulders drawing in. Thrusting my hips up while using my hand on her ass to push down and meet my cock fucking her. She comes with a cry, her ab muscles tremble with release as her skin breaks out in goosebumps. Every orgasm she gives me further cements the fact that she's mine, fucking mine. I pull her down to kiss her hard, my hands now gripping her hips as I fuck her fast.

"Fuck me Dornan, fuck me," she pleads, she knows I love when she dirty talks and so she continues.

"My pussy loves it, loves your perfect hard cock slamming into me, it feels so good, making me wet and needing your come. God Dornan, give me your come. I want to feel it, feel it filling me and spilling out of me," she begs.

"Fuck, fuck, fu-" my breath catches, my muscles flex and tighten as I fuck her as hard as I can.

"Tell me this cock is mine. Tell me you're mine," she demands.

My eyes open to meet hers, and see how intense she is. How much she wants to claim me as I do her, shoots a lightning bolt through my chest.

"My cock is yours. I'm all yours. Take it all. Fuccckkkkk," I groan.

My jaw tightens before I groan into her mouth, realizing she's also coming again as she gasps against my lips. Her nails dig into my flesh, her pussy soaking my dick as our come mixes and is forced out onto our thighs and my lower stomach. Slowly our bodies calm and with chests heaving, she lays down on top of me. Taking her hand in mine to lace our fingers together, lifting them to kiss her palm. We lay there, half-awake, half asleep. Our breathing's the only sound in the room, her body still trembling from orgasm.

"Are you feeling better?" I ask in a gruff voice, my throat dry from exertion.

Her body stiffens, tensing against mine before relaxing a moment later.

"Oh, earlier...yeah, just a headache and I didn't feel up to driving home," she replies.

She tightens her muscles around my cock still inside her, and I start hardening in her again. Lifting her leg from across my hips, I fall free from her sopping wet pussy. She raises her head to look at me, her fucking gorgeous eyes meeting mine. I run my palm down her cheek, tucking some hair behind her ear.

"I missed you today," she sighs closing her eyes and reveling in my touch.

"I miss you every day, even when you're in the office and I'm in the clubhouse. I miss you when I'm in bed and you're in the bathroom. I miss you when I can't touch you like I want, or...I miss you a lot."

I stop talking because I know I'm sounding like a total fucking idiot, the more I talk the worse it sounds in my head. All I want is for her to know what I feel, she's always gotten me though, even when I can't get the words out. Her eyes open as she smiles, her fingers trailing patterns on my chest and the ink there, as she rises onto an elbow. Running her nose along mine, she presses soft kisses to my face before finding my lips, gently pecking them then slowly running her tongue along my lower lip. I let her tease me as I attempt to deepen the kiss, but she smiles and pulls back to look at me before returning to teasing again. Essentially making me crazy and turning my cock to granite. She pulls back again and this time I place a hand on the back of her head, bringing her lips to mine, kissing her hard and fast. My other hand moves to the one she has on my chest at the same moment, forcing her hand down to grasp my erection, and guide her fist up and down. My hips push up to meet her hand while she begins to dry hump my thigh, pulling her leg up over my waist to rub her clit against my hip bone.

"Put your mouth on my cock," I demand with my lips on hers. With a moan she sits up, bending onto all fours beside me so I can see her profile, as her hand continues to pump me. I love how eager she is for me, again, like she's made to suck my cock. I arrange her hair so it falls over her other shoulder, to give myself an unobstructed view as she takes my cock deep into her mouth. The moonlight casts shadows on her curves and defined body as one arm holds her up, her heavy tits hanging down plump and full. They sway along with the movement of her arm, her nipples hard and raw from my sucking. My eyelids flutter and I sigh, as her mouth takes all of me until she gags.

"Fuck yes," I groan. "I love when you choke on my cock, you want it so bad don't you? You want all of it," I growl because the idea that she can't get enough of me calls to some caveman part of me.

My hands tangle in her hair and rest on the crown of her head, not pushing or guiding just yet, but there. She moves her hand down to press my balls against the base of my cock, when she pulls me deep into her throat this time, she slips her tongue out to lick my balls. Her mouth is full of me, her tongue lapping at my ball sack, and I shudder as a trail of spit slides down my balls and ass. My entire body tenses, as I start to guide her speed and depth with my hands on her head. The sound of her vigorously sucking me is wet and loud, loving the sound that comes from the back of her throat, as I hit there repeatedly with the head of my cock. V moans and moves to lie on her side, spreading her legs wide while reaching down and rubbing her fingers over her clit. I watch mesmerized at her show for me as she dips her middle finger inside her pussy. Even in the low light, I can see wetness coating it as she pulls out, spreading it over her folds. Her fingers move in fast little circles, her lips and mouth still fucking my cock.

"Shit V... touch yourself babe, yes," my head falls back. "Make yourself come thinking about my cock coming all over you."

She moans again with her mouth stuffed, and I watch her stomach tighten, her chest heave as she reaches for an impending orgasm while also working to get me there. But I want this orgasm, I want all of them. I don't ever want her to get herself off when she has me for that, and although hot to watch, I want her come all over my face. My hands reach for her hips, and I have to sit up slightly to grasp her fully. The movement makes my dick slip deeper into her throat, causing her to gag again as pre-come shoots into her mouth. I take her small frame and lay back, bringing her with me and positioning her pussy onto my face. Her hand strokes me as she moans from my tongue lapping her, sucking her lips and folds, as fingers move to spread her greedy cunt for my all too willing mouth. She puts me back into her mouth and we're fighting each other to bring pleasure, matching the other in intensity. Her taste is like no one else's, she's sweet and savory, and the smell of her makes me drunk.

My lips latch onto her clit and her back arches, her mouth leaving my cock once more as she grinds down onto my tongue. Wrapping my arm around her waist like a band to hold her against my lips, I feel her muscles tighten. My own orgasm speeds up like a fucking freight train, beginning in my spine and pooling in my balls. Her hands pump me as she chants 'oh God' and 'holy shit Dornan, so good' all her words of praise bringing me closer and closer. Sliding a hand up her spine, between her shoulder blades, I push her down and mouth back to my dick. She moans long and hard as she comes, my tongue pushing in deep and fucking her as it ripples around me. Her flavor spreads over my lips and chin, lapping it all up, like a bear with a honey jar.

With a grunt I begin to spurt inside her mouth, my thighs tightening and hips bucking up, her lips sealing around me like a vacuum. Even after coming for long moments, my body still contracts with orgasm and I know I've never come as intensely or as hard as I do with her. V takes all of me, swallowing and gasping, her lips gently pressing a kiss on the sensitive head once I've finished.

She rolls off me, and I can see how wet and pink she is between her legs. I grasp the foot she can't manage to move off my chest with my hand, and kiss her ankle, running my fingers up and down her calf. I sit up and move to lie between her thighs, kissing my way up her torso before sliding my cock inside her snug swollen pussy. Her eyes are closed and as my body moves above her, she trails her fingers up my chest to meet around my neck. We just lay like this, me inside her not moving, her legs tangled around me. Kissing her neck up to her ear, causing her to hum and sigh.

"The best thing I ever did, was allow myself to fall for you," she whispers and I smile against her skin, because it's so fucking true.

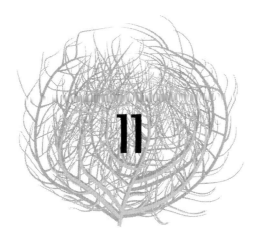

MAVEN

I wake before Dornan and get ready for the day quietly, as he lays passed out in bed. We'd fallen asleep, but he woke me up with his cock moving inside me or his mouth licking my pussy several times. I make sure to throw my overnight bag in the trunk of my car, so I won't have to explain how I had planned ahead of time to pack for a random headache. The thought of why we stayed the night at the club, makes my stomach sour. Just like it did when I'd gone to Dornan's apartment that night, and had to walk past the spot where Brayden assaulted me. Dread overwhelmed me, and it dawned on me that the incident has left a permanent mark on me, which didn't occur to me before then. My brain just can't deal yet, I need to process what happened in order to move on, and I'm just not ready to go there yet. Now to think that Brayden, or at least his club, is possibly lurking around my house, possibly knowing where I live now... pisses me off. What the fuck is the point of him coming to my house? I don't have anything there that's of value to him, unless he wants to scare me, which, mission accomplished. He already has a power over me that

159

I don't like since the night at the clubhouse, and I'm not going to give him anymore by having me not stay at my house or live my life. I'm a strong woman who owns a gun, and has no problem with self-defense. He caught me once at a weak moment, but it will never happen again.

Dornan's still sleeping when I place a cup of coffee on the night stand, and kiss his cheek. He doesn't budge, so I go to work. There isn't anyone really in yet, just Rocket and Chain standing under the open garage doors. They drink their coffee as they talk bikes, and both nod at me as I walk past.

There's not much for me to do yet, I worked pretty late last night finishing everything on my desk, so I decide to call my dad. Normally an inmate has phone privileges, but they're usually the ones making the calls, not being called. But I'm being optimistic, hoping since it's early that maybe I'll speak to someone who's feeling a bit generous, and get me through to him.

After being transferred to three different people and sitting on hold for half an eternity, I'm finally told that my dad's been put into solitary and has no phone or visitor privileges for the next three weeks. With a groan I hang up, not even asking what he did. It's not like they'd tell me and I'm sure it's because of something stupid, which will further anger me. As I waited on the phone, the shop began to fill with staff, customers, and cars. In perfect timing with me getting off the phone, there's a disgruntled tow truck driver who's given shit to Skye before, who happens to start yelling at her. Needless to say, I'm able to take out my annoyance on him.

We go at it pretty hard, back and forth, using curse words Missy would be proud of. Taking everything out on this guy, from my frustration with not getting to talk to my dad, to the shit going on with Brayden.

Eventually, Sven has to break up the verbal assault taking place in the garage, and in front of an audience. Smokey is smiling his ass off the entire time as he holds his cellphone up, and knowing him, recording the entire altercation. Instead of going back to my office, I start for the clubhouse. Halfway there the front doors open and Dornan, followed by Joey a few steps behind, walk out heading towards the shop. I'm breathing hard still, my fists clenched at my sides. Dornan immediately smiles at my fiery disposition, which makes my eyes narrow and nostrils flare.

"Rough day at the office dear?" His smile widens as I get closer, fairly sure word's gotten to the clubhouse about the argument.

My hand flies to his arm, and I begin yanking him back to where he just came from.

"Oh shit," Dornan groans in understanding that I'm actually pissed.

"What the hell, we missed it?" Joey asks as we walk past.

"I'm sure Smokey will be happy to show you," I snarl as Joey chuckles and shakes his head.

He continues towards the shop, as I lead Dornan by the bicep towards the clubhouse. A Bad Company song is blasting throughout the clubhouse, while a few guys loiter around the pool tables. But they don't seem to notice us, as we pass and head for the apartments.

"What happened?" I can hear the smile in Dornan's voice as he asks, thinking it's so funny when I get pissed.

"I tried to call my dad and he's in solitary, then that asshole-" I pause when we reach his apartment.

I open the door, pulling him to the bed and forcing him to sit down on the edge. Before kicking the door closed. He looks up at me, willing to hear me vent. But as I reach down to peel off my shirt and unclasp my bra, his eyes change in understanding. Dornan licks his lips and stares at my nipples before returning his eyes to my face, his hands reach for me but I take a step back.

"That asshole who I keep telling your dad we shouldn't use anymore, because he's unprofessional and is a complete bastard, keeps saying he'll take care of it. Then turns around and tells me there's nothing he can do, I told him if that company refuses to fire that jerk, we'll just stop using that company he's all buddy-buddy with."

Pausing again to kick off my boots and peel down my jeans, Dornan's eyes now shoot down to my bare pussy. His lips part and I can see his breathing increase, his hands tightening on the comforter beneath him.

"But nooo, instead he'd rather us deal with this fucker because he doesn't have to, but Skye and I do," pointing a finger at my chest. "I'm so sick of these motherfuckers thinking they can talk down to me, like *I'm* the moron," I huff.

Slowly, his eyes trail up my torso to meet mine. I can see even without asking, he knows this is so much more than my dad, or that tow truck driver…and this is why I love him.

"What do you need me to do?"

His voice is low and rough, torpedoing all the right spots inside me to make me wet and my clit pulsate.

"I need you to make me stop thinking," I reply quietly.

He reaches out a hand in silent agreement, seriously, this man. As soon as my fingers touch his, he yanks me onto his lap. His hands tighten on my hips as he moves us further onto the bed, his lips hungrily devouring mine. The movements so fast and perfect, I gasp and press myself into him, wanting to consume him. Once he settles us with my body on top of his, hands move to my hair and neck as he delves deeper into my mouth. I'm totally naked and he's fully clothed, and there's something so sexy about that. It turns my want into a hunger I've never known before, my legs fall to his sides and I shamelessly begin to grind down against the thick ridge in his jeans.

We both groan, as his hand in my hair tightens. He bites my lower lip, and begins pushing his hips up to press against me harder. Sitting up, I pull back and fumble with the fly of his jeans. My lips feel swollen and puffy, and I suck the lower one in between my teeth as I look up at him through my lashes.

"You're so beautiful," he groans.

His hands move down to help me with his pants, his erection trapped inside his boxer briefs as we tug. The anticipation of wanting to see his dick, causes me to growl with impatience deep in my throat. The thwack sound his fat thick cock makes when it falls back against his abs, makes me nearly come. He's so hard, skin so tight, veins bulging. The head nearly reaches his navel, his balls already shrunken up and ready to release, and my mouth waters to taste the glistening liquid coating the head.

"You want my dick in your mouth?" he asks.

I look up and nod eagerly, but he gives me that side smirk and a shake of his head. Seconds before he has me flipped onto all fours, and is sliding inside. My pussy sucks him in, wanting more, wanting harder and faster and all of him. I look at him over my shoulder, catching our reflection in the mirror above the dresser in the process. He's still dressed aside from his jeans pulled down, his ass flexing as he pushes in and pulls out. He looks huge behind me, and this seems so dirty. It doesn't bother me that it might look like a sweet bottom to an observer, because I know the difference is I'm in as much of control of this as he is.

"Fuck me," I order.

"I am," he teases, his cock taking shallow stabs at my entrance,

"I've seen Rocket nail girls harder than this, and he's what, sixty years older than you?" I retort.

A strong hand grabs the back of my hair, lifting my torso back against his chest.

"You want me to fuck you? You sure about that?" he asks, his cock still slowly teasing me.

"Yes," I gasp. "Fuck me with that huge cock of yours so hard that I forget everything."

"Shit," he groans and reaches down to roughly stroke between my legs with his fingers.

"Fuck me like you love me," I groan.

He pauses, but only for a second. Releasing my hair and not too gently pushing my torso down onto the bed, positioning my hands flat above my head. I watch in the mirror as he stands, removing his shirt and pants, before returning to the bed and pushing my legs wider. Rough fingers run up and down my wet pussy, before smacking my ass and positioning himself at my entrance once more.

"Don't make a sound other than screaming my name when you come."

Just as the words register, he slams inside me. His cock so thick and so hard, relentlessly fucking me. My teeth sink into the back of my hand to muffle my cry, my breath coming out in a rush, like his cock is literally pushing the air from my lungs. Wet flesh smacking, as I let out a muffled whimper I can't control.

"Shhh," he whispers with his lips against my ear.

Reaching back through my legs, my fingers tease his balls and he groans. Sucking in a sharp breath between his teeth, as my fingernails gently rake the retracted flesh. Then his hands are on my biceps, yanking my arms towards him to clasp behind my back, holding them in place and pulling me back by my wrists. He fucks into me with abandon, his moans and groans are loud, savage and animalistic. I love that he's using me to find release, knowing he's not hurting me and that this is also what I want, just him as he is. I'm whimpering and because I feel possessed, I can't stay quiet anymore. I start begging him, begging for his cock and begging him to never stop fucking me, all while I'm coming and keep coming. I orgasm so hard my knees give out, my throat hoarse from shouting his name over and over. His thrusts break rhythm as he frantically seeks for his own orgasm. His chest pressing onto my back, his forehead against my shoulder as he comes, holding himself deep as I feel him fill my channel with semen. Warm breath beats against my skin, my heart pounding and all the things that had been picking away at me, are gone.

"Thank you," I sigh.

Dornan lets out a low laugh before pressing his smile and then a kiss on my shoulder, then another on the back of my neck. "I'll always take care of you."

12

It takes us a while to re-emerge from the apartment, there's nothing more I wanted than to lay in his arms talking and living in our bubble, not having to deal with the outside world. When we finally do return to the real world, there are some old ladies and kids inside the clubhouse, cleaning up for a pool tournament we're having tonight. It's just our club this time and sure to be fun, we play for dollar bills but usually manage to accumulate a large sum of money, which we donate to the local children's hospital. This year a portion of the raised money is also going to help with Smokey's medical bills. Dornan holds me close with an arm around my waist as we walk out into the sunshine, his fingers caressing under the hem of my shirt just an inch, but that inch does everything to fire up my libido again.

"You keep touching me and you're about to meet the business end of the top of my desk," I whisper in his ear as we walk past the guys sitting out front.

"Promise?" he growls against my lips, pressing a kiss there before we walk into the garage.

I roll my eyes when I see that indeed a bunch of the brothers are watching the video Smokey took on his cellphone of me and the tow truck driver getting into it.

"Hey Dornan, want an insta-boner?" Smokey laughs and shakes his head at me. "Always killin it V, there's nothing better than when you make a dude shit himself."

I narrow my eyes and curl my upper lip in a snarl.

"Maybe I will take you up on the desk sex," Dornan answers as he walks over to watch the video.

He did eventually come to my office in hopes of getting that desk sex, because for whatever reason he also enjoyed watching me go toe to toe with a man, But I was swamped. There was an accident on the freeway and three of the cars had come here, all the insurances needed to be dealt with before I could head home.

Even though I was only gone one night, it's an odd sensation walking into my house. There's a slight unease, like the boogeyman's about to jump out at any second. But Dornan's presence and Bagheera running in and out of the back door, helps settle me. I jump in the shower as Dornan makes dinner and everything seems right again, my fear from the day before nonexistent. I'm heading out for some girl time with Missy, Gwen, Katie, and Emily before the pool tournament. I'm excited to get out and do something, it's been a while since I've spent time with them, and a cycle of the flu meant the last few Sunday dinners have been cancelled.

Entering the bedroom after my shower, my eyes land on a black strapless mini dress draped over the bed, noticeably absent are any under garments. A pair of burgundy peep toe heels with a dainty strap at the ankle, sit at the end of the bed, remembering that Dornan told me he liked them once before. I shouldn't like that he picks my clothes out, but I do, there's something about it. He doesn't pick things that make me feel like he's trying to cover me up, he picks things he likes seeing me in.

After blow drying my hair in loose waves, I apply my make-up, choosing gray smokey eyes as opposed to my normal brown eye shadow and liner. The outfit's sexy, with a short tight skirt that shows off my long legs. The top just barely covers my cleavage to reveal plenty of neck, but with my hair down it covers a majority of the open back. When I go downstairs, Dornan's sitting at the table eating with Bagheera at his feet. When he looks at me, the fork stops halfway to his mouth as his eyes trail up from my heels to my eyes. I smile and pose against the doorframe like a centerfold, noticing his throat move to swallow before he snaps out of his trance and begins eating again. Just then, a horn honks outside and alerts me to Missy's arrival.

"Thank God," Dornan sighs. "You stay here any longer, and we're not going anywhere for the next few weeks."

I walk over and place a kiss on his cheek, then begin towards the door. Before I can get too far, he pulls me back to plant a hard kiss on my lips, smacking my ass as I stand. I shoot him a pout as if I'm unhappy about his actions, but can barely contain my smile as I grab my purse and open the front door.

"Shit, maybe I should've picked something else."

I glance over my shoulder to see Dornan mumbling to Bagheera, an afterthought now that he's just gotten a view of how short this dress actually is. I'm the last to be picked up, so Missy's cars already loud and full. The passenger seat's been left open for me, thankfully I don't have to climb into the back seat and show off my ovaries.

"Damn girl, Dornan know you're leavin' the house like that?" Katie teases and smacks my shoulder from her spot in the backseat.

"He picked this for me to wear," I smile looking ahead as the whistles and 'oohh's' begin.

"He's the only man I swear that wants guys to see how hot you are, if I thought about wearing something like that, Smokey would cut off a guy's future kid's dick for looking at me," Emily says causing us all to laugh.

I think most women would feel like Dornan wanting me to look sexy, meant that he didn't care if men check me out. But it's the opposite, he wants every guy to see what they aren't getting, just one of the many ways that shows me how confident and alpha he is.

We head to the tavern and proceed to drink and sing karaoke. Although I opt not to drink tonight, since my last experience with alcohol is still too raw to want to go down that path again anytime soon. I manage to still go on and sing my butt off, and have a blast. It's around midnight when an intense Aretha Franklin battle ensues between Missy and me, and only after Missy can't spell R.E.S.P.E.C.T, we decide to call it quits and head to the clubhouse. Since I'm the designated driver for the rowdy drunken bunch, I decide to drive thru and get some burgers in hopes of sobering the girls up slightly. Knowing that none of their husbands will appreciate how shit face drunk they are. Reasonably drunk and playful are states of inebriation they like, not these sloppy ass messes.

Regardless, when we pull up and park in the lot, Gwen swings open the passenger door and they all begin climbing out of the car, falling all over while laughing like lunatics. I'm chuckling but just about over them when Joey walks out of the club to light a smoke, and Katie nearly falls into his arms. His mom Gwen smacks his cheek in a meant to be loving way, that turns out to be a little bit more aggressive by the look on his face.

Gwen and Missy walk into the club arm in arm, Emily follows as she fixes her hair while nearly tripping over her own feet, stumbling in her heels. Deciding I should leave Joey and Katie who are now making out, I head inside. Smoke and the stench of beer thick in the air, along with the sounds of The Doobie Brothers. The voices and laughter of about one hundred people fill the clubhouse, and it's times like this I really miss my dad being here.

I ignore the pang in my chest, the sadness that follows knowing my only parent will never be free again. So I search for the only person who always takes that pain away. My eyes scan the faces for Dornan, but can't see over the crowd. Knowing he'll be at the pool tables owning the tournament with Sven, I head in that direction. As I navigate my way through, my name's called and hello's are exchanged. But I keep pushing forward, the need to see Dornan overwhelming me. I can't explain it, but it's almost like nothing seems right if he's in the same vicinity but not with me, close but not close enough. At first I feared the feeling, not wanting to be so dependent on someone that I couldn't live my life without them by my side, but it's not that. He's my other half, he's the part of me that contains my heart, and without him I'm barely able to feel like a complete person.

My eyes finally land on Sven who has an arm slung around Missy's shoulders as she whispers in his ear, his other hand posted up on a pool stick, but still no Dornan. As I get closer, Sven smiles and gives me a chin tip. I notice Smokey and Chain are also there with their wives hanging on them.

"Doesn't V look absolutely beautiful?" Missy asks Sven as I stand in front of them.

"She always does. But yes, she is looking particularly beautiful tonight."

Sven gives me a smile, like how my dad does when he's trying to be sweet and feels a little uncomfortable showing his softer side.

"Thanks, where's Dornan?" I ask.

They all look at me and smile, like they know something I don't. I open my mouth to ask what's so amusing, when big warm hands slide onto my hips, Dornan pressing his lips on my bare shoulder. I turn my head to breathe him in, running my nose along his cheek, as he turns to press against my lips softly. He gives me a moment of kisses before standing to his full height, pulling me back against his front. Even with these sky high heels, he's still taller than me. Everyone's still looking at us with dumb smiles, and I feel my cheeks heat slightly in embarrassment. Slowly it turns into a hot flush, when I feel Dornan's thickening cock press into the curve of my ass. Eventually everyone begins to take their attention off us, and start talking amongst themselves.

"Where were you?" I ask, turning my head and smelling his neck again.

"I had something to do really quick, did you have fun?" he asks, his fingers flexing against my hips.

I shrug, "it was fine. You guys winning?" I ask.

"We just got knocked out when my mom came up and jumped on the old man's back, he missed his shot."

I smile and shake my head slightly.

"I want to show you something," he says into my hair.

I turn in his arms and look up at him, my brows raising.

"Come on," he gives me that sexy side grin, at the same time linking his fingers with mine.

I watch his ass in those jeans that fit him like the maker used a mold of his body to design them, wrapping my other hand around his strong forearm. We walk down the apartment hallway, when he suddenly halts and turns to me. I lean forward trying to kiss him, but he steps back and smiles. Oh he's going to tease me? He reaches into his pocket and retrieves a black bandana, folding it before raising it to my eyes. I pull back while raising a hand, intercepting the material just inches from my face.

"It's a surprise," he replies, still holding the bandana up.

I gave him a pointed look, before relenting and closing my eyes. Like I can ever resist him, even if I don't really like the idea of being blindfolded. He presses a quick kiss to the tip of my nose, placing the cloth against my face and tying the ends behind my head. He links his fingers with mine again and I hear the heavy back door open, then slam behind us as we go outside into the warm night air. Dornan leads me with care and acknowledgment that I'm in four inch heels as we walk, I have a feeling I know where we're going, especially as we keep walking and the music from the clubhouse gets further away. Hearing the breeze blowing in the leaves, alerts me that we're going to the tree house for sure, but it's still unclear why we're going there exactly. I don't say anything, just bite my lower lip and try to hide my grin over the thought that he's planned something for me. Then we stop and Dornan lets my hand go, the air shifting as he turns to face me.

"So I'm sure you know where we are...can you do the stairs in those?" he asks.

Knowing he means my shoes, because we've climbed up the ladder many times blind to our movements at night. I nod and reach out, Dornan assisting me in finding the sides of the ladder. Once my foot hits the first step, I easily find the rest, feeling Dornan's hands on my hips and ass making sure I get up safely. Once reaching the top, I straighten fully and move over slightly to allow room for him to stand beside me. Still not understanding why I need a blindfold for something I've seen a million times. He guides me in front of him, his hands at my sides, splayed on my ribs and under my breasts. His warm breath delicately plays with my long tendrils, before he sweeps a hand across my shoulder and gathers all my hair over to one side.

"There were so many times when we hung out in here, that I wanted to ask you out."

He places a soft kiss on my neck, sending chills over my skin.

"That I wanted to kiss you," another press of his lips.

"Touch you," he whispers and I feel my body push back into his, a sigh escaping my lips as they part.

"You did?" I pant.

Dornan runs his knuckles down my arms, before his hands start touching me all over, almost frantically.

"Now that you're mine, I want to do all the things I spent days and hours thinking about doing to you."

A tremor shakes my body slightly, excitement charging through me and awakening all my wants and needs. The bandana loosens and falls free, candlelight filling the small space as my eyes flutter open. There are hundreds of candles set up all over, along with twinkle lights strung up and hanging from the walls. The gesture's simple, yet so sweet, I feel the backs of my eyes begin to burn.

"This is perfect," I gush.

Dornan places a hand on my cheek, his thumb swiping away the tears. My emotions reflect in his eyes, as he leans in to run his nose along mine.

"You deserve nothing less than perfect," he says softly.

My insides become jelly, my heart swelling. I want nothing more than to make love with him right here, to show him how he also deserves nothing less. He motions for me to sit on pillows I've never seen before, arranged on the floor. Not only has he spruced the place up, but I realize then that when I got to the clubhouse and he wasn't there, that he must've been out here lighting all the candles. He sits down beside me but seems anxious, and I don't know if it's because he maybe thinks I'm not surprised. It's then I hear music and glance over his shoulder to see my iPod on its dock in the corner, Stevie Nicks and Don Henley- "Leather and Lace" is playing. The song's perfect for me and him, his rough manliness and my softer woman side, this song is just…us.

Dornan turns away from me and I look anxiously around at the lights and candles, because for the first time in his presence, he's making me nervous. Maybe because this is a place I never associated with feelings other than friendship with Dornan, and now here we are, lovers. A chill runs through me, and I bring my knees up to my chest, wrapping my arms around them. Dornan faces me again but his eyes focus on something in his hands resting in the center of his lap, something wrapped in cloth.

"I have this for you," he says softly, his eyes still downcast.

I look between his face and his hands a few times, before I dip my head down in hopes of bringing his eyes up. Which works and he flicks those beautiful blues to me, I can sense apprehension or a tension there, something worrying him.

"Here," he says, placing the cloth in my palm.

There's no preamble or explanation to why he's giving this gift to me, which is so Dornan's style and I smile. Bringing the gift closer to my chest, as I pull back the cloth. My breath catching as my heart pounds faster in my chest, my eyes taking in the gift.

"Dornan," I whisper because I'm honestly shocked.

It's a hand stitched patch, one I know Gwen's made since she makes all the club's personal patches. This is of an infinity knot, and like nothing I've ever seen. Muted silver like the color of our Warrior of the Gods crest, with mine and Dornan's names interwoven in the threading. Most guys give their old lady's a patch that says 'old lady' or 'so and so's girl' because they're property. By Dornan giving me this, it really means he wants me to be his equal. That those hadn't been just words he told me to get me to stick around, he truly meant it and wants everyone else to know it too. This must've been why everyone at the club was smiling at me like fools, they knew Dornan was giving me this tonight.

"Wear this?" he asks.

The fact that he's even asking me, causes a smile to spread over my lips as I look up at him and nod. The tension in his eyes vanishes as he smiles, leaning in closer. I wrap my arms around his neck, pulling him into me and kissing him breathlessly. We kiss for a long while, until the small space is no longer cold, and I'm panting with the need to move things along. When I add tongue he plays for a second, before retreating and pressing soft kisses on my lips.

"I want to act out every fantasy I've had about you in here."

"Yes," I reply cupping his cheek.

He smiles, seeming cool and calm, not at all about ready to jump out of his skin like I feel. We're sitting side by side, our hips parallel, both our legs bent as we begin kissing again. His knuckles graze up the inside if my thigh, and I startle a moment at the unexpected contact. He coo's softly against my lips, instantly relaxing me. Feeling the rough texture of his large hands against my delicate skin, causes chill bumps and my breath to hitch. He's whispering things in between kisses, as he teases the soft skin between my legs. My head falls back and causes my hair to cascade down my back, giving him all the skin from my neck to my cleavage to play with.

"You feel so perfect, I could touch you for a lifetime and never get sick of it. I can feel how hot you are for me without even touching you there."

I let out an aggravated whimper, opening my legs wider, luring him in, needing him there. Instead, his hand runs smooth over the top of my thigh to the outside hem of my dress. Pushing the fabric up to my hip and over my ass, before moving to the side closest to him and repeating the motion. Cool air hits my wet skin as he kisses my neck, sucking and licking, causing my legs to tremble and quiver.

His lips and teeth graze over my jaw then my collarbone, as his nimble fingers run over my breasts, circling my nipples through the fabric and causing them to harden. My breath is sputtering and quick, I'm grinding my hips towards nothing in hopes the motion will bring some relief to the ache there. Still he teases my nipples, cupping my breasts and kissing them over my dress, adding a bite of roughness against my skin.

Reaching down I grab him, running my hand up and down his length which is straining against the thigh of his jeans. He groans and finally pulls down the front of my dress, sucking my nipple into his mouth, lapping his tongue over the budded flesh. I'm tempted to use my other hand to rub my clit, but it's currently the only thing keeping

177

me from falling. I scoot backwards slowly, sliding my butt across the floor to press my back against the wall and Dornan follows. Changing his position to kneel between my spread knees, his lips never leaving my skin. My fingers touch my wet folds for a moment, before Dornan's hand's there and pulling them away.

"No," he says gruffly and I whimper.

"Dornan, touch me there," my brows furrow as I begin to beg.

"Is that what you want?"

His eyes dart up to mine as he gives a long lick to my nipple, before blowing a stream of cool air against it. I'm trembling with excitement and lust, biting my lower lip and groaning as he does the same to my other nipple.

"You want me to touch you here?"

The calloused fingertips of his index, middle, and ring fingers begin to rub against me.

"Yes," I breathe out, eyes closing as my head tilts back and thuds against the wall.

"I wanted to do this to you so many times, we'd be up here alone. You'd be laying at my side, and I fought to reach over and slip my hand down the front of your pants."

His face is right there, his nose teasing mine. I can barely remember to breathe, as his fingers do wonderful things to me.

"To feel how soft you are here, to smell you, to hear you say my name when you come," he whispers against my lips.

The same moment he extends his middle finger down to retrieve the wetness coating my entrance, before gliding back up onto my clit. My head lulls to the side, resting my cheek against one of my quaking shoulders, and realize just how tightly wound I am. I also realize he's maneuvered my hands away from his pants and to my sides, they're balled into tight fists against the floor as I hold myself upright. He's watching his fingers rub my pink wet flesh fast and steady, and I become transfixed on the motion as well. The quivers in my belly become stronger, the tightening of my pussy before I come, and his lips are on mine. Both our lips are dry from breathing heavy, the kiss is soft and sweet and the perfect balance to the supernova that's rocking my body with violent shudders and spasms. Dornan leans up on his knees, his eyes blazing as he quickly pulls his shirt off. My hands immediately run down the tight, toned muscles of his chest and abs, to the V at his hips to help him undo his belt and jeans.

Our eyes lock and I can see there's something he's containing, the need to fuck me until we break this tree house down. My hand wraps around the velvety skin of his hard shaft, feeling him pulsate beneath my fingers. He pushes my hand away and leans down, guiding his cock towards me as I use my fingers to spread my lips and ease his entry. I can feel every inch as he slides in, stretching me and pushing me almost to the point of pain, but never fully taking it there. I feel him filling me, his body looming over me with his broad shoulders. His want for me so hot, that he's barely pushed his jeans down on his thighs. He makes me feel like a goddess, like he planned things one way, but once he got me going he couldn't control himself and needed to be inside me, and that's such a powerful feeling.

His hips spread my legs wider, hooking my knees over his forearms as he braces his upper body. His muscles tighten and flex with every stroke, as he pushes me harder against the wall. The feeling of being virtually immobile as this beast of a man fucks me in a raw, animalistic way, makes me need him even more. His eyes never leave mine, our ragged breaths fill the air and the space between our lips. Even though he's moving hard and quick inside me, he's still making love to me. Whispering things to me again about how good I feel, how our bodies fit, how good my tits look when he fucks me hard and they bounce along with his movements.

My arms wrap around his shoulders and as I feel my orgasm roll through me, pressing my forehead against his chest. Gasping his name as he pushes in twice more, before slowing and holding himself deep. He shifts us away from the wall so we can lay, he's still inside me and we're both trying to catch our breaths. Pressing soft kisses on my face as he often does after we make love, showing me tenderness after fucking me, taking care of his mate like a lion. He sweeps his hands over my forehead and cheeks, moving the hair that's stuck to my skin with sweat. I kiss his palm and look into his eyes, showing him how I feel, his eyes close slowly as I bring his face closer. Kissing his forehead, before resting his head on my chest.

****

The next few days are busy with club activities, we're working on something for The Steel Axes and a third party buyer, this time a 'legitimate' deal. Legit as in the buyers are using us and The Steel Axes to work out money, pick up, transport, and delivery of the guns. Basically, we're the middlemen. This also involves actual business, no breaking in anywhere or stealing guns.

I'd sat down with Sven for about seven-hours yesterday working out the deal we would propose to The Steel Axes, who'd take it to their buyers and negotiate our cut. When we finally reached an agreement,

Sven called gathering where he laid out the plan and all the details, the runs going to be two days from now on Saturday. This is a big job for us, we're moving a lot of goods this trip and making a seventy thousand dollar profit. Since we've worked with this buyer before, we felt comfortable asking for a larger cut than last time, which they agreed to an upfront amount on top of a smaller portion to come after the transaction.

I expressed my fears to Sven that the deal seemed too good, they only had come back to us once with a counter offer of a smaller amount which we denied and then they agreed to the original asking price. It seemed that they weren't really negotiating, surely they could use other clubs for a cheaper price. They didn't even try to push us or make us wait, just agreed. All our legit deals, are done in person, but this one was done over prepaid phones. Sven did the talking and even though untraceable, I don't like business done this way. Regardless, he doesn't seem to agree with my worrying and assures me everything is fine, that Chilly has eyes on the buyers and everything they've told us checks out.

I'm late getting up that morning, since Dornan woke me up early to tell me he was leaving for the club and taking Bagheera with him, before falling back asleep. This gives me some alone time, so I pull on my running clothes and head out for a much needed long run. Even though it's been almost a week, I still get giddy inside over the patch Dornan gave me. It's currently residing on my dresser at the moment, since Gwen won't be able to sew it on until next weekend. But I like seeing it there, since I don't wear my cut every day. The suns blazing, but the sweat feels so good and I can't remember the last time I had such a good work out...minus Dornan that is.

I'm just heading back into Plantain from the foothills of the canyons that outline the south side of town, when I hear a car slowing behind me. Glancing over my shoulder to see Milton in his squad SUV. I slow to a walk as he pulls up beside me, his forearm resting on the door frame of the lowered window.

"Morning Maven," he says.

"Milton," I nod, my hands on my hips as I try to regulate my breathing.

"I need you to come with me."

I sigh and squint at him, the sun shining over his truck blinding me. "Why?" I ask.

He stops and so do I, raising a hand to shield my eyes from the sun. I don't see Milton all the time to know his tells or read his body language well like I can with most people, but it's not hard. He appears agitated, maybe a little apprehensive, like he doesn't want to be doing this right now. There's nothing I can think of that warrants me needing to go to the station, but something tells me by his expression, not to question him.

"Maven," he says quietly, his eyes scanning the area around us. "If you don't..." he pauses and shakes his head slightly. "It will just be easier this way."

His demeanor's getting my back up, putting my senses on full alert. The not having any clue what this can be about, worries me.

"I'm all sweaty, can I shower and meet you there?" I offer.

"This won't take long," he counters.

I hesitate a minute, before reaching for the door handle to the backseat and getting in. Seconds later, Milton's pulling a U-turn to head us away from town. I set my iPod down on the seat beside me, lifting the bottom of my tank top to wipe my face, trying to tamper down the 'what the fuck' feeling inside me. Alarm bells ring as we drive further from Plantain. Something tells me not to ask where we're going, that part of me who needs to act like I'm not freaking out. Pretending I'm not worried in the slightest that I don't have anything but my fists to protect me. Milton avoids my eyes in the rearview mirror, and I curse myself for the first time at not bringing my cellphone on my runs. Milton however makes me think that nothing's going to hurt me. I know he'll protect me, even if he doesn't want to.

He pulls into a driveway, the beginnings of a subdivision in the desert. We drive past workers and sounds of construction. Pulling down streets that have frames of houses, towards fully built unoccupied homes. It's eerily quiet back here, away from the commotion in the front. Milton parks in the driveway to a massive two story house, your stereotypical prefabricated house in a sub. My confusion level rising because I don't see any cars nearby, the house looks locked up with no signs of life. Milton lets out a weary sigh as he unfastens his seatbelt and exits the vehicle, then opens the door for me. I hop out and follow him towards the front door, and it takes everything in me not to crack a joke thanking him for taking me house hunting, just to break the tension. But the tension only grows as we enter the stuffy house, vacant of any furniture. He leads me into the dining room, a large six-person table with only two chairs occupying the space. At the same moment I comprehend that someone's sitting in one of them, as my stomach drops, seeing it's Justice.

13

What the fuck? He's just sitting there, leaning back in a chair, a smile on his face. My head begins to flip, why has Milton brought me to Justice? Why didn't Justice call me if he wanted to meet? It's been a week or two since we last talked, chatting about the building of the club and only work related topics. But more importantly, how the hell do these two know each other?

I look over at Milton, who gives me an apologetic look before nodding towards the vacant seat opposite Justice. My brows furrow before I look back at Justice, who's watching me with a twinkle in his eye at my confusion.

"As you probably can guess, I'm not a contractor...I'm a federal agent."

Justice shrugs slightly, and I feel my stomach flip. Although shady and I knew something was up with him, never did I think it was this.

"My name really is Justice Tanner, that part's true," he raises his hands. "But I did lie to you about a few things. Again, not a contractor. I lied about my intentions with you by asking you out, I'm sorry for that."

He looks at me with sincerity in his eyes, was this guy for real? Like he felt bad for leading me on or something.

"Oh and I'm not from Montana, I'm from-"

"Georgia," I answer softly before he can finish.

All the weird things that happened at lunch that day, suddenly make sense now. He took me out in hopes, I'd what? Tell him my life story? He gives me a knowing smile, which widens as he shakes a finger at me.

"It just came out at lunch, I wasn't thinking, but you caught it. Granted my accent is pretty hard to cover up," he smiles playfully. "But of course you caught it, you don't miss much, but you didn't show you noticed my slip up that's for sure."

The warmth I used to see in his eyes is gone, even though his demeanor seems jovial and relaxed, it's a facade. He's trying to seem at ease, in hopes it'll actually put him at ease. But the way he keeps looking at me, seeing my blank expression, is making him edgy.

"So, I really have you here, because we need to discuss some things."

He glances over at Milton for a moment, before reaching to the side of his chair to retrieve something from a box on the floor. I also look at Milton who again nods towards the empty chair, so I sit. He steps back towards the entryway, leaving us alone.

"This is your file that the Plantain Police Department has on you."

Justice holds up a manila folder before setting it on the table, opening it to read the contents aloud.

"Maven Gypsy Lofgren a.k.a V, a.k.a...Voodoo Child," he raises his brows and looks at me. "Voodoo Child...like the Hendrix song?" Justice asks, amusement in his eyes

"Hendrix song?" I cock my head, confusion in my tone. Playing completely clueless as I usually do in interrogations, which always annoys the person questioning you. I'm not about to tell him that people call me V not because it's short for Maven, but for my road name, Voodoo Child. I'm also not about to tell him this is my road name because when I was an infant, my dad claims that was the only song that would get me to stop crying. Aside from that, I'm still too confused as to what the hell is going on to even talk.

"Cute," he answers with sarcasm and a wink, before looking back down to the papers in the folder.

The fact that when men do little gestures like that, thinking it would piss me off, actually let me know I was a challenge. I've been questioned by the best, and I know for certain, Justice has nothing on them.

"Minor offenses in vandalism until age thirteen, then six months in juvenile hall which seemed to do the trick...nothing after that," he says looking up and raising the two sheets of paper from the folder in each hand.

"Now this," he pauses as he reaches down again, bringing up a binder and making a thud as he drops it on the table.

"This is your official file, my file," he smiles.

The binder is no measly little thing, the three rings holding the papers together is barely closing...fuck, FUCK. I look from the binder to meet his laughing eyes, and I want to smack that stupid look off his face. Instead, I keep my eyes on his, my face void of any reaction. His jaw ticks slightly, and a vein begins protruding in his temple with frustration that he got zero reaction from me.

"You were off the radar until five years ago, five years ago your dad gets locked up for murder. You either patch into Warrior of the Gods, or simply take his place."

The way he says this, I know he's not quite sure which it is himself.

"The day I took you to lunch and told you I had a disagreement with an associate…my boss told me if I didn't get you to incriminate yourself at that lunch, then the case was to be left alone and revisited at a later date, when we had more on the club. Of course you didn't say anything, you lied better than I thought. So, I made Milton pick you up and bring you in. I was the one behind the mirror. Again, you gave nothing away... and we were about to call it quits when we hit pay dirt." he smirks.

He pulls out a set of photos of us sitting by the window of the diner that day, and now it makes sense why he made us go there and sit where we did. Photos to prove in court that we met, he probably was also wired as we spoke. With the binder still open, he retrieves a paper and sets it in front of me. My eyes not leaving his, as he looks between me and the paper.

"You'll want to look at this Maven."

My eyes don't budge, and again his jaw ticks.

"We found your prints in the Durango compound, on a door knob."

Fuck…fuck…fuck. Again, I'm instantly aware of my body. Remaining stock still, my breathing slow and calm. Trying to not allow the artery in my neck to thump wildly in sync with my heartbeat. The Feds had to have been watching us, how else would they know about Durango? It's not as if someone reported that their illegal semi-automatic guns were almost stolen.

"And?" I ask.

Justice smiles wider and shakes his head slightly, sitting back in his chair.

"You don't get it Maven, *we got you.*"

I narrow my eyes.

"What do you want?"

There's no point in denying my involvement with the MC at this point. I want to know what this is all really about, knowing full well I'm not who Justice actually wants. I'm a no one in the scheme of things.

"We're willing to grant the release of your dad from prison and to not press charges or investigate further into the Durango robbery...if you provide us detailed information about Warrior of the Gods and other clubs."

"Information?"

Justice's jaw begins to tick again, as he crosses his arms over his chest.

"The guns, the drugs, other shit. We want to catch the big dogs, Sven Fredricksen, Judas Watson, all the Presidents."

"Why me?"

"Because when I met you for lunch, you lied on the fly better than I've ever seen anyone lie in my career. Not just your words, but your reactions, you don't have any tells."

His brows raise as he leans forward, and begins flipping through the papers in the binder.

"You said you didn't go to college, but you graduated high school early and went to UCLA, graduated with honors with business and accounting degrees in three years at the age of nineteen. You made up that bullshit story about your neighbor, and him getting you into bikes instantly. You didn't even blink when I mentioned the Warrior of the Gods. It's like lying comes easier to you then telling the truth...and that's why it has to be you. I know they won't suspect you of being an informant because, you can just lie."

Justice acts like he's had some eureka moment, I shake my head and let out a humorless laugh.

"Those guys, they know me better than anyone...they'll know I'm lying."

Especially Dornan, and the instant thought of him and doing this, makes my heart hurt.

"Maven, if you don't agree to this you're lookin at twenty-five to life for what I have in this binder," he states placing a hand on it. "Now, I know this is a shock, you need a little time, we're giving you until tomorrow night-"

"You're giving me as long as I want, because you have no case against the MC without me. So you go ahead and press charges against me for my fingerprints being on a door handle, along with hundreds of other people's at an attempted robbery scene, and good luck proving I'd never been in that building before. It doesn't sound like that's the real case you want, Justice."

He just looks at me, fuck, I hope I'm right on this one. If I go to trial and they have all the circumstantial evidence he claims is in his binder, a lawyer could convince a judge or jury that I was at the crime scene, and past history would nail me to the cross.

"There were items taken from the scene. Assault rifles that would have no problem finding their way onto your property if necessary."

This fucker was going to set me up. I begin to stand when he raises a hand for me to stop, his eyes looking at me with intensity.

"There's something else I want you to see before you leave," his voice taking on a somber tone.

He digs to the center of the binder, freeing a separate thinner green folder. Setting it down, before sliding it closer to me across the table. He looks back up at me before opening it, and my eyes trail down to see a dead woman, naked, with long dark hair covering her face and breasts. She doesn't look like she's been dead very long when these were taken. Her hair's tangled, her skin dirty, and she looks beaten and bruised. I narrow my eyes, and look back up at Justice in confusion.

"These are the remains of your mother Maven. In a shallow grave, W.G. carved into her forehead. The club killed your mom Maven, she did *not* leave you."

My heart plummets into my stomach, bile crawling up my throat as I literally feel the blood drain from my face. I begin to shake my head frantically, covering my mouth with my hand as my eyes tear.

No fucking no, stop Maven. Pull it together, not here, and not in front of them.

"Jesus Christ," Milton growls as he stomps into the room, slamming the file shut, and shoving it back across the table at Justice.

"The club isn't your family, they killed your mother and they will kill you too if given half a reason. Think about this, is this who you'll go to jail for the rest of your life for?" Justice says in a rush because he knows I'm about to bolt.

He tosses a stack of photos onto the table, scattering them everywhere. Pictures of my brothers, my dad, Sven, Missy, and the one that lands closest to me...Dornan. I stand quickly, the chair falling back onto the floor with a clatter.

"You used to be a good person Maven, before the club. I know you can do the right thing," Justice adds calmly.

"Take me home," I order Milton.

He nods and walks towards the front door, I'm right behind him when Justice grabs my arm.

"Here," he says, handing me a business card. "Take this, call me at this number when you decide, the number you have for me now will no longer be in service. We don't have much time, but I will let you think about it."

I jerk my arm away, walking out of the house behind Milton. I take several deep breaths outside in an attempt to push the burning acid rising in my stomach, and back down my throat. I can't breathe, the world's spinning, and I can't navigate what's real and what isn't. Milton opens the truck door for me and I climb in. What the fuck just happened? Has my whole life been a lie? My mom didn't abandon me, but was murdered. Did I have family out there? Her family that never knew me. Dad said she was a runaway, but now I question everything. Did everyone know she was dead but me? Not only the club, but the whole fucking town? There are no secrets there. Did my grandmother know and hide it from me? I lean down and put my head between my knees, bringing my arms over my head as the cool air Milton's blasting through the air conditioning pours over me.

"You knew this was gonna happen? All the times you questioned me was for him? He was behind the mirror and you knew and didn't fucking warn me?"

I don't ask him if he knows about my mom's death, because fuck him. I sit up and look at the back of his head in front of me, wanting so badly to hit him or do something to vent this rage burning inside me.

"I'm a cop Maven, he's a federal agent!"

"Fuck that! My dad saved your aunt from being brutalized, and you lead me into this without any warning-"

He cuts me off, "My father helped your dad so don't you forget that. That was their shit not ours-"

"Oh wow he withheld evidence, my dad is still gonna rot in prison the rest of his life. My dad killed that son-of-a-bitch for your family, that goes beyond the bullshit you and your fucking father ever did for us."

My palm slams against the top of the seat, before I grab my iPod and shove the earbuds in, and cranking the volume up. I don't want to think, or feel, or accept any of this.

Milton drops me off where he picked me up from, hesitating to leave me at the side of the road, before he finally peels out after a long moment. I'm in a daze, a daze getting home, a daze in the shower, nothing seems real or right. There's no way I can go to work. Now the MC that once felt like family and my most trusted companions, seem like enemies. A group of people who aren't protecting me, but using me.

I need answers, and of course my stupid dad is still in solitary fucking confinement. Part of me wonders if he'd even tell me the truth about my mom if questioned. The reasons he avoids talking about her, or having pictures of her anywhere, I always thought was anger over her leaving. But what if it's anger over something else, something that made him so angry he killed her? I feel not like myself, like my whole identity, who I thought I was, is no more.

Checking my cellphone on my bed, I see Dornan's texted me several times asking if I'm okay and when I'm coming in. Clasping the phone in my hand, I pull down the covers and crawl into bed. Not only does my body feel exhausted from my run, but my mind feels like mush and all I want is to go away for a while. Before I doze off, I text Skye that I'm not coming in. At first I don't want to message Dornan because I know he'll come home to check on me, but I don't want him to think I'm avoiding him.

"Hey babe, headache again, going to lie down, maybe come

into work later.”

I silence my phone and throw the covers over my head, sleep finding me fast.

Something's stroking my cheek, running over my hair and back again, my name being said softly. I inhale sharply with awareness, and breathe in Dornan's scent, I moan slightly as he presses his lips on my forehead. My head's killing me, like a nails being hammered into my temple over and over. I raise my hand and press my palm against the side of my head, my eyes barely able to open, they feel puffy and swollen.

“Shh...sorry to wake you up, do you need something to eat or more medicine?” he whispers.

My eyes flutter open and then close, expecting harsh sunlight, but it's dark. I squint trying to make out the features of my love, he's kneeling at the side of the bed as he continues to run his fingertips soothingly over me in comfort.

“What time is it?” I ask.

“Nine.”

“Fuck,” I moan, I slept the whole day.

All at once, the morning's events come back. A heavy weight engulfs me, encompassing all of me. Suddenly, Dornan's touches are painful, my body not wanting him here. He hasn't done anything, he didn't kill my mother, he's not been approached by the Feds and asked to be an informant. Yet, I still feel just tense with him here.

“I brought you water and some pills,” he whispers, pressing his lips to my forehead again.

I slowly sit up, my eyes still struggling to remain open. Which I don't fight because I think that when I actually look at him, I'm scared of what my reaction will be. He knows me too well, I can't just lie and say I'm fine, he'll see right through it. His fingers place my hands around the glass, then there's something at my lips. I part them as he slips in the headache pills into my mouth, guiding my hands up until the glass is there. I take a long drink before finally looking down at him. He's studying me, his brows pinched together slightly as his hands resume stroking my hair and face.

"Where were you?" I ask, because something had to have been keeping him from getting to me immediately after receiving my text.

"I went on a run with Joey to meet with The Steel Axes this morning, didn't you read my messages? I sent them before you said you weren't feeling well."

Dornan talks in a calm, soothing way, and all I can do is watch his lips, my eyes not being able to look into his. There's such a pain of guilt and shame resting inside me, like a brick sitting on my stomach. I want to tell him what happened today, that Justice isn't a contractor, they have my fingerprints, what Justice wants me to do for them...about my mom. But I can't, the fact that I know what I'm going to do, fucking kills me, but it's what needs to be done to end all of this.

"You've been sick a lot lately with the headaches, maybe you should see a doctor."

Dornan leans up and rests his forehead against mine, his hands cupping my face. I feel my lip quiver slightly before I swallow and nod.

"Yeah I will," I whisper.

I bring my arms up and wrap them around his shoulders, comforting him because I know this is worrying him. When Missy was diagnosed with breast cancer, she had symptoms that she kept playing off and ignoring. When she finally did go to the doctor, the cancer was so advanced she had to have a double mastectomy. I know this, my headaches, that he's thinking the worst, and by lying earlier makes me feel awful. Although now I really do have a headache. He nuzzles his face into my neck and inhales deeply, his arms wrap around my torso and pull me close.

"What do you need me to do?" he asks.

"Will you put some music on and lay with me?" I request.

After a few beats, his arms leave me and he stands, retrieving my iPod from downstairs while I snuggle back into bed. My heads too foggy with emotion and overloaded with everything, that I don't want to think anymore tonight, the music and Dornan will help. The opening song to Bob Seger's -Night Moves album comes over the dock speakers softly, causing me to smile since Dornan knows this is my favorite album. He strips his clothes off and moves into the bathroom, I hear the shower turn on and I picture him naked, wet, and soapy, rubbing his body as the water runs over his skin. My heart cracks a little, I have to stop this. This isn't going to work, not now and certainly not after knowing what I have to do. But I can't just push him away, he won't go and he'll know there's something I'm not telling him.

By the time the song "Night Moves" comes on, Dornan's back in our room, naked. The pale moonlight shines in, highlighting the contours and cuts of his muscles and tan skin. I roll onto my side as the bed dips, as he positions himself behind me. He gently slips the hair-tie from my ponytail and his fingertips begin rubbing my scalp as he sings the words 'she was a black haired beauty with big dark eyes.'

I bite my lip hard as my eyes slowly glass with tears in remembrance of only a few months ago when Dornan lay here with me and sang those same lyrics. If I only knew then what I know now...would I still decide to be with him? Would it have changed my heart from falling in love with this man? My decision about what I'm going to tell Justice is going to kill me, but I know it will ruin Dornan. He won't trust me anymore and I'll crush everything he ever thought about me. I can live with the effect my future will have on me, but I can't deal with what it will do to Dornan, and so I can't think about it now. Instead I lay with my back pressed to his chest, his hands and voice caressing and loving on me, lulling me into a restless sleep.

14

I wake early, sleeping like shit the whole night and decide to head into work before Dornan wakes. He looks so beautiful laying here, totally naked and edible. But rather than waking him up with my mouth on his cock, I kiss his cheek and head out. The normal early birds are already at the shop, Rocket and Chain talking as usual out front as they drink their coffee. Boo-Boo and Smokey are also standing around the punch clock and coffee maker, not really saying much, but both nod hellos to me as I walk past. The stillness of the morning dissipates, when I jump slightly at seeing Sven sitting at my desk. My body tenses, does he already know about Justice and he's here to confront me? He's never, ever here this early, fuck. He's sitting with his back to me, leaving the seat behind my desk unoccupied.

"Hey," I try to say as casual as possible.

"Sorry to scare you," he says, turning his head slightly and showing me his profile while raising a hand.

I move around to the side of my desk, dropping my purse into a drawer as Bagheera sits on his doggy bed behind me. Sven seems casual, a leg up with an ankle resting on his other knee, coffee in hand. But his brows are furrowed like his sons do when he too is stressed.

"What's up?" I ask, sitting down.

I have to mentally assess my features, making sure my face is blank, my fingers aren't fumbling, or my legs not nervously tapping. Can I be looking at the man who possibly killed, or helped kill my mom? I know two sides of Sven; just like I know the two sides of every other man in this club. The person they are day to day, and the person they are during business. I know Sven's killed before, and has done so in front of me. A hardened member who knows the game, and has opted to kill numerous people so Dornan, Joey, and even I didn't have to. Even though I know this side of him, I've never seen him kill an innocent person, a woman, definitely not someone he knew and was his best friend's wife. But people do things sometimes we can never imagine, circumstances and emotions cause reactions from people in moments of chaos. Still, knowing what I know and taking things into account, I just can't get past all the things he's done for me, especially in the absence of my dad. Maybe it's due to guilt from killing my mom, or knowing my mom was killed. I just can't see a heartless killer past the good man I've always considered a second father.

He leans forward and nods once towards the landline phone on my desk, which is pulled closer to him from its normal resting place. The red light blinks, meaning someone's on hold. He presses the button, then clears his throat.

"Go ahead Chilly."

"I think...yeah, I think we have a snitch," Chilly's gravelly voice crackles over the speaker.

My breath hitches, my heart taking a fast track to my stomach.

Sven's eyes remain downcast, like this is something he doesn't want to believe but has no evidence to think otherwise.

"What?" I ask in disbelief, a cold wash of dread enveloping me.

"The deal we worked out the other day with The Steel Axes, and the third party buyer," Sven begins. "Sent Chilly to check out the drop point and pick up, just to let us know of anything we might need to be aware of."

Sven lifts a shoulder. This is normal practice, even when we use the same locations repeatedly for business, Chilly always goes ahead of time to check things out.

"Chilly went there several times and every time, there were black unmarked vehicles in the vicinity."

I lean forward with my forearms flat on the table.

"Another crew?" I question.

"Not sure," Chilly replies. "I wasn't able to get a positive ID or legitimate confirmation on any details, and when I tried to trail them it was like they vanished. I got the sense they were trying to prepare for the day of the drop, where to hide, shit like that."

"Someone from the Steele Axes?" I ask.

"No one in that crew knows the drop point," Sven replies somberly.

We sit in silence. Did the Feds have another member under the same deal as me? I don't even want to voice anything about law enforcement, because at this point it will only raise Sven's suspicions. Chilly knows my guard is up with them since my phone call to him. But did he tell Sven of my suspicions?

"Who do we have that's got a beef?" I ask.

"Hard to say."

Sven runs an old weathered hand over his face, up over his slicked back hair.

"I mean, of course we always have prospects thinking they can find a better crew, since they get treated like shit. Drag still might be ticked about Dornan roughing him up, and being put on long distance runs lately. But he's good people, I don't think it's him."

"For sure the guys would've caught word if any of the prospects were talking shit, or not happy with the club," I offer.

"I'll talk with Dornan, see if he's heard anything. I want to go to gathering as soon as everyone gets in."

I nod and sit back. Fuck, this shit is just getting crazier by the minute. To me, this has to be the Feds, just the way the job was done over the phone, and the way they didn't seem to negotiate the payment. Maybe they really did have someone else in the club who is snitching, but then why would Justice be needing me?

"The club will be alright if we push back this job?" Sven asks in reference to money.

"Yeah, we're good," I reassure.

"We need to be smart about this, keep your ears and eyes open." Sven's looking at me, his eyes piercing mine and I keep eye contact, not letting my nerves get the better of me.

"Pres, can I talk to you off speaker?" Chilly asks.

It feels like my mouth's full of sand, I can't actually swallow. I want to look away, but instead I watch Sven grab the receiver and press it against his ear. He's looking down at his coffee cup, listening, when his eyes meet mine and narrow slightly. Holy fucking shit, he knows, he knows I've been asked to snitch. What am I going to say if he confronts me, tell him the truth? Deny everything? Finally, he nods and says, "I'll get back to you after gathering."

He sets the phone back into its cradle, his eyes remaining on me. "Have you heard from Brayden?" his tone and look softening.

The question stutters my brain for a second, not at all what I thought he was going to say. I shake my head, remembering the last time I saw him.

"No, not since..." I stop, swallowing down the sand finally.

Sven nods in understanding and as if he doesn't want me to finish the sentence, both of us knowing the last time was when he attacked me.

"I hope you know that the club would never let him get to you, never. You don't have to be scared or worried, he and his club can't touch you."

I know that Chilly's told him my concerns, but they think it's because I think Brayden's after me. Okay, I guess that's sort of how it is but, not that I think he will hurt me again. Brayden's after something, I just don't know what yet, it can't possibly be revenge on me. Again, the feeling that Sven looks after me like a daughter, nudges the feelings of the situation with my mom back just a little further.

All I can do is give him a small smile, watching as he stands and appears more troubled now. Like he thought I'd have some insight or information to dismiss the idea of the snitch. The sinking guilty feeling ever present, is now lodged in my gut, I wait until moments after Sven closes my door and is far enough away before I begin to sob. The pressure eating at me, the guilt like a ball and chain around my neck, and I can't keep it bottled up anymore.

After spending an hour or so in the bathroom, crying so hard I'd started throwing up. I finally make it back to my desk, resting my head in my hands. I'm on the verge of calling Justice to meet up, because I feel like I can't do this one second longer. There's a soft knock on my door and I know it's Dornan, not even needing to look. Bagheera walks over to greet me, and begins whining at my disheveled state. Dornan's rough fingers coax my hands away gently, as he pulls me up and into his arms, setting me on his lap as he takes over the chair. I inhale his scent and my breath hiccups as it's still trying to calm after vomiting. As he runs his hands over my clammy skin, along my sweaty hairline, there's concern in his voice when he asks, "Could you be pregnant?"

"No."

I shake my head and want to ignore the flash of disappointment in his eyes. But it's there, and the idea of having babies with him lightens my heart. Before that bitch reality comes back, and my hopes of that future is gone.

"Do you think this is something-a result from when Brayden assaulted you?"

The pain in his eyes at even mentioning the incident, spears me like a dagger. I fucking hate lying, but I can't tell him, I just can't.

"Maybe," I whisper, resting my head in my hands as I close my eyes.

His arms wrap around me tighter as he begins to stand, "I'm taking you home."

"No, we have gathering."

"I don't give a fuck, you can barely keep your head up."

As if to prove him wrong, I raise my head and open my eyes, trying my best to get myself together.

"I'm fine."

He shakes his head and looks away from me, and I take his face into my palms.

"I'm fine. I'll go to gathering and then the doctor's."

He gives me a look like he doesn't believe me, but I widen my eyes in assurance before he sighs.

"Promise me, after gathering you'll go, okay?"

"Promise."

We make our way over to the clubhouse, Dornan protectively walking with me with his arm around my shoulders. Entering the large room to see most everyone already sitting around the wood table, only members allowed to this meeting and no prospects. No one's talking, as if they sense, like I had earlier in my office, that by Sven's demeanor there's something major going on. Dornan and I take our seats and Sven begins, telling everyone the details of Chilly's surveillance and asking if anyone's been getting bad vibes from the not present prospects. Following with a warning that if one of the snitches is us, that we won't ever get to enjoy the deal that's been offered to us in return for ratting out the club.

Of course all the brothers voice their opinions that it has to be Children of the Reaper, since we now have a beef with them, no one even brings up law enforcement. My stomach's in knots and all I want to do is be away from this place, I feel like I haven't taken a deep breath since I arrived. Sven orders us to not tell anyone outside the room about what we've discussed, and for everyone to be on high alert. As soon as Sven says the meeting's over, I'm the first out the door and on my way to the parking lot, when a hand wraps around my upper arm. It's Smokey, seeing him surprises me, and I stop in the middle of the lot to turn and face him. The other members are all milling about the entryway to the clubhouse, smoking and talking, but no one seems to pay any mind to us. Dornan and Joey must still be inside, because they certainly would be eying the two of us.

"V," his voice low. "Fuck, I don't know how to say this." His eyes scan around us nervously and I've never seen him looking this way before.

I feel my cellphone begin to buzz in my back pocket, but I ignore it.

"Yesterday when Dornan couldn't get a hold of you, he sent me to find you running since I don't know where you live. I caught up to you in the foothills, I was still kind of far back when I saw Milton stop you."

Fuck. I close my eyes and exhale a long steady breath.

"I followed you. I saw that Justice guy leave the house after you, and I'm assuming he's not a contractor."

"Smokey," my voice a plea.

His fingers wrap tighter around my bicep, not to hurt me to bring my attention to his words. My cellphone's going off again, but it barely registers with what's happening right now.

"You saved my ass at Durango, and I told you I owe you one. I'm not gonna say anything... for now."

The breath I've been holding whooshes out.

"I know you V, I know you're not gonna do something stupid and put the club in danger or whatever, but you have to tell Sven or...I don't know. But I can't keep this a secret for long, figure your shit out and tell him."

"Everyone in the clubhouse!" someone yells from the doorway, and we both look to see guys quickly making their way back inside. Smokey lets my arm free, giving me a long look with raised brows.

"I will."

Slowly I follow towards the clubhouse, my cellphone buzzing again and finally I reach for it, reading the display is a number I don't recognize.

"Hello?" I answer.

"Maven, this is Officer Milton."

I enter the club to see all the guys standing around the bar, looking up at the three flat screen TV's and all I see is fire and firetrucks.

"There's been a fire, the strip club and the new club you're building," Milton says.

Sure enough, I see both scenes of the fires flash on the screen. Our established club in flames, along with the construction site for the new club.

"Goddammit," Dornan growls beside me. "Those fuckers are dead," he adds.

I look up at him, his eyes narrow, jaw tight. He knows this is Children of the Reaper's work, we all know it. The Feds wouldn't do something like this.

"Justice wants to meet you somewhere," Milton says.

I pull my cell down and end the call, slipping it into my pocket again. I steady my features, to not show how fucking insane my instinct to just blurt out the offer Justice has given me is. I need to meet with him, I need to give him what he wants. I want to know what happened with my mom, *to* my mom, and I'd hoped to be able to find answers before turning myself in. But I don't want to deal with it if I'm being honest, not wanting to be told that my whole life's been a fucking lie.

Dornan and Sven are now talking, and I know this is my time to go while everyone's distracted. I need to sneak to my house, get Justice's card and call him to meet me. Everyone's talking in raised voices as I back towards the door, making sure no one notices me. Once I push through the doors, I bolt to my car. Making it to my house in record time, I rush over to the fireplace mantle where I put Justice's card under a flower pot. My heart begins to pound harder than before, as my fingertips graze the small paper. I'm gulping in air and close my eyes trying to psych myself up, I can do this...I *have* to do this.

"Maven."

The sound of my name startles me and I whirl around, bringing my hands behind my back to hide the card. Dornan stands in the entryway to the front room, breathing just as hard as I am.

"Jesus," he lets out in a rush, walking to me and cupping my face. "Fuck, you can't just disappear right after we find out the club's burnt down...fuck," he sighs again.

"I'm fine," I whisper as the words catch in my throat.

He's looking at me like he knows otherwise, and then I realize he's noticed my hands behind my back. Slowly he steps away, running a hand through his short hair as he turns his back to me. I take a deep breath ready to confess all the shit that's been going on, but he starts first.

"Is this about us? You've been acting fucking weird lately and I'm over pretending it's nothing, and don't tell me it's nothing or the headaches because I can see some shit is bothering you."

"Dornan-"

He shakes his head, a signal for me to stop talking as he turns to face me. I see the worry in his eyes and the difficulty he's having at confronting me. How can he even question me about how I feel for him? Then it dawns on me that this is what I need him to think, it'll be easier this way if he thinks I don't want to be with him anymore.

"Don't even fucking tell me some shit Maven, I can read you like a fucking book and I know you're not feeling this. You haven't put the patch I gave you on your cut, I'm the one making all these steps to make a future with you. So if that's not what you want, then just fucking tell me that."

The way he's looking at me is shattering my heart and I just can't bear to look at him and say it's over between us. Slowly and with shaky hands, I bring my arms around to show him the business card. He glances at it, but I know he's too far away to read what it says.

"The Feds want me to snitch out the club," I state.

His eyes switch from anger to confusion, and I immediately know what he's thinking.

"I'm not the snitch Sven's talking about," I rush out. "The contractor Justice is an agent, and they have my prints from Durango. I don't know with all the chaos of Smokey getting shot, but...when we got back to the club my gloves were gone." My voice trembling as the words tumble from my lips.

Dornan just stands there, looking at me, his expression one of shock. My stomach sinks and I'm not sure what to say or do. My fear that he'll walk out right now and never look back is at the forefront. I almost want to die at the feeling of utter loss that will take over me if that happens. Isn't this what I need to happen though? For him to be pissed and leave me, to not look back? Just as I'm about to speak, saying what I don't know, he starts for me, his hands cupping my face hard.

"Give them me. Give them everything on me."

The breath from my lungs comes out in a sob of relief that he's touching me, and looking at me like I've never seen before. I close my eyes as the tears scorch my cheeks, the pain in my chest slowly easing. This man, this man is my everything and I can't let him go.

"They don't want us; they want all the MC's. I think if I don't give them anything, and they have to settle for me, that they'll go after someone else. That it can be okay."

As I'm rambling, he's shaking his head and his grip tightens on my face.

"You can't chance that; I won't let you. You're not going to prison. I'll make it better."

He rests his forehead against mine and we both close our eyes, exchanging breaths as my hands wrap around his wrists. The boy who said he'd never make me promises, is pledging to me that I won't have to do what I know I need to. Deep in my heart I know he's my partner in this, the relief of confessing my predicament, only allows the pain of what I've learned about my mom to slam into my heart.

"Do you know what happened to my mom?" I ask.

"Of course Maven-"

"No," I pull my face back to look at him. "Justice showed me a picture of her, dead, Warrior of the Gods carved into her skin...he said our dads killed her."

"No, that can't be. My parents talk about your mom like she was the best, my mom still talks about her all the time. Club business or not, she wouldn't be cool with my dad having part in killing her best friend."

"Dornan, what if they did? That means everything I know about her is a lie, she didn't abandon me, they took her away."

My voice raises and I feel the years of a life I thought I knew, begin to change into something I don't like. A lifetime of being lied to, made to feel she was a stranger who walked away from me. When in reality she was taken away, that she loved me.

"Let's talk to my dad," Dornan states.

"I-how can we ask him without saying where I got this idea from all of a sudden?" I ask.

Dornan runs his hand down the side of my hair.

"Don't worry about that. Trust me."

And I do, I trust him with my life and always have, it's time I really prove it.

"What if they did kill her, am I ready to hear that?" I ask somberly.

"I'll be there; you won't be alone in this."

He takes my hand and fishes his cellphone from his pocket, pressing it against his ear.

"Dad, is Mom home? Can you meet me and Maven there right now?"

We get into his car as he ends the call, I try to buckle my seatbelt but my hands are shaking so badly that Dornan has to do it. We sit silently in the car, Dornan's hand linking with mine. The fact that when I told him what I'm up against, what's really going on, he's all in, not letting me deal with this on my own. Feelings of overwhelming love and loyalty fill my heart and I want him to know, even if the words don't compare to the expanse of how I feel.

"I love you."

His fingers tighten around mine and I look over at him, he's doing that one sided grin that lights me up. A moment later we stop at a light and he turns to me, his smile growing as he leans over and crushes his mouth against mine. For a small moment all is right, none of the crazy shit that's going on around us matters. All that matters is that I love this man, and now he knows it.

15

We're sitting at the dining room table, and it's obvious Missy can sense something's up. Other than offering us a drink, we haven't spoken, so we somberly sit at the dining room table in silence. I wonder what she's thinking, she knows it's something serious since she's heard the clubs burnt down. All Dornan told her was that we want to talk to her and Sven together, so here we sit in silence.

Dornan takes my hand under the table, resting our clasped hands on my leg to stop it from bouncing. I hear the rumble of a motorcycle as it begins down the street and shuts off beside the house, notching up my fear every second. Sven enters the room and looks between the three of us, then takes the seat beside Missy, opening his hands.

"Well? Don't tell me y'all are announcing you're getting married, while we got serious shit going on with the club that you pulled me away from."

We both remain silent, until Dornan takes a deep breath and starts.

"We want to know what happened to Maven's mom."

I see Missy's face pale, looking shocked as she crosses her arms over her chest while glancing over at Sven, whose demeanor hasn't changed.

"We know she was murdered; we want to know what happened."

I love that he's saying 'we' and not 'Maven,' like we really are in this together.

I stare at Sven, waiting. Waiting for a reaction, waiting for him to speak. Finally, after an eternity, he clicks his tongue and nods towards Missy, who abruptly stands and leaves the room. Now I don't know what to think, did she leave because Sven's about to tell me he killed my mom and doesn't want his wife to hear? But he still doesn't speak, just looks at me. Missy returns to the table with a shoe box, placing it on the table in front of her. She opens the lid, shuffling through the contents before pulling back her hand, a photograph between her fingertips. She gives it a long look before setting it down, and sliding it towards me. I know immediately that this is my mom, the instant connection I feel to her causes me to inhale sharply. She's beautiful and radiant, and… alive. Compared to the only other photo I've ever seen of her, courtesy of Justice and his crime scene photography.

"When your dad met your mom, she was dating another biker named Jasper. He was the son of one of the four who founded the club with your granddads. From the start he and your dad never got along, always competing even when we were kids. When Jasper started bringing your mom around we all loved her, her and Missy became best friends and even though she'd never been exposed to the biker life, she adjusted and became part of the family. None of us knew that her and your dad had started something and that they wanted to be together. Your dad didn't care about Jasper's ideas on the matter but your mom didn't want to hurt him, I think she was scared from things we knew that happened between them. Jasper was a hot head and she was too forgiving. So, your dad gave her some time to break it to him, but one-night Jasper caught them in your dad's club apartment and he went ballistic. He ended up leaving the club and starting his own club in Utah, and your mom and dad got married and had you. But apparently the fucker never got over it and our club ended up taking business from him, which caused his club to go bankrupt and he owed everyone."

Sven stops and runs a rough hand over his mouth, reaching into his vest to pull out his soft pack of smokes. Lighting one and inhaling deeply, we sit and wait with baited breath for him to continue.

"Missy had been trying to get a hold of your mom all morning, but she figured you were keeping her busy. So she decided to take Dornan with her to check on you guys. When she got there, you were alone and crying, the house was trashed and there...there was blood on the kitchen floor."

Missy covers her face with her hands as she begins to softly cry, like remembering what she'd seen all those years ago still affects her. Sven wraps his arm around her shoulders, pulling her into his side.

"There was a note pinned to your diaper from the person who took your mom. When Missy called me I knew immediately who was responsible, and when I told your dad he knew it was Jasper too. The note had a time and place so, of course we got the crew together to ride out. When we got there, Shine was dead in a hole in the ground, the clubs' initials carved into her head. Your dad lost it, he tried to kill himself with his gun right there."

I feel the emotion thick in my throat and pooled tears burn the backs of my eyes. Dornan puts his hand on the back of my neck and squeezes gently, reminding me he's here for me.

"For days your dad and I looked for that asshole, or anyone associated with his fucking club. But it turned out he was still here, hiding in plain sight. We think maybe he was planning on taking you too, taking you and your mom separately would only drive your Dad more insane. To take everything away that your dad loved, since that's what your dad did to him. Jasper was staying in a motel outside the city, shocked as shit when we showed up at his door," he says somberly and cuts his hand through the air, saying what he won't aloud. That they killed him.

I nod and think of what he's just said, that they thought Jasper was going to take me, to kill me, to kill everyone my dad loved. My chest's so tight, like I need to cut it open to relieve the pressure.

"Your dad was gutted about what happened with your mom, took down all her pictures because it hurt too damn much to see her. You two started spending more time at your grandparents', avoiding anything to do with your mom. Your dad said being in your house, the memory of your mom, it was too hard. When you started asking where your mama was, he told you she was gone and you assumed he meant ran away. So in an effort not to destroy you even more, he just agreed…and so did we. It was never meant to hurt you girl, only to protect you."

The look Sven's giving me, it's so genuine it makes my insides ache even more. The fact I ever doubted them, the fact that I believed a stranger for one minute, instead of giving my family the benefit of the doubt, pisses me off.

"I have some more pictures of your mom I'd like to show you," Missy says clearing her throat.

I nod and feel my breathing begin to slow as relief washes over me, to finally know the truth. At the same time, it saddens me to think of what kind of life or how different I would be if my mom was still here. These thoughts I've never had before, since I was so resentful in thinking she didn't want to be a part of my life all this time. An even deeper sadness fills my heart, knowing my dad suffered the loss of my mom alone, and I didn't even know.

"Son," Sven says as he stands. "Let's give them some time alone."

Dornan nods and leans over to kiss my forehead, before following his dad into the den. Missy and I look through all the pictures, and I love hearing all the memories she recalls with each picture. So many road trips, crazy nights at the clubhouse, my parents' wedding day, the day I was born. Mom's always smiling, and the way she looks at my dad, you can see how much they loved each other.

"And this, I'd hoped to give you one day."

I look down to see my mom holding a two-year old me, we're both smiling and she's looking down at her mini me with such pride and happiness, as I look up at her with nothing but love. Missy sniffles, her brows furrowing as she speaks.

"I'm so sorry Maven, that we didn't tell you the truth before. You have to know that it wasn't to lie, but to make sure you grew up happy and didn't know how cruel the world could be just yet. No one ever intended for you to not eventually find out, but as the years went on, it got harder and harder to confront you with the hard truth. Just know that we all love you, your mom loved *you* very much."

I take her hand and kiss the back, before curling my fingers around it, sniffling as I clear the tears from my eyes with my free hand.

"If she couldn't be here, I'm glad you were, I know that's what she would've wanted for me. Thank you for loving me unconditionally and taking care of me like I was your own, you'll never know how thankful I am for that."

Missy covers her face as a small sob tears from her throat and we hug for a long while, eventually breaking apart to wipe our faces and get ourselves together. I love this woman as if she's my mom, but I'll never forget the spirit of the woman who brought me into this world. I ask to take some of the other photos, ones of my mom and dad together, and another of the three of us. Missy removes one photo from the box, one of her and mom and gives me the rest.

Dornan and I head out about an hour later and I'm all smiles, forgetting again about the shit going on that's bigger than us, wanting to remain in this bubble a little longer before I have to burst it.

"The only option my dad can come up with is Drag as the snitch, shit's been tense between us for a while, and he wants me and Joey to take him on the run tomorrow."

"Is he back in town?" I ask.

Drag's been doing all the cross country runs. At first I knew Dornan had been putting him on those just to get him away from me, still pissed that he'd come onto me at the bar. But then for some odd reason, Skye turned up one day engaged, and Drag started asking for the jobs. I want to tell Skye that I think it's more than a coincidence, but have too much of my own shit going on to get involved in that.

"Tonight."

"Did you tell your dad about Justice?" I ask.

He shakes his head in the negative. "You and me need to figure out what we need to do about Justice, before we go to dad with it," he states.

I look out the window, knowing I have it set in my head that I'll turn myself in, no matter what Dornan says.

The clubhouse is packed, and everyone seems to be dealing with the club's burning down by drinking. They too don't want to worry about how we're going to make up for the lost income. We know we can rebuild and Sven's never let finances get to where we can't bounce back, we will just find another way until we're back on our feet.

Dornan leads me through the main room and towards his apartments, holding the door open for me as we enter his. The sun's setting, bathing the room in orange and pink. I set the box of pictures on the dresser, and let my fingers linger over the top for a moment. Dornan slides his hand across my cheek to turn my face towards him, his lips pressing mine into a kiss. His mouth continues to meld with mine, as we begin to remove one another's jackets, not rushing but savoring. It feels like this time together is limited, that there's a countdown to me leaving. As if he can sense my mind whirling, he pulls back and looks down at me.

"I want you to be here with me, get out of your head and let me do the thinking."

I nod as he slides both his hands into my hair and tugs slightly.

"Do you understand?"

"Yes," I moan.

He bows his head and begins kissing my neck, and collarbone while he moves his hands towards the bottom of my shirt, kneeling down in front of me. I stare down at him, his fingers running under my top to caress my stomach, planting small kisses on the exposed skin. From there, his hands move up over my bra to my breasts as he grabs them roughly. His teeth nip at the top of my jeans, as he lets out a little growl.

"I can smell your pussy, drives me insane."

My head lulls to the side as my hands move to his shoulders, his fingers pinch my nipples as I push my hips against him. I yank my shirt and bra off, before hastily unbuttoning the fly of my jeans and roughly jerking them down my thighs, as he buries his nose in the cleft of my pussy. His tongue slides up my clit and my skin breaks out into goosebumps, a full body shiver jerking my body and I groan.

"You want me to taste your beautiful cunt?"

His eyes look up at me, as he takes another long lap with the flat of his tongue.

"God yes...please Dornan, eat me out," I whimper as all the heat pools where his mouth is.

His big hands brace my hips as he brings me to the bed, forcing me onto all fours. Since my jeans are barely pushed down over my ass, the material forces my legs to stay together. He begins to devour my pussy from behind, lapping and feasting on my drenched opening and plump lips. Using three fingers he rubs my clit hard and fast and I'm coming, my body clenching around his tongue inside me.

That orgasm propels my need for him even more, and I can barely contain my smile as he pulls my jeans off, flipping me onto my back. I'm biting my lip, watching as he removes his clothes, my eyes zeroing on his thick hard erection. He runs a hand up and down his shaft, while crawling on the bed to straddle my face. His hand guides his cock down and I lean up to take him in my mouth. The thick head pushes past my lips, over my tongue and into my throat. Even though he's on top of me and he's in my mouth, Dornan's holding back. I guess with all that's going on, causes him to think I need him to be gentle. But I want him to lose control, to fuck my mouth and not be so hesitant. He remains still with his entire cock lodged in my mouth, his eyes closed and chest heaving. Even though I can't breathe, I want this, I swallow around him and he groans.

"Oh fuck, take all of my dick, fucking love it."

As he pulls out slowly, inch by inch retreating, I gasp for air and grab him by the hips to repeat the motion. His abs contract, his arms shaking with restraint. My fingers curl around the tightness of both his ass cheeks and force him to fuck my mouth. He groans with every thrust of his hips as he curls his upper body over me, bracing himself with one hand on the mattress, the other gripping the back of my head as he controls my motions. This is what I want, for him to take me over completely. Suddenly, he stops and pulls back, my saliva dripping off his cock and onto my lips and chin. He drags his wet dick down the center of my chest, down my stomach, to rest on my clit. Spreading my legs to cradle his hips, I'm so wet I feel it on my thighs. Taking his cock into his hand and giving my clit a few slaps with the head, before he shoves inside me, causing a squelching noise as he impales me fully. I gasp and claw my fingers into the sheets, while he watches our bodies joining. White noise fills my ears, and colors dance behind my eyelids. Every pleasure point inside me being stroked and massaged, to an elevation of pleasure I've never experienced before.

My eyes are closed when he shoves his index and middle fingers into my mouth, and instantly I suck and wet them. Dornan's body blankets me as he lays completely over me now, his wet fingers sliding into my asshole, forcing my lower body up into his thrusts while he fingers my rear.

"Jesus," I gasp, my nails digging into his sides. He's touched me there before, preparing my body to one day take him, which I have a feeling will be soon.

He's suffocating me with his massive body but I don't care, it adds to the intensity building inside me. He scissors his fingers while his cock pistons into me and I'm screaming his name, losing my mind with an orgasm that's never ending.

When I emerge from the haze, I'm on my stomach and the head of his cock is pushing into my ass. He's either spit on me, or used my cum to lube my entrance. He's there and pushing in, and I whimper before he's rubbing my sensitive clit softly. His teeth sink into the skin between my neck and shoulder blade, before forcing through the tight ring of flesh with a hard thrust. My body tenses, and instinctively I pull away.

Dornan lets out a long groan into my ear. "Shhh, relax and feel me."

His fingers rubbing my clit helps me ignore the sharp pain, slowly allowing it to vanish and my body to soften. His cock feels so good there and I can't explain it really, but I know it's making me feel different than anything I've ever felt during sex before. This act so intimate and so beyond having sex. I truly feel like I've given him every part of me now, that we're cemented and permanently bound to one another. A wave of emotion crashes over me, when everything clicks and feels perfect and meant to be. But before I can be completely overwhelmed and overtaken by the feeling, he's moving, hard and fast into me. His fingers begin to quicken, and I'm coming again. This time more intense than ever before, and warm liquid drenches my thighs, pouring out of my pussy. I have no idea what's happening due to the supernova rocking my senses, but shit, it feels out of body.

"Shit, shit, fuck babe you're squirting…fuck, don't you dare stop, I want every last drop."

Dornan orders against my ear while rubbing the flat of his hand all over my wetness, he pulls out and pulls my ankle as I roll onto my back. My ass hitting the drenched sheet from my orgasm. His tongue licks my flavor off his hand while the other begins to jerk hard on his cock, moments before warm spurts of ejaculation land on my skin.

He chants, "I love you, I love you, I love you."

My body's trembling with aftershocks, the feel of him in my ass is still prominent and leaves me feeling decadent and sexy. Dornan's still breathing hard as he lays down on top if me, his semen slick between our hot skin as he kisses my face, and holds me like he's never going to let me go.

16

The apartments have never been updated from when they were built in the 60's, the wood paneled walls make the room seem dark. But when I wake and see a sliver of sunlight peeking through the yellowed sheers, I at least know it's morning. Possibly my last morning waking up to this man I'm currently wrapped around like a vine. My eyes sting as I look up at him sleeping, his face perfect. Even though small scars mar his skin in several places, he wouldn't be Dornan without them. I run my fingers over them, placing kisses there afterwards. I can't control my emotions, and have to bite my lip to hold them back. He'll get over me, he'll have to. I can live knowing I gave this man a life, one that he might not have unless I do this. My plan is to sneak out and go to my house, get Justice's phone number, and turn myself in. That plan being chucked out the window, when Dornan's eyes flutter open and he squints up at me, his arms tightening around my torso.

"What are you doing? he sighs, closing his eyes again.

"I was gonna go home to shower and change," I whisper.

He gives my butt a spank, before palming the entire cheek and squeezing.

"I'll come with you."

"Don't you have that run with Joey and Drag soon?"

He sighs again and opens his eyes, blinking a few times to clear the sleep away. Lifting his hand to run it over his short hair, before leaning up to meet our lips in a soft series of kisses.

"Shower with me before you head home."

I nod and sit up, my insides feel like they're having a tug of war, and I feel on the verge of vomiting. My head knows what it needs to do, but my heart is fighting like a panther with that bitch. It wants to tell Dornan to fuck the run and go with me somewhere, anywhere, ride our bikes into the sunset and leave all this shit. But I know we'd be leaving the shit for the club to deal with, and who knows what could happen then.

"You okay?" he asks.

"Yeah, of course," I smile.

But I know he senses that all this is weighing on my shoulders, there's only so much fucking we can do before reality comes knocking. Before I start to cry, I get up and head to the bathroom, turning on the water and testing the temperature. I'm already in the shower when Dornan joins me, his front to my back, while his big rough hands run over my slick skin with soap.

"I told you I would never make you promises," he says softly into my ear. "But you won't go to prison, I will do everything in my power to make sure that doesn't happen."

He runs his hand down my wet hair and I close my eyes. God, I love him for thinking this can be any other way. But he can't keep me safe from this, he can't control the uncontrollable. Someone has to give the Feds something, and since they came to me, I'll give them that.

We finish showering, and other than Dornan's proclamation, we remain quiet. I throw on my jeans from the day before and one of his t-shirts, which is long and smells of him. Taking a seat on the bed, I watch as he gets dressed for his trip, and drink in everything about this perfection before me.

"Call me when you get there." I tell him as we kiss and he wraps me in his arms so tight I can barely breathe, as we stand outside in the middle of the lot.

"I'll be back by morning, and we can talk about meeting with Justice, yeah?"

I nod, my eyes watching my fingers run over his necklace. Using a bent finger, he raises my chin to meet his eyes.

"Yeah?" he repeats, his brows raised.

"Yes," I sigh, squinting up at him as the morning sun shines on us.

He kisses me once more before he heads over to Joey and Drag, who are already sitting on their bikes waiting for him. Joey gives me a nod while Dornan starts his bike, and they pull down the driveway and out to the street.

"Maven!" Skye shouts at me from the entrance to the shop and I turn. "Accident on I-9, five car pile-up, I need you."

I'm about to ask what the E.T.A is, when the first of several tow trucks enters the lot. I guess heading home will be delayed a few hours. As I work on the accident claims and all the shit that goes with it, I show Skye step by step the process. I think she thinks I'm irritated that she needs me for this, or that she doesn't know how. But really I'm showing her so when I'm not here and probably in prison, the shop won't be affected. Even though there's a lot to it and I'm on full work mode, I can't help but think of Dornan's run. I forgot to ask him how he and Joey planned on finding out if Drag's the snitch. But knowing them like I do, I assume it will have to do with brut force.

Finally, things begin to slow. Skye and I are sitting in my office and I'm showing her how to fax an insurance company through the computer, when my cellphone rings, with a number I don't recognize.

"Hello," I answer putting the call on speaker.

"Ms. Maven Lofgren?" a woman asks.

"Yeah, this is she."

"Hello Ms. Lofgren, this is Officer Daniels-"

My first instinct is that Dornan's been in an accident, oh God, no. This thought overwhelms me so much, that I miss what the lady on the phone says.

"Ms. Lofgren?"

"Yes, I'm here."

Skye's looking at me with wide eyes, her mouth agape.

"Did you hear me?" Officer Daniels asks.

"No sorry."

"Your father's been killed."

The blood leaves my head, and dread fills my belly.

"Wait, my dad- what happened?"

Skye gets up and hurries from the office.

"He was attacked in the dining hall yesterday, expired this morning-"

"Why wasn't I called last night? He was alive and you didn't call me?" I ask in disbelief.

"Ma'am...per the guidelines of your father's incarceration, he does not have the same rights that patients would normally get."

"What about my privilege of being with my dad before he died, you stupid bitch!"

"Ma'am..." she begins, but I'm out of my mind.

Skye returns with Sven who grabs the phone and takes it off speaker, before placing it to his ear. Skye kneels down next to me, talking but I can't hear her. She's wiping my face repeatedly, am I crying? I can't *feel* anything. She tries to get my hands around a water bottle but they won't function, giving up, she grabs my jaw, spreading my lips while pouring the cold water into my mouth. My heart's pounding and I can't breathe; I can barely manage to swallow the water. I'm shaking and can hear myself trying to gasp for air, suddenly I'm pushed down from behind, my head goes between my legs and finally I can breathe.

"Fucking bitch," I hear Sven curse as he tosses my phone back onto the desk.

His big warm hand's on my back, he's the one who forced me into this position.

"Call Missy," he orders Skye.

Not like she can get here fast, because I know she's already left for a weekend trip out of town with Gwen. Sven crouches down beside me, as Skye leaves to make the call.

"Maven, Maven, breathe," he's telling me. "Maven, it'll be okay."

And I know he's talking about my dad, but I can't help but think he's comforting me for all the shit going on. I slump off the chair and into Sven's lap, his arms cradling me, rocking slowly as he sits back onto his butt and just holds me. I know we sit awhile, and I know I'm in shock. I'm blank and empty, no tears or thoughts. When my body kicks back into reality, we're still in my office but there are more people around. I hear Smokey and Chain, while Sven barks out orders.

"Maven, Spiney's going to take you home, and Missy will come get you. She's going to bring you to our house until Dornan can get back, we're still trying to get ahold of him, or Joey and Drag."

I don't respond but feel him stand, holding me until my feet are planted on the floor. He firmly holds my arms, waiting for me to get my bearings and not need him any longer. My head's foggy and I feel like I've been beaten up, or drugged, I can't focus. There's a vague sense of being guided to a car, and being buckled in. Then Spiney's driving and looking nervous and worried, looking over at me and back to the road several times.

"We're almost there," he repeats.

By the time we pull into the driveway, I'm able to get myself out of the car, but need him to help me up my porch steps. My legs feel like jelly, that at any moment they'll go out on me. Bagheera's at the door and going crazy, barking and pacing. He knows something's wrong, and also doesn't like that Spiney's here. Sure he recognizes him from the shop, but since I never have people here, he's on high alert.

"Go lie down and I'll take care of Bagheera," he says.

On autopilot I make my way to my bedroom, and all I want is Dornan. I want him to tell me my dad didn't suffer, that he loved me and forgave me for taking so long to mend our relationship. I need him to shoulder this pain, to hold me and kiss me, and assure me life will go on.

"Get yourself together, get to Missy's and Dornan will come," I tell myself out loud as a mantra, along with several deep breaths.

I pull off my pants and the long sleeved shirt I'd put on over Dornan's t-shirt, and I don't know why. Once the smell of him on the shirt hits me, I understand my logic, as it gives me a small sense of comfort. A noise downstairs makes me pause, it's Bagheera and he's...whining?

"Spiney, what's going on?" I shout.

No reply, yet Bagheera keeps whining and now it sounds further away.

"Spiney!" I say a little louder and move towards the top of the stair case.

I listen and it sounds like the whimpering's coming from the basement. What the fuck? Still out of it, I hold onto the railing tightly as I go down the steps on wobbly legs. There's no sign or sound of Spiney, what the fuck is happening? I pause right outside the basement door, and sure enough I hear Bagheera behind it. Reaching for the door handle, my arm's suddenly yanked away and pulled behind my back, a hand and cloth placed over my face. I try to fight, to pull my body away. But the harder I struggle, the sooner I realize I'm losing consciousness with every inhale. Some chemical must be on the cloth covering my nose and mouth… and all goes black.

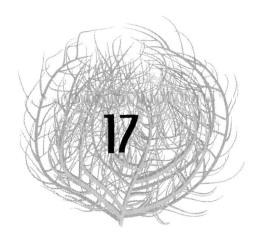

17

"Wake up honey."

I moan. Honey? Oh God, please no.

"Honey...come on, you need to wake up."

My eyes feel plastered shut, my head spinning. I'm moving but that can't be, because I know I'm not upright. I'm lying on something hard and hot, and wherever I am smells of a combination of fuel and sweat.

"I said wake up!" an angry voice growls and then my cheek stings, realizing I've been slapped. I now recognize the voice *is* Brayden's. Slowly my eyes open to see a foggy version of him, right in front of my face. He slowly comes into focus, my eyes dry and burning, as he kneels down in front of me. I can make out Spiney standing beside him, and another guy I recognize as one of Brayden's brothers, but don't remember his name. We're in some sort of trailer or back of a small cargo truck. The drugs I inhaled to knock me out have left me even more fucked up than before, and the urge to vomit is creeping up my throat.

"There she is," Brayden smiles sinisterly, showing me an unearthly demon in his expression.

My head hurts from trauma, my wrists burning, and the zip ties holding them behind my back are digging into my skin. I'm only wearing Dornan's t-shirt and a pair of panties, which I've sweat through and stick to my damp skin. The air inside the trailer is stifling, which adds to my nausea. I hear a whimper and look towards the front of the trailer, Bagheera's lying on the floor, a rope tied to his neck that's attached to a lever above him. If it wasn't for him making noises I'd think he was dead, my heart aches seeing him lying there in obvious distress. I wonder if this is it for us, there's no way I'm in any shape physically to get us out, and the sorrow that my dog will be hurt or killed, fills me with anguish.

"I guess I should tell you what this is all about," Brayden says reaching behind me, grabbing the back of my hair and yanking my head towards him.

"Since your club decided that they're pussies and have your back over club business, we decided our club needed to take out yours. In order to dismantle the Warrior of the Gods, we recruited your prospect here."

He tips his head back towards Spiney. It's then I realize how Spiney knew where I lived without asking me. Granted Sven could've told him, but now I think that's not the case.

"Me and some brothers went to break into your place, we were gonna put this plan into motion then...but your fucking loser boyfriend was there and your neighbor was watching us. So we decided just to get a lay of your house... no security system," he tsks. "Stupid for you of all people."

Brayden smiles like the devil he is, I then feel something warm on my forehead and under my nose, and know it's blood.

"Burning down the strip clubs, that was just the beginning of this. Your death and the death of your Pres and his only heir to the club is the end. Resulting in the club's dismantle, and the beginning of The Children of the Reaper becoming the largest MC known to man."

I'm not scared for some reason, I've never feared that my death would come from being a part of this club, due to the things I've done. I've killed people, hurt them, lied, stolen...I deserve whatever is about to happen to me. But knowing they plan to kill Sven and Dornan, the impact that will have on not only the club, but Missy, it will ruin her.

Brayden's just looking at me, trying to see if his words have caused a reaction. Of course my outward appearance doesn't allow one, but inside, I'm shattering. It's then I notice, I hear no traffic, no other cars around us and I wonder if we're out in the desert. There are stretches of road out here, that sometimes you don't see another vehicle for miles. Brayden slaps me again with his free hand, while pulling my hair harder with the other.

"Do you understand?" he asks through clenched teeth. "We're taking you to the desert, gonna call your man and get him and his old ass dad out here. By the time they get to you, you'll be dead- not even in a grave, just right on the fucking ground. You won't even get a shallow hole like your bitch mom."

My eyes meet his and I can't help but show him the spark of shock there.

"Oh yeah, didn't know I knew that, huh?" His brows raise.

"Judas was there when she was killed, said she cried like a fucking baby when they had a knife to her throat. Pleading that she was a mom and you needed her, pissed herself too. You think you'll do that?"

I let out a long shaky breath, clenching my jaw, and stare into the eyes of a man I once thought I loved.

"You think you're so fucking hard, but I know you, better than you think I do."

He doesn't, he doesn't fucking know me. He knew the me before I found the love of Dornan, the man who truly, with every cell of his being loves me. He knew me as the shell of a person I'd become because of him, with Brayden I was someone else. Weak inside, thinking I deserved the little slice of anything this married man had for me. I allowed him to treat me like I was nothing, like I didn't matter, or even have feelings. But thanks to him I can appreciate the man I love now, the man who's always loved me and never stopped, even when my time was wasted with this piece of shit before me.

When I don't say a word, I can see the anger build in him, and the moment his patience and self-control snaps. His fist makes contact with my jaw, before slamming the back of my head into the steel trailer wall. He keeps hitting me until he's knocked me onto my back, I can taste the metallic flavor of blood before he puts his hands around my throat, squeezing. My legs are kicking at nothing as I try to loosen his hold somehow, his hands only grow tighter as his eyes darken. He constricts harder and harder and I hear the bones in my neck cracking, my eyes flutter and fill with white light. It's almost a sense of euphoria, that this is death. But that feeling of tranquility only lasts a moment before he's smacking my face, bringing me back from the brink.

"I'm not done with you yet."

My eyes open as I groggily try to focus once more, then his hands are there again, strangling me. His eyes are filled with hate and rage, sweat rolling down the tip of his nose as he shakes with the strength he's exerting. Part of me hopes he will snap my neck, instead of slowly suffocating me. He does this several times, making me black out from lack of oxygen, before reviving me and repeating. I'm praying or at least pleading to some higher power to not let me wake up next time, for him to break my neck or just give up. I can't even fight him, my body's limp, but I feel tears and blood pouring down my face. I know Brayden's enjoying this, seeing me like this. He even laughs when I wake up, happy he can continue his torture. There's a part of me, the part that can still think, that pictures Dornan finding my body in the desert and I hope for his sanity he doesn't. I hope they never find me, so he won't have to live his life with that memory. I want to scream for Brayden to just kill me, but I have no voice. Suddenly, I hear pops and the trailer begins to bounce on flat tires, the driver yelling back to us.

"Fuck! We're hit!"

18

DORNAN

Joey, Drag, and I were heading back to the club when I got the call from Chilly. I usually don't answer my cellphone when I'm riding, but something caused me to pull over and answer it. I knew once we got started on the run, that Drag wasn't the snitch. Something didn't seem right to me about it being him to begin with, but it still didn't stop me and Joey from taking him out to the desert and confronting him.

When Chilly told me that he was following a truck on the freeway, that Brayden, Spiney, and Max had taken Maven from her house and thrown her lifeless body into a trailer truck, my heart stopped. When he told me he didn't think she was dead, it allowed some solace. I have something to hold onto, something to get me to her faster knowing she's alive.

Chilly said he assumed they were using her to get to me, and my blood boiled. The thought that whatever they had done to render her unconscious, reaffirmed that by the end of the day, Brayden would be dead.

I asked Chilly how he even knew she was taken, to have witnessed what was going on. He said she'd called him a few weeks ago, telling him she thought The Children of the Reaper were trying to collect personal information of our members. He said it didn't sit well with him since Maven rarely ever called him personally. That he heard in her voice that there was something she wasn't saying, like they were trying to get information on her, and not the club. So he decided to keep an eye on her ever since, installing cameras on the light post outside her house and on the garage. Why she didn't tell me she thought she was in danger, I don't know, and I don't have time to think about it.

I see the texts from my dad that Maven's dad is dead, that she needs me to come back. I can't imagine how broke down she was at the news, knowing Spiney took her home, and how Brayden's plan unfolded. Spiney probably called Brayden and told him he was bringing Maven home, that I was gone, that they could get her. My sweet girl who was most likely in shock over her dad, hurting, her defenses down. That's the only way Brayden's ever been able to roll up on her, because when she's at her best, no one can fuck with her. The three of us are speeding through the desert, on the same freeway as Maven. They're thirty miles ahead of us, but we're closing the distance. We will get to her. We will get to her before anything more can happen to her.

The adrenaline pumping in my veins is like I've never felt before, not ever. Not even when being shot at, or seeing Brayden trying to rape Maven. I'm on a whole other level that's only growing in intensity as the miles go by, and I know we're getting closer. I can see the dust ahead from the truck tires, and it slowly begins to come into focus.

The sun's beginning to set, and I feel like its rays are scorching through my cut. The heat reaching unbearable, and I can only imagine how hot it is in the fucking trailer. I've come up with a way to stop the truck, I just hope it doesn't kill her. The three of us catch up to Chilly who's been following the truck from a safe distance, the four of us becoming a horizontal line and I feel for my gun underneath my leather jacket. The truck begins to speed up and the dust being kicked up from the tires is almost blinding, as I press the throttle and speed past the truck. As I pass by, the driver fires at me from the open window, the bullets tinging off the metal of my bike. Still, I speed ahead and continue on, getting about a half a mile ahead of the truck, before I stop at the side of the road and position myself for the truck to pass. The driver is still attempting to shoot at me, as I raise my nine mil and focus. My heart beats in my ears as I squeeze the trigger in rapid fire, hitting the left front and back tires, instantly they hiss and pop.

The driver starts to lose control as he veers off the road and towards a grouping of rocks, the speed not slowing. The vehicle kicks up even more dust, before the entire thing rolls twice before landing on its side. The engine's smoking and I hear coughing as I take off running towards it. The dust blankets everything but as I get closer, I can make out the back of the trailer and the door is pushed up half way open. I'm running and hear the boots of my brothers behind me, but there's smoke and dirt thick in the air and I can barely see. I look inside the trailer to see Max lying lifeless, but I shoot him anyway, the shot loud in the cavernous space. I hear another shot from outside and as I move to the driver's side of the truck, Joey's pulling back with his gun from the window. I don't see the others, where the fuck is Maven? Maybe Chilly's wrong, and maybe this isn't the right truck.

"D!" Drag yells and I move around to the other side of the vehicle,

Spiney's standing there with his face bleeding as one of his arms hangs lifeless at his side. Then my heart stops. Brayden is holding Maven up on her knees by the back of her hair, her wrists tied behind her back, with a gun to her temple.

She's dirty and bloody, but her eyes are open and she's looking at me. God, she looks strong and aware, even though the whites of her eyes are blood red, and it enrages me that she's only in my t-shirt. When our eyes meet, I'm stopped from my frantic pace and I just…look at her. I want nothing more than to take her into my arms, to clean her wounds and kiss her, to protect her. Then the asshole starts to speak and I look up to see his nose is broken, blood's pouring down his face. They both look fucked up from the crash and Maven even more so, like she's been hurt prior to the crash, dark blood on her forehead and nose. Her neck is covered in red marks, from rope or… hands.

"Don't come any closer asshole," Brayden says.

We outnumber him, but he knows no one will fuck around with a gun at Maven's head.

"What do you want?" Joey asks.

"I want this bitch dead, and that fucker too," he says, lifting his chin towards me.

"Problem is, there are more of us," Joey says.

"I got people out there, they're coming, and you won't follow us. You won't come until I call. But how about you two join Children of the Reaper, your shit club is about to be taken over, probably best to convert while you still can. Come on, you two have put in enough work, kill these two with me and you have my word I'll make you V.P.'s."

I grind my teeth and return my eyes to Maven's. She looks calm, albeit in pain, but she's not panicking. How does she do that? I know I look a fucking mess, because I *feel* a fucking mess. She's staring at me like she won't ever see me again, well that won't fuckin' happen. The longer we share the connection, her eyes slowly start to water and she's pleading to me with them. She's not worried for herself, but for me. Well *fuck that*.

"How about fuck yourself," Drag replies to the offer.

"Stupid," Brayden laughs.

The dust's still everywhere and I know I can't get a clear shot, but I have to do something. I'm sure as shit not going to let this asshole take her from me. As I begin to take off running towards Brayden, knowing he will shoot me and not her, then Joey can fire at Brayden. From out of nowhere, Bagheera comes running from behind the truck and bites Brayden on the upper arm, causing him to drop the gun and fall onto his back. Joey runs to Maven as I move towards Brayden and begin to hit his screaming face with the butt of my gun, before I drop my gun and begin hitting with my fists. Bagheera's biting and yanking and growling, and I feel as much of an animal as he is. I feel no pain in my hands, nothing but ruthless, savage, revenge.

I keep hitting him until he's lifeless, a bloody smashed mess. Bagheera has his teeth clamped on Brayden's neck, then suddenly he releases, limping over to Maven. I stand and follow, Joey's freed her hands and she's sitting on the ground. She looks so small in my shirt, while Bagheera licks her face and cleans her. I fall to my knees and instantly our arms wrap around one another, tears sting my eyes as I bury my face into her hair and inhale. Behind us, Joey and Drag have their guns pointing at a kneeling Spiney, one hand in the air in surrender. I close my eyes and savor the embrace of Maven, hearing her breathe and her heart beat. Shots ring out and echo, then a thud hits the ground as Spiney falls, followed by a vehicle coming to a quick stop bedside us, kicking up even more dust into the air.

"Dornan, we have to go!" Milton yells and I turn to see him in a black SUV, getting out of the driver's side, as he takes in the scene before him. He doesn't say anything, just takes in the carnage.

"Does she need a doctor?" he finally asks looking down at Maven, I pull back and run my battered hands down her hair, taking in her bloody and bruised face.

That fucker deserved more than what he got for doing this to her. One of her eyes is beginning to swell but she looks up at me and shakes her head, wincing before grabbing the back of her neck.

"No," I tell Milton.

"Then we have to go."

Joey, Drag, Chilly, and Maven are all looking at him with confusion, not getting why a cop is trying to get us away from a murder scene.

"Do you have everything?" I ask Milton.

"Yeah, it's all in the truck, we gotta go. Justice sent out a call on the radio that Maven was trying to run, I'm only ten minutes ahead of them."

I stand Maven up and Milton takes her hand, leading her towards the SUV. Bagheera following closely behind them, as I walk to my brothers.

"Follow us," I tell them and they all nod.

"Joey, get my plates-"

"Got it bro," he says as he opens his knife blade and heads towards my bike.

Maven's in the backseat, slumped against the window. I sit beside her and pull her into my arms and onto my lap, as Bagheera jumps over the backseat to occupy the space beside us. He's covered in blood and I raise my hand to pet his head, while Maven tucks her face into my neck. We take off, and I look back to see our brothers following.

I know that I can't save her from the world, I almost didn't save her today. But this is one thing I can do, and we will run for as long as we need to to keep her safe. We drive for hours, and it's past midnight by the time we stop. Maven's been in and out of sleep, but she assures me she's fine, even if she can barely get the words out. Her voice is gravelly and weak, and I have a feeling that the red marks around her throat have something to do with that. Milton checks us into a motel in the middle of nowhere, and I leave Maven in the car as I walk over to Joey.

"We gotta stay here for the night, head over to the Devil's Backbone clubhouse, they know you're coming."

"What about you brother?" he asks.

The three men look exhausted from sitting on their bikes this entire time without stopping, but they're our brothers and we would follow each other into hell for eternity if one asked.

"Maven and I will leave in a few hours. I can't tell you where we're going, but I'll contact you when we're settled."

"What about him?" Drag asks. "What got up his ass to help?" Looking beyond me at Milton walking back to us from the motel office.

"Family history."

I carry Maven into our ground floor room and set her on the bed, Bagheera following. I take a set of keys and two duffel bags from Milton, shaking hands as he also gives me a manila envelope. I don't really know what to say since just thank you seems useless. I don't really care if he only did this because he felt he had to, he still did it, and I'll never be able to thank him enough.

"Take care," he offers before getting into his SUV and pulling back onto the freeway.

I grab the ice bucket and fill it with water in the bathroom sink, setting it on the floor for Bagheera, who begins to lap at it until it's gone and I refill it. Then I turn on the water in the tub, pulling the cheap plastic shower curtain out of the way. Maven's laying on the bed, not moving from the position I'd set her down in. After removing her clothes, I place her in the tub, her head falling back against the rim as I rub the bar of soap over her skin, removing the dried blood that's caked on. The gash on her forehead and a cut under her eye are the worst, I think they might need stitches.

The water's almost black when I'm done cleaning her, and I wrap her in a towel. Grabbing a shirt from her bag and slipping it over her head. Then laying her down under the covers after brushing her hair.

I clean Bagheera off the best I can, checking his body for any injuries. Other than some chunks of fur missing from around his neck, he seems fine. He settles on the floor in front of the motel door before resting his head, then it's my time to shower. I feel I've lived a thousand lives today, having to really think back on how the day started, with Maven in my bed. My hands hurt like a son-of-a-bitch, and I open and close my fingers several times under the hot water to sooth the ache.

Most of the night is spent sitting up watching her sleep, making sure no one pulls into the motel that isn't checking in or staying. The sky's just turned to blue in the beginning of the sun rising, when Maven finally wakes. Her eye's swollen more, but the cuts on her face have finally stopped bleeding. When she looks up at me, I know that I'd follow her to the ends of the earth and never regret anything, just so she can wake up next to me. She sits up and presses her palm against the wound on her forehead and winces, I lean forward and kiss her cheek, moving her hand to my shoulder before cupping my face. We stare into each other's eyes, exchanging all we can't verbalize.

"I want to shower," she says with a hoarse voice before getting up slowly from the bed.

"Do you need help?" I ask as she stands to get her bearings, shaking her head stiffly, knowing he must've done a number to her neck.

The rage simmers in me even though there's some relief in knowing that asshole's dead, and that I'm the one who did it. I doze off while Maven's showering, then wake to her sitting on the bed. She must've used something to seal the large gashes on her face.

"I went to the office and got some super glue," she says, answering my thought. "And I made sure no one was around when I left the room, took your gun too."

I sigh and sit up, looking her over, taking in all her cuts and bruises. The skin around her eyes are peppered with the redness of blood vessels being broken, the whites of her eyes clouded with blood. My fists tighten in wanting to know, and not wanting to know what the fuck he did to her.

"I'm fine, we're alive Dornan," she says running her nose along mine.

All I want to do is touch her and feel that she's really with me, that she's alive and so am I.

"When did you pack bags for us?" she asks in confusion.

"Last night, after we made love. I waited until you were asleep and went back to the house."

She nods slightly, before asking,

"What do we do now?"

I kiss her lips gently, trying not to disturb a small split on the plump part of her lower lip.

"So when you told me about Justice and that you were going to turn yourself in, I asked Milton to return the favor that your dad did for his family."

I can see a flicker of pain in her eyes at the mention of her dad, but she doesn't move her eyes from mine.

"He got us new identities, dug into the database and gave me two names and social security numbers of a male and female who died in the 1950's. Then proceeded to make licenses, birth certificates, and all the documentation we need to...not be us."

As I'm talking, her mouth slowly opens as her eyes widen.

"I told you I was going to do everything in my power to not let you go to prison Maven."

She swallows and looks down at my lips, before nodding and looking back up at me.

"But, you-you don't have to do this with me-"

"I will go anywhere, be anyone, so long as I'm with you...nothing else matters."

A single tear falls from each of her honey colored eyes, before I swipe them away with my thumbs. She nods again, sniffling and blinking back the other tears threatening to fall.

"Where are we going?"

Epilogue, Six Years Later

MAVEN

We've been in Alaska for five and a half years, the first six months on the run, we did just that, run. We weren't sure where to go, Dornan had planned everything about us getting away, and even a car was at the motel we stayed at that first night waiting for us in the lot. Yet we didn't know where to hide, nowhere felt safe, and every time we contacted Chilly he said my name was still hot on Justice's list. We went to Dornan's sister Kendall's ranch in Montana from there, but then the fear they'd find us there was so overwhelming that we left after three days. Finally, we ended up in Alaska, where it seemed like most people go to run from something. Where the people there don't ask many questions, and accept that you're not from around there.

It took a while to get used to the weather, freezing cold, daylight for months or nighttime for months, all took its toll. Besides all that, we had new identities, not only new names but not being able to tell our coworkers or neighbors anything personal about us, caused us to seclude ourselves. Every time we heard or saw a motorcycle we'd both watch. I knew Dornan was longing for that freedom as I was, but it was something we couldn't chance with buying bikes.

The first year was the hardest, I felt like my old life and everything I knew besides Dornan was dead. Sure we talked with Chilly, but even then, Dornan didn't contact him until we'd been settled for seven months. The absence of being able to contact anyone ourselves, or to maintain the relationships we had, felt final.

I grasped at any information about our friends and family that I could, even if the conversations with Chilly were limited. Sven had a stroke two months after we'd left, but with rehab and therapy he recovered. The stress at not being able to see him was one thing, but it felt terrible that Dornan wasn't there for his family. I felt guilty that I not only lived this 'life,' but that Dornan had chosen to go along with me. Why anyone would decide to leave everything for one person, mystified me. Yes, he loved me, but to give up everything for a life of uncertainty never made sense to me.

Depression set in and I stayed in bed a lot those first few months, watching the sun rise and set, not eating or sleeping. Just lying there, day in and day out. I couldn't even listen to music anymore. What once brought me solace and memories, did nothing but cause pain. Dornan picked up odd jobs and kept himself busy, while I could barely manage to shower daily. I knew my state ate away at him, plaguing him with the idea that maybe leaving was the worst thing he could do for me. I wanted to reassure him, that yes, he did the right thing but that selfish bitch side of me couldn't talk to him about it. Until one night when Dornan got sick of my pity party.

"You've been in here all day again? he asked, walking into our bedroom.

He was fresh from the shower after being gone all day, helping a coworker on their home renovation. I remained on my side of the bed, looking out the window at the sunset. He let out a long sigh, the drawer to our dresser opened and closed and then I heard him messing with something on the bedside table. When the music from my iPod started just as he yanked the blankets off me, I rolled onto my back about to yell at him, when he gave me a look I knew meant to keep my mouth shut.

"You have to stop this Maven," he said looking down at me, naked and still slightly damp and God if his body wasn't better than it had ever been. He'd been working out more since we didn't have much else to do, his muscles hard and shadowed in the light provided by the side table lamp. I opened my mouth to speak but he stopped me.

"Shut up."

My mouth closed instantly.

"I know this shit's been hard, but you're not even trying to make it better. We can't change that we're here, we can't go back. So today is the last day you do this shit. Hit me, yell at me, fuck me- whatever you have to do to end this."

I felt my eyes burn and I looked down at the bed, his rough hands wrapping around my ankles as he pulled me towards him, positioning me at the side of the bed with my legs spread around him. Running his hands through my hair as I sat up, he kissed the top of my head and I closed my eyes. He gently stroked me several times before pulling a handful of my hair, forcing my head up to look at him.

"You done with this shit?" he asked.

I grit my teeth but don't answer.

"Are you?" he asked again, his voice rising.

251

"No!" I yelled and my voice cracked. I kept repeating, my throat tight with anger and sadness. "No, fucking no, I don't want to live like this, but I don't want to face reality."

Dornan stops my screaming by punishing my lips with a kiss, his hand gripping my chin as he sucked hard on my mouth and tongue, and I bite his lower lip every time he sucked my upper lip. I'm crying and whimpering, but it was because I needed this, I needed *him*. With his free hand he grabbed my hands, bringing them to his raging erection, wrapping my fingers around it to feel how hard he was and I grew wet and achy with the thought of it in my mouth and pussy.

"Are you gonna stop this?" he growled against my lips.

I shook my head, just because fighting with him felt good, I wanted him to be rough with me and be Dornan with me. He released my face and pried my hands off him, pushing me back by the shoulders. I bounced on the mattress before settling on my back.

"Fuck you!" I yelled. It felt good to scream and I felt like I was yelling at the gray cloud that had taken over my life.

Dornan smirked as he wrapped his fingers around the base of his dick, his other hand rubbed over the head. He was hot and swollen and fuck he was touching himself, and I wanted that to be my hands. I was so wet now, my juices slicked my inner thighs, as I bent my knees and pressed my legs together. He stopped stroking his cock to pry my legs apart, to yank down my pajama pants, revealing my wet pink panties. Dornan slid his thumb down my clit hard one time, before he returned back to jerking himself off.

"Stop!" I try to yell, but it came out as a moan.

"You said 'fuck you'...that's what I'm doing. I'm not fucking you 'til you stop being fucking ridiculous!"

"Shut up, just shut the fuck up!"

"No, you shut the fuck up-" he growled back.

I sat up and began to beat my fists on his chest, trying to push him away. He takes every punch, and of course barely budged as I released my anger out on him.

"Give me everything you got babe...I love you, I'll take anything you give me."

And with that, my anger goes and I began to cry. Slumping against his chest as the tears came, he wrapped his arms around my shoulders and kept telling me he loved me. I raised my head and began kissing him, this time not so rough. He kissed my lips, then my cheeks, my closed eyes as he removed my shirt. Laying me back onto the bed and slipping my panties off, before crawling over me. I wrapped my arms and legs around him like a vine, holding on so tightly it was a wonder he could even move, but he pivoted his hips and slid his big beautiful cock inside me. I let out a shaky breath and pressed my face into his neck, he moved slowly inside me and whispered into my ear.

"You're so fucking sad, it's gutting me. I can't see you like this anymore, I want you to listen to music and run everyday...I want you to smile again."

I rested my head on the bed and looked up at him, his eyes were wet and the emotion in his voice was like I'd never heard from him before.

"Everyday I feel so guilty that you're here, that you did this with me-" I hiccupped.

"I don't ever regret the decision I made for us, because I get to wake up next you, to fall asleep inside you, fold laundry with you, have dinner with you, share space with you. That's all I've ever wanted, ever since I was a kid, was to just be with you. So don't *ever* think this isn't the life

I wanted."

I bite my lip before I leaned up and kissed him, my tears fell as the intensity built inside from his hips moving faster. He linked our fingers and brought our joined hands above my head, telling me he loved me as we both come. He rolled us so I was on his chest as the song, "Wild Horses" by the Rolling Stones came on. Dornan let me cry into his chest as he played the song over and over again and I finally talked to him.

After that I felt lighter, freer, like the dark cloud that had been hanging over me is gone. Eventually, we move out of our apartment and get a house, after Dornan gets a steady job working construction and I start work as a secretary at an elementary/ middle school. I wanted to use my degree in accounting, but since I wasn't Maven anymore and had no degree, I settled. The house is nothing like mine in Plantain but it's nice, and it's something we can call our own. I often think about my house, after putting so much hard work into it. Chilly told me that it's being taken care of by Joey and Missy, which offers some comfort that it wasn't sold.

Seven months after moving we got a shock, we were pregnant and both of us we're happier than we had been in a long time. Needless to say I went through a roller coaster of emotions, we'd isolated ourselves, afraid to make close friends. So we spend all of our non-working hours together, which causes us to fight...well, me to fight with him. I yelled at him for leaving his dirty clothes out, for stealing too much of the covers, I even accused him of checking out other women when we were at the grocery store. All of which sent me into tears and apologies, but one thing I always cried about was the fact that we weren't married. I don't know why it bothered me so much, it's not like we by any means lived by the rules of society. Something about not being able to legally marry the man I love, that we would be marrying as two strangers who weren't named Dornan and Maven, hurt me even more.

Dornan however would always reply, "You belong to me and I belong to you, we're married in every meaning of the idea. We don't need a judge or witnesses to tell us you're my wife."

Which of course made me cry harder. But in true Dornan fashion, he bought me a silver band to accompany the ruby ring I already wear that he'd given me back in Plantain. He proceeded to get us naked and in bed before slipping the ring onto my finger and vowing his undying love. But he didn't need to, he killed someone for me and got us here, that's more than love. Even with the love of this man, I still can't help but be sad going through pregnancy alone. With no mom, no Missy or Gwen, no baby shower or advice.

At two a.m. on a rainy morning, my water broke. I sat in the front room, rocking in a chair by the window. Timing my contractions before waking Dornan, who needless to say, was in a panic. He rushed around the house making sure we had everything, as I stood calmly by the front door with my overnight bag in hand. My labor and delivery was stressful watching Dornan losing his mind seeing me in pain. On top of not having anyone we knew to lean on, in addition to experiencing the actual pain, was overwhelming. "You're doing so good," he kept telling me.

I'd been in labor for thirty-six hours, and was beyond exhausted. The fear was secondary to the need to get the baby out. To see Dornan barely able to look at me due to the pain I was in, to be so connected to me that it was almost as if he felt everything I was going through. He held one of my legs as he kissed my temple and told me, "You're so strong, you can do this, it's almost over."

I bared down and pushed until I couldn't hold my breath anymore, continuing to push with everything I had. Feeling my lungs burn, and telling myself to hold it just a little longer. Then my body relaxed, and I heard the doctor announce:

"It's a boy!"

I let out a long breath and rested my head back.

"A boy, you did so good babe, so fucking good."

Dornan continued to kiss me, and by the warble of his voice I knew he was crying. Having him with me my entire labor made our relationship even stronger, but not having visitors to see our newborn made my heart hurt. Not being able to even send photos to our friends and family, to not share all the things you go through as new parents with anyone, sent me into tears daily.

Legally their last names were fake to match Dornan's, but we named them Nolan Sven Fredericksen, who was born in August. While Wyatt Owen Fredericksen was born thirteen months later in September. Even without family, both boys helped me even more from breaking through the depression, and reaffirmed that Dornan and I had done the right thing by running.

Now they're two and three. We never talk to the boys about family, and they are young enough not to know about grandparents and aunts and uncles. But soon they will be in school, and I don't know what to do if they ask me about those types of things. We don't want to tell them that they don't have any, the thought of one day being able to go back home is the reasoning behind that.

But not a day goes by that I don't think about my parents, having kids of my own put in perspective everything about my life until this point. The thought that my mom pleaded for her life because of me, how

I would do the same now as a mom. How I resented my dad for getting me involved in the club, but because of his actions he led me to Dornan. Not saying that he and I wouldn't have eventually ended up together, but still. The regret that I had about the way I felt about my dad while he was in jail eats me up, but I only hope that in his last moments he knew I really did love him, more than anything. It isn't that I hated him, I hated what he'd done and that he'd put the club before himself and lost years with me in return. But now, Dornan and I have done the same, sacrificed relationships for the safety of others.

It's Saturday morning and it's my thirtieth birthday, I can hear Dornan and the boys downstairs in the kitchen. He's a great dad, but still learning to not get irritated with the little things.

"Wyatt, stop putting your hand in there," he says. "Nolan, give that back to your brother!"

I smile to myself picturing the scene, imagining Dornan collecting himself as both boys begin to scream at each other. Quietly, I sneak into the master bedroom's en-suite bathroom and jump in the shower, taking solace in the calm before the toddlers. I barely get a towel around me when Nolan comes bursting in the bathroom, his mouth rimmed with some brown substance.

"Mommy!" he smiles as I bend to kiss his head.

"I said leave Mommy alone, she will be out in a minute."

Dornan appears in the doorway carrying Wyatt, followed by Bagheera.

"Sorry," he says while trying to get Nolan out of the bathroom.

"It's okay, I'm done anyway."

Dornan stops and looks at my body from toes to the top of my head and everything in between, his eyes smoldering. He growls deep in his throat as he leans over to kiss me, Nolan runs out of there as Wyatt squirms and Dornan lets him down before he takes off too. Now with free hands, Dornan cups my ass and pushes our pelvises together, I bite his lower lip and groan as I feel his erection pushing through the denim of his jeans. With having no friends, we rarely ever go out and don't have anyone we trust to watch the kids, so we have to take advantage of alone time.

"I'm going to make you come thirty times tonight," he says against my lips.

I roll my eyes, not that I don't think he can, but more due to the fact that a night never went by without one or both of the kids coming into our room for something, doesn't allow much time for that. A loud pop jerks us apart as Wyatt starts crying. We enter the bedroom and I see balloons and chocolate chip pancakes sitting on the bed, Nolan holding a deflated balloon.

"I sorry Daddy."

Dornan scoops him up, "It's okay buddy."

"Did you eat the chocolate chips?" I ask Wyatt as I pick him up and tickle his stomach, causing him to giggle.

"Happy birthday babe," Dornan says.

"Happy Birthday Momma!" Both the boys shout.

"Open your prizes," Wyatt says pointing to a gift that the boys obviously helped wrap.

"Presents," Dornan corrects as I reach over and grab it, setting Wyatt onto the bed. I tear open the wrapping to see two small hand prints set in plaster with the boy's names carved underneath.

"Aw...oh my God, I love it!" My eyes water as I kiss both the boys then my husband.

Later in the afternoon I go out for a run, and on my way home I receive a text from Dornan asking how much longer I'm going to be, figuring the boys' are driving him up the wall. I don't respond since I'm only two blocks from home, but my trot slows to a stop when I see a black SUV sitting in the driveway and my heart begins to pound. Fuck, we've been found out. I enter the house expecting to see Justice there with cuffs to arrest me and Dornan in front of our kids. But when I enter through the back door, both boys are sitting at the kitchen table coloring, and Bagheera lying down between the two chairs. Due to his lack of alert makes me wonder even more who's at my house. I kiss the top of the boys' heads and ask, "Where's Daddy?"

"In there," Nolan answers not looking at me but pointing down the hallway.

I head for the front room, my pulse pounds, and my hands shake as I take a long breath and walk to the entryway. Dornan's sitting with his legs spread wide, his elbows rest on his knees, running a hand along his mouth. He sees me and sits up, I walk further into the room and see, Milton. He looks older now but still very much like a cop.

"Hi Maven," he says and I look between the two men.

"What's going on?" I ask as Dornan reaches out a hand for me to come to him.

"He has something to tell you," Dornan says.

I sit down beside him and grasp his hand with both of mine, I can't tell by his expression if this is good or bad. But since seeing me, his posture's become more relaxed.

"I don't know how to say this without just saying it...your dad isn't dead."

My throat tightens, my pulse jumping.

"What do you mean?" I can barely get out.

"He made a deal with the Feds to snitch on Judas. He had years of intel from their dealings together and what no one knew was Judas was present at your mom's murder. Not even Sven knew and how your dad knew-we have no idea, Judas didn't even know your dad was aware. But ever since he did find out, your dad decided to get close to Judas and document all the deals and the inner workings of The Children of the Reaper. Justice didn't think the government should settle for just one President, he thought he could get all the club Presidents. That's why he went after you, but when you ran, the Feds knew they couldn't blow an informant like your dad, someone they knew for certain would get them a President. Your dad decided it was time to divulge this information when Justice told him they were coming for you, he became a rat to save you. In return for his information he made a deal that he would remain in witness protection and that no one could go after you or the Warrior of the Gods when they finally brought Judas to trial...and that day has come."

I hear the words, but I can't believe them. This must've been what Dad meant when he told me all those years ago, that someone was going to try and talk to me but to not talk. That he had a deal he was working on.

"So what does all this mean for us?" Dornan asks.

"It means...you can go back home, you can go home as Maven and Dornan."

A giggle sob burst from my lips as I cover my mouth with my hands, my eyes become watery with tears. Looking over at Dornan, he too has a huge grin on his face, tears in his eyes. I throw myself towards him and our arms wrap tight around one another. We're going home, home! Back to a life I thought I hated but now want nothing more than to be a part of.

This brings us to current day. I'm sitting in Wyatt's room, at his small desk writing a letter to my dad. We've been home for months now and I finally came to terms with what my dad sacrificed for us, knowing he took away probably any chance to ever see us again. The trial against Judas has started, and my father's deposition and testimony was apparently doing what my father had intended, and it looks like Judas will be going to prison for a long time. I went to court the days my father was testifying, although no one was allowed in the courtroom other than lawyers, the judge, and the jury. Still I hoped to get a peek of him to and from the courthouse, unfortunately that didn't happen since when the van arrived transporting him, went straight down to the underground entrance. Knowing he was there though, alive, and maybe he could see me in the small crowd grouped in with the media, gave me the gratification of being there.

I've been thinking about what to write him for a while now, ever since I heard of what he'd done. How do you tell the man who raised you how much you love him in words? How much you appreciate what he did so you can have a family that he might never know?

But today is a monumental day for me. I'm about to become Mrs. Maven Frederickson officially this afternoon in our backyard. Something's shifting in me today, not as if I don't feel the connection to Dornan and our children already, but it's going through the transition of being someone's wife. There's something in the tradition of father handing daughter over to husband, little girl becoming a woman. Today though, my sons will be walking me down the aisle towards their dad. I wrestled with the idea of asking Sven, but something didn't feel right about it knowing my dad is alive. Sven knew of my dilemma, and told me he was honored to even be considered for such a task. But suggested the boys, and I finally agreed.

The day we came back to Plantain was emotional and bittersweet in a sense. Finally coming home for Dornan and me, meant a new place filled with family they didn't even know existed for the boys. I guess since we hadn't formed any strong ties in Alaska made it somewhat easier for them, but having to give them an entire family tree and names of our friends and their kids, just seemed too much for them to comprehend.

Everyone was waiting for us outside our house, and all the worry about coming back was discarded once we stepped from the car and were immediately embraced by Missy and Sven. Who aside from looking a little older, and Sven looking a little weaker from the stroke, it was like no time had passed. Missy burst into tears when she hugged Dornan, kissing his cheeks and cupping his face to get a good look at her baby boy. When we stepped back, the boys at our sides looked up at two strangers, only for a moment did they hesitate before both raised their arms and greeted their grandparents. This sent Missy into a set of fresh tears, my eyes watered too and even Sven wasn't lacking a little wetness in his eyes. Dornan and I then moved towards our friends to allow his parents and the boys some alone time. Katie practically jumped into my arms as Joey and Dornan hugged, slapping one another's backs. Smokey and Emily had two more kids since we'd been gone and when I saw Drag standing off to the side, something about him caused me to walk to him when I had always avoided him like the plague.

"Maven," he smiled. "Glad you're home."

Even the way he spoke was different. He was looking into my eyes and not ogling my body.

"Drag, looking good," I baited.

"You're just saying that because you're married."

He was teasing me, and not in a creepy way, like a normal flirty person, I was going to have to get to the bottom of this transformation. Dornan sidled up beside me and outstretched his hand, Drag accepted with a nod.

"Brother," Dornan said.

Just like with everything in this crazy club, all was forgiven. Dornan forgave Drag for hitting on me, just as Drag forgave Dornan for beating him up. But regardless, they both had come to get me that day in the desert. Both had killed for our family that day, so all was forgiven.

The boys love their new life and love our massive property my grandma's old house is on, which now really does feel like our home and not hers anymore. Dornan and I filled it with two crazy boys and of course Bagheera. We also took over having the Sunday dinners, filling the house where I used to like to keep it to myself. The biggest shock of all since our return, was to find out that the MC had gone legit, no illegal anything anymore. Sven had figured we made enough money with the collision shop, the two used car dealerships, the several gas stations, and if we reopened one of the strip clubs that we would be okay financially. I was shocked and I think Dornan was too. We'd never thought to not do illegal things as a bike club, but with all the shit that went down, Sven didn't want to lose any more family or even risk the possibility of going to jail once he caught wind of what the Feds had been up to.

The entire time we were gone there was an overhaul in the club, not only rebuilding a strip club, which none of them had ever done before, but also losing many members that didn't want to live the outlaw life. We had a lot of new prospects and recently patched in members who I was still trying to learn the names of. I was also surprised to learn that around the time we'd left so had my secretary Skye. This whole time I thought for sure she'd be doing my job and running the business, she had been on the west coast, but she was here for my wedding and I couldn't wait to finally hear that story.

Smokey had taken over my job, apparently it was rough for a bit but he managed to not send the club into bankruptcy, I thought he'd want to remain in the position and I was going to have to find something new to do for work, but telling me the job was mine were practically the first words out of his mouth when we reunited.

I found out that Drag had done the nomad thing for a few years until his brother, who he was close to, died tragically. He really had matured, albeit still flirtatious as fuck, but not lewd and obnoxious. He became someone I liked spending time with and often stopped by the house randomly to see the kids and stay for dinner. I was glad he and Dornan and Joey had become a closer unit since it seemed as if the death of his brother was taking its toll on him.

Sven decided to step down as 'boss' and handed over the reins to Dornan, which meant he was my boss at work now. That did not go unnoticed by him, he liked to remind me usually three or four times everyday at work. It was strange how he and I melded back into our old lives as new people. We were now parents, returning to a place where we had left it as lovers. He was back to laying clothes out for me most days, I was running in the mornings before we took the boys to school and then drove to work together. We'd kept my Mustang but traded Dornan's Charger for an SUV which was way better than a minivan, and opted to use that vehicle over our bikes most days. But we did often take the bikes out into the desert and ride for miles when the boys would stay over at Missy and Sven's.

My love for Dornan has only grown over the years, as we've both transformed and become the people we are today, and I can only imagine how much stronger our love will be as we morph into the people we will become. He still turns me on like he did so many years ago, but even more now seeing him with our kids and seeing him as a boss at work. Our lives are just beginning, for the third time together.

I finish the letter and fold it into thirds, before tucking it into an envelope. Milton's assured me he will be able to get it to my dad, and I don't question how he's positive he can. I hear voices outside the house and the boys trying to be wrangled downstairs by Sven, as I walk down the hallway. Wandering into my bedroom, I see my wedding dress lying on the bed. It's simple, a white satin slip dress that's long, and I decide I will go barefoot. The only accessories I'm wearing is the ruby ring Dornan had given to me at sixteen, along with the wedding ring he'd given me when he married me in bed. I leave my hair down in long waves, covering the low cut back of the dress and the spaghetti straps that delicately lay on my shoulders. I apply minimal makeup since it's what Dornan prefers. I also decide to forgo any undergarments, since that's also what Dornan prefers.

"It's time," Skye says from the doorway and I look over my shoulder towards her.

She's always been thin, but seeing her today, she looks sickly small. Her hair's longer and pulled back into a low bun, a navy and cream maxi dress hangs off her body and my heart breaks a little for her. She still looks beautiful; her bright smile never wavers as I inspect her. Walking closer, she hands me my bouquet of flowers I'd grown around the property, a mix of hydrangea, lilacs, and tulips. Her fingers linger on the petals, as my hands wrap around the base.

"You should come visit for longer next time," I say.

Her eyes are downcast and I've never seen her so reserved. I don't like this girl, the one who seems so far removed from the happy go lucky girl I knew from years ago. I guess we all grow up and change, but this is different, it's like the light in her eyes is gone, and a weight is literally causing her shoulders to droop.

"Yeah, maybe this summer," she raises her head and smiles.

"Skye," I say, trying to get her eyes to connect with mine.

There's an unspoken communication going on between us, she knows I know something's going on, even if she didn't say it.

"If you ever need us, we're only a phone call away…and know that we would drop everything to get you," I say.

I watch as she sinks her teeth into her lower lip as her eyes well up, she nods before looking at me and smiling.

"Thank you," she whispers.

"And you can live with us until you get on your feet," I add.

Her eyes dart to mine and she lets out a long breath.

"Thanks Maven," then she adds. "You look beautiful, absolutely stunning."

I smile at her and my excitement returns. I can't wait for the wedding, but can't wait even more for our honeymoon. We're not going anywhere since we both feel we've been gone from home long enough, so Missy and Sven are taking the kids for the weekend. I look out the huge bay window in the master bedroom and see the guests are seated. Dornan, who's wearing a black dress shirt with the sleeves rolled up, black dress pants and his hot as hell black boots, stands at the arch at the end of the aisle, waiting for me.

"Maven, it's time," Missy says entering the room.

Instantly her eyes water as she looks me over, Skye moving aside to allow the only mom I've ever known to take me in as I'll soon become her daughter-in-law officially. She begins to cry as I walk over and wrap her in my arms, trying myself not to cry. We pull ourselves together and begin the walk towards my husband.

Stopping at the entryway to the backdoor, Skye and Missy go ahead to take their seats as I take my sons' hands on either side. Of course Wyatt doesn't want to walk and before he throws a temper tantrum, I sling him up onto my hip. We walk out and everyone stands, Dornan's eyes locking on me, he looks me up and down and I can't help but grin like a lunatic as we walk towards him. His eyes grow darker the closer I get. God, he looks devastatingly handsome, and the urge to run and jump into his arms before making out with him is overwhelming. As he reaches for me, I set Wyatt down, and both boys stand beside us.

"Wow babe, you look stunning," Dornan says quietly.

I feel a little shy at the attention, and glance down at myself.

"Please tell me you have something on under that?" he mumbles.

I give him a playful look before the priest begins and we became man and wife.

After the ceremony, Dornan kisses me silly as we're announced as Mr. and Mrs. Dornan Frederickson. Now, it's party time. Sven, Chain, and Rocket barbecue as the old ladies finish cooking in the kitchen, bringing things out to the many picnic tables we have set up. It's a beautiful summer day and the suns beginning to set, and the night feels like a dream. Never have I imagined my life turning out this way, that I would be my best friend's wife, that we'd have two beautiful children, back in our hometown and simply…happy.

Our first dance together is like a movie of memories as we sway along to, "Night Moves." It's funny how I can't remember anything regarding that song before Dornan sang it to me in bed that first time, as if my life never was anything before he was mine. Dornan's all hands and gets to feel that indeed I'm naked under the silk of my dress as he runs a hand along my ass cheeks. The urgency he has to take me upstairs is laughable, until I realize he's being completely serious. With much pleading that I want to enjoy or reception, he relents, but continuously through the night attempts to grab my ass. It's easily eleven p.m. before the last guests go home, and Dornan's parents leave with our sleeping boys. Even though exhausted and in need of sleep, I sneak off for a shower, as Dornan tells the prospects all they have to clean up from the wedding. When I enter our bedroom afterward, he's sitting on the side of the bed. His shirt's off but his pants and boots remain, as if he just sat down. He looks up at me in the doorway, clad only in a towel.

"I wanted to peel you out of that dress," he says.

"I can go put it back on," I offer with a tilt of my head.

"No, no...I want to fuck you now," he says in a low gruff voice.

"Oh yeah?"

"Mhmm...do you want me to fuck you?"

He's looking at me with that fire in his eyes, his hand moving to his lap to palm the thick bulge on his thigh through his pants.

"Yes," I whisper breathlessly.

"Take off the towel."

I release my fingers holding the two ends at my chest, letting the fabric fall to the floor. Already with just him looking at my body, my nipples harden, and the pull between my legs begins to pulse.

"You want me?" he asks.

I take one step towards him, before he says, "Crawl to me."

My insides flutter as I sink to my knees, my palms making contact with the floor as I move forward. My eyes never leaving his as I slowly prowl closer, and Dornan lets out a groan as he watches. I move between his legs and sit up onto my knees. I bite my lip and run my hands up his thighs on either side of me, feeling the thick ridge of his cock. I reach the button of his pants, slipping the fabric and zipper down easily. He sits up enough to allow me to pull his pants and boxer briefs down his hips, his cock emerging and standing hard and leaning to the left. I lick my lips before tracing the tip of my tongue from his balls to the flush head, returning back down and repeating the motion several times.

"Oh fuck," Dornan groans and I grab my breasts, plumping them in my hands then teasing my nipples, he licks his lips as I lean closer. My lips hover over the tip of his dick and I let a thick deposit of saliva slide down his long shaft to his balls.

"Jesus."

I place my cupped breasts on either side of his cock, allowing the hard flesh to slip between them, while I lean up and Dornan grasps my chin as he kisses me. I move my tits up and down and Dornan's body tenses, groaning as he attacks my tongue, his hands tangling in my hair as I move faster. Moments later he breaks from the kiss and lifts me, turning me so my back is to his front and I'm sitting on his lap. My ass grinds into his hips, his cock between us as he spreads my legs. He begins to rub my clit, his lips kissing along my shoulder and neck, causing my eyes to flutter shut.

"Now that you're my wife, when you gonna let me put another baby inside you?" he asks directly into my ear.

I grind against him, my sex pushing into his hand and his lap. I'm about to lose my mind before the words register as to what he's said.

"You already have," I groan.

His motions stop, as if he's processing my words. Swiftly he rolls me onto my back before he moves over me.

"You're pregnant?" he asks.

"We're pregnant," I smile and lean up to kiss him.

And that is the story of Dornan and me, albeit somewhat fucked up. It's our love story, and I wouldn't change a thing.

MAVEN'S LETTER TO HER DAD

Dad,

I hope that this letter finds you, Milton's assured me that he can get it to you so I have to believe that it will. There's so many things I want to tell you, too many for a letter I'm sure. I know that my words can only give you a peek into what my life's become and who I am now, but it's better than nothing.

I'm now a mom and soon to be a wife. Nothing could've prepared me for motherhood, but I never imagined how much it would change me and how much I love it. Wyatt and Nolan are better than I ever could've dreamed. We're expecting another baby which I haven't told Dornan yet, but I know he'll be thrilled.

Everyday I see my kids, I can't help but imagine myself as a child and how you and mom would've done anything for me. You both proved to me that you did, even if it took me years to understand. I know that even as Mom was being taken from us, that my welfare was her greatest concern, and I know that feeling now as a mom. I know you sacrificed yourself for me in so many ways, and I'm sorry I didn't get the chance to tell you in person. I love you so much Dad. When I thought you'd died, it caused a pain inside me I never felt before. The pain that I never get to see you again, that we never really mended the rift I'd caused to get so big.

It guts me that my kids will never get to meet you, that I'll never get to hear you laugh or feel your arms around me again. But everyday I'm reminded of you and mom in my kids and the things they do. Nolan has a sense of humor like yours and they both have my eyes, which I know are like mom's. Missy gave me photos and it wasn't until then, that I know how much I look like mom. I hope to one day find her family and hope to learn more about who she was.

Knowing that it caused you so much pain to have photos of her in our house, or even to tell me about her, I understand that. If I lost Dornan I couldn't imagine how I would carry on, but I would for my kids, as you did for me.

Oh Dad, I miss you constantly, especially today. I'm about to be married in a few hours, and I wish nothing more than to have you walk me down the aisle. There are so many things we will have missed out on together, but there is a glimmer of hope inside me knowing you're out there in the world somewhere.

I hope you find happiness and love in your new life, that you know how much you are missed and loved in this life. I love you Daddy, I'm enclosing a photo of your grandkids and I hope you will know them one day.

Love, Maven.

AMELIA OLIVER

℘LAYLIST

Jimmy Hendrix- Voodoo Child
Steve Miller Band- Livin' in the U.S.A.
Golden Earring- Radar Love
Gregg Allman- Midnight Rider
Eddie Money- Shakin'
Billy Joel- Always a Woman to Me
Motley Crue- Girls Girls Girls
Van Halen- Hot for Teacher
The Who- My Generation
Led Zeppelin- When the Levee Breaks
The Eagles- Life in the Fastlane
Doobie Brothers- Listen to the Music
Tom Petty and the Heartbreakers- Breakdown
Bad Company- Bad Company
The Rolling Stones- wild horses
Van Morrison- Into the Mystic
Nazareth- Hair of the Dog
Ted Nugent- Stranglehold
Led Zeppelin- All of My Love
AC/DC- Back in Black
Heart- Magic Man
Stevie Nicks and Don Henley- Leather and Lace
Bob Seger- Night Moves

Plantain Series

The next book in the series is Skye and Drag's roller coaster relationship. Their story begins in the past, and takes them on a journey to our present day where Running with the Devil leaves off. I can't wait to take you on their journey or heartbreak, growth, tragedy, and love.

ACKNOWLEDGMENTS

Thank you to all my girls who read, and re-read, and re-read this masterpiece to make it perfect. Tiffany, Joanne, Rose, Laura, Paula, Theresa, Brittney, Meghan and Tali, I appreciate you all more than you know. You all helped motivate me, and didn't let me give up when the journey got a little too rough. For that, I will always be indebted to you all. Ellie for putting up with my endless questions, my annoying, slightly bullying, on the verge of harassment, neurotic texts, you are a unicorn goddess of wisdom and insight. Tali Alexander, and B.B. Easton for helping me with questions, and fangirling over models with, thank you. Thank you Haris Nukem for the amazing cover photo, you have no idea how grateful I am for you. Thank you Jess for turning my cover into another level of art. You all gave me the confidence to make my dream come true, I love you all with every part of me.

Thank you to the readers, can't wait to hear from you.

You can contact me at:
authorameliaoliver@gmail.com

You can also follow me on Instagram at:
@authorameliaoliver
&
@men_w_ink

Made in the USA
Monee, IL
07 February 2022

90865137R00155